BLOOD OF THE SONS

A MAFIA CRIME THRILLER

THE CONSENTINO CRIME SAGA
BOOK TWO

VINCENT B. DAVIS II

For my mother

It's easier to find enough words to fill a book than to find the words to express how grateful I am for you.

Thank you.

The Bureau is your connection to Vincent's growing library of crime thriller books. It's like having a direct connection to the Chief of Police with top secret clearance where you get the inside scoop in real time.

Just scan the QR code below!

PART I

1

SONNY

Poughkeepsie, Dutchess County, New York- October 17, 1930

Ninety-three days had passed since Sonny swore the oath and joined the Honored Society. But he still didn't find this kind of work any easier.

He frisked the captive, finding only a wallet, a pistol, and a pocket New Testament in Italian.

The wallet contained a license belonging to "Francesco Siragusa," as well as papers to prove his citizenship.

Sonny concealed the man's pistol in his jacket. "You just get off the boat?" Sonny asked, realizing the man hadn't been in the States for more than a year.

The captive squared his shoulders and kept his lips shut in defiance. A frigid breeze wafting in from the Hudson River shook the old barn, causing the rotten wood to creak. The shack was dark and secluded, just as intended, far enough away from Wappinger Falls that no one would hear any gunshots or screams.

Continuing to dig through the wallet, Sonny noticed a studio photograph of a pretty young woman. He admired her and stepped to the captive to cut his restraints. He returned to a chair across from him.

"I wouldn't do that," Sonny said, noticing the man was contemplating whether or not to run. Sonny pulled back his suit to reveal his own revolver. "Is this your wife?"

"Don't speak of her." The man spit at Sonny's feet.

"I mean no disrespect. She is a beautiful woman. I'm sure you'd like to return to her." Sonny looked up and ensured the look he gave Siragusa conveyed empathy. "It would be a shame for you to die looking at something ugly like me when you could go back to someone like her," he said, reaching across to return the wallet and its contents to Siragusa.

"What do you want from me?"

While the man spoke in broken English, Sonny turned his attention to the New Testament. He flipped through the pages, and found a verse underlined. "You know what I want. I need to know where Steve Ferrigno is," Sonny said.

Ferrigno was the target Mr. Gagliano gave to Maranzano's family. Sonny asked to avoid being involved in any more murders, so he offered to find out a location instead. Siragusa was a known associate of Ferrigno's, and he was the best place to start. Siragusa's penchant for late night gambling made him an easy target.

"I'm not going to tell you anything. *Vaffanculo.*" Siragusa again spit, this time hitting Sonny's shined Oxford shoes.

Sonny took out a handkerchief and cleaned them. He returned his attention to Siragusa's New Testament.

"I love this verse." He pointed to the Scripture. "My

father read it to me often as a boy, when I would have nightmares."

"What verse?"

"Are you afraid, Mr. Siragusa?" Sonny looked the captive in his eyes.

"No. I am not afraid," he replied, but his darting eyes and fidgeting feet betrayed him.

Sonny read from the Gospel of Luke, Chapter 12. "'And I say unto you my friends, Be not afraid of them that kill the body, and after that have no more that they can do.'"

Siragusa finished the verse in Italian, "'But I will forewarn you whom ye shall fear: Fear him, which after he hath killed hath power to cast into hell.'"

Sonny looked up impressed. "You know your scripture. I appreciate that."

"That is why I do not fear you," Siragusa said, "Because you cannot cast me into hell." He jutted out his chin.

"You are right. I cannot. Nor would I want to," Sonny said. "But unfortunately, I have the power to bring hell to you." Sonny stood and nodded to the shadows. Antonello stepped out with a leather bundle in his arms. He sat it on a table between Sonny and Siragusa. Unfolding the bundle, he revealed the contents. Hammers, screwdrivers, and various other tools were placed inside.

Siragusa squirmed in his seat.

"I have tried to treat you with respect, Mr. Siragusa." Sonny opened his palms in a gesture of goodwill. "I have no quarrel with you. In fact, I don't even have a quarrel with your boss."

"What are you going to do?" Siragusa's chair squeaked against the concrete floor.

Sonny stood and began to pace. "I don't want to kill you, Mr. Siragusa. Nor do I want to kill Mr. Ferrigno. I am simply to find out where he is and pass that information along to those who care to know. Will you help me?"

"Go to hell!" Siragusa swore.

Sonny stood and stepped between Siragusa and Antonello, as if to say that this was the last time he would be able to pacify his violent friend.

"I bring you here without a bruise on your body. I have not threatened you, hurt you, mocked you. You spit on my shoes and tell me to go to hell." He stepped in and grabbed Siragusa by the shirt. "I even cut your restraints. Now, if you don't tell me what I need to know, I'm gonna have my friend cut off your hands. We know you're involved. My information came from a source that doesn't make mistakes, and the .38 in your pocket confirmed my suspicions."

Antonello stepped closer to Sonny, a pair of sharp sheers in his hands.

"What makes you think I know anything about Ferrigno? I'm nobody!" Siragusa began to weep, his face contorting like a characterized clown.

"It's too late to play foolish, Mr. Siragusa." Sonny stepped aside, and Antonello took his place. "And you will talk. You will tell me. The only thing that remains to be decided is how much hell you would like to endure before you do so." Sonny nodded for Antonello to proceed. Siragusa fought back but at half Antonello's size, was easily restrained, and the violence commenced.

Sonny retreated a few steps and turned his back. He didn't want to watch, and he didn't want Siragusa to see weakness in his eyes. Sonny's own hands trembled while he lit a cigarette and tried to block out the sound of the screams.

By the time Sonny was halfway through his cigarette,

Siragusa was relieved of a few fingers and a pint of blood, and he wanted to talk.

"Step away, Antonello," Sonny said, pushing aside his friend. "I hope we can end this now." He helped Siragusa from the floor back onto the chair.

Sonny pulled out another cigarette, lit it, and placed it in Siragusa's lips. The captive puffed gratefully.

"Don Ferrigno has an office in the Bronx," Siragusa said. "He has been working there since Joe the Boss put out notice that your people were trouble."

"Where in the Bronx?"

"I don't know."

Antonello grabbed a hammer and hoisted it over his head.

"Okay, okay," Siragusa covered his face with mangled hands, but Sonny reached out to stop Antonello. The captive continued, "It's in a Jewish neighborhood, where he figured he wouldn't be seen."

"Which one?"

"Pelham Parkway. That's all I know, I swear! Give me my Bible, and I'll swear an oath on it."

Sonny patted the pitiful man on the shoulder. "That won't be necessary." He turned and showed Siragusa his back again. "Let him finish his cigarette," he said to Antonello.

Antonello nodded and bundled up his tools. When Siragusa stamped out the cigarette, half unconscious from the pain he'd endured, Antonello grabbed an empty cement bag and wrapped it over Siragusa's head.

Sonny kept his eyes shut until the man's feet stopped thrashing against the floor. The job didn't take long, but it was too long for Sonny.

They had an address. That was good. They had been

successful. But knowing that location meant more people were going to die. And Sonny was still trying to understand what that meant for him. He rubbed the back of his neck and exhaled along with Siragusa's last breath.

"All right, it's over," Antonello said.

"Thank you, Antonello," Sonny said, and meant it. He was glad he didn't have to do it. Francesco Siragusa didn't kill his father after all.

Sonny recovered the wallet and tried to ignore the smell that now filled the barn. He pulled out the license and handed it to Antonello.

"His address is on there. Have flowers sent to his wife."

"Got it."

"Then afterwards take off the bag and lay him down with the New Testament in hand."

Antonello scratched his head. "What? I thought we was gonna drop him in the Hudson?"

"We just widowed a woman," Sonny said. "At least we can give her a chance to see him one last time."

"Seems dangerous." Antonello shook his head.

"Let's give his mother an open casket, huh? That's why I told you not to shoot."

"Consider it done." Antonello smiled. "Just make sure Old Caesar hears about how good I done."

Sonny didn't return the gesture but nodded and turned to leave the barn.

Little Italy, Manhattan—October 18, 1930

. . .

Sonny had not walked the streets of Italy in a long time, except to pick up his vigs from the shopkeepers under his protection. He wasn't supposed to be here at all, actually, but decided to accept the risk and make a quick visit to the St. Patrick's Cathedral. It was unlikely Masseria's boys would show their face on Elizabeth Street, but he still couldn't be too careful, so he kept his collar up and his fedora low.

There were churches in Brooklyn he could have attended, in Harlem, too, but Mass never felt right outside of the cathedral his father raised him in.

"Hey, mister! You're a big shot, ain't you, mister?" A few children ran up from behind him. Worn out old newsboy caps, stained white union shirts, and hand-me-down suspenders. They reminded Sonny so much of himself and his brothers that he had to laugh.

"I don't know if I'd say that, pal."

"Gee, you got a dollar, mister?" one of the kids asked.

Sonny considered it for a moment, keeping his eyes on the faces of the boys, as he brandished a roll of dollar bills and slid each of them a two dollar bill.

He had seen important men make charitable gestures like this all his life and had been the recipient of it a time or two himself. He beamed with pride.

They lingered, analyzing the dollar with wide-eyed amazement, turning it over carefully like it was the Declaration of Independence.

"You boys stay in school. Don't listen to anyone if they tell you to quit. And always trust your parents. Understand? Your mother and father know what's best." He had never been in a position like this before. He felt, if he could speak more frankly, he really would be able to impart wisdom on these kids. But there was only so much he could say.

"I wanna be just like you when I grow up, mister," one of the boys said.

Sonny's stomach dropped. "No, you don't, pal. Go on, you're going to make me late for Mass."

They nodded and practically skipped away, already shouting about what they'd do with the money. Sonny waited until they were out of eyeshot before he shook his head. There was a lot that kids don't know. And thank God for that.

The early Mass began and ended, but Sonny wasn't ready to leave, even after a few hours. Bonanno was probably wondering where he was, and Maranzano was more than likely waiting on a report or call. But Sonny had not received what he had come for, and he desired to remain until he did.

He wanted an answer. He wanted God to speak to him and tell him what he should do. He felt lost, felt like he hadn't heard God's voice in so long. He rubbed the beads of his father's rosary and said the prayers he was taught, but never heard a reply.

The sun was just beginning to set over Mulberry Street, and it shun through the stain glass windows, sending rays of purple, blue, and green light throughout the church. Sonny looked up and fixed his eyes on the image of the risen Jesus and wondered why he couldn't hear him.

"You doing all right, fella?" came a voice from behind Sonny. To his surprise, he found that the voice belonged to someone wearing the white collar of a priest.

"I didn't see you there, Father. I'm okay," Sonny replied as the priest settled into a pew.

"No worries. Just figured I'd check in. You've been in prayer for awhile and wanted to let you know I'm here to pray with ya."

The priest had a rugged handsomeness and had the thick jaw of a heavyweight boxer. He looked younger than the other priests, but already developing some grey in his otherwise jet black hair. He was clearly Italian and looked like any number of the guys on Maranzano's crew.

"You from around here, Father?"

"Houston Street, born and raised," the priest said.

Sonny turned and tucked the rosary back into his shirt. "Then you probably know about guys like me."

"I didn't make no assumptions." He leaned forward and propped up on Sonny's pew. "I'm dyin' for a coffee and a pastry. Want to join me?"

"I probably shouldn't right now, Father."

"It'd be some ruthless gangster to kill you when you're eating breakfast with a priest," he said.

Sonny was surprised at how well the Father seemed to understand. "I gotta get back though."

"*Capiche*. No worries. My name is Father Russo, but if you call me Sammy I won't alert the Pope. Come back around some time, eh . . . what did you say your name was?"

"Sonny."

"I know about a million of them." The priest laughed.

"Sonny Consentino."

Father Russo stood. "All right, Sonny Consentino. Let's grab a bite next time you're in Little Italy."

"Yeah, I'll do that, Sammy."

Bronx, New York—October 21, 1930

. . .

Sonny knocked on the door of the second-floor apartment building, holding nothing but a single suitcase. This apartment would be home for the foreseeable future, by Maranzano's orders. He was told he didn't have to pull the trigger when Ferrigno was found, but Maranzano wanted some of his own people to be there with the soldiers Gagliano had sent.

A short man built like a bull cracked the door.

"Yeah?"

"Old Caesar sent me," Sonny said. The man opened the door and allowed him to step in. As he entered, Sonny choked from the amount of cigarette smoke that greeted him.

Two beds, a table, and a small stove took up more than half the tiny apartment.

"I'm Joe Cargo." He offered Sonny a drink.

"No, I'm fine." Sonny turned his attention to the other two men in the room, sitting on the edge of the beds. Despite the unmistakable scar under Enzo's eye and the dimple in Vico's chin, they were like strangers. They hardly resembled the twins he grew up with.

Since discovering that Enzo and Vico were involved in the war effort against Masseria, Sonny hadn't been able to talk with them much about it. He wouldn't even know what to say. Enzo had only whispered to him that no one knew they were brothers, and that Vico went by his boxing name, Bobby Doyle.

Other than that, they didn't address the situation. Enzo avoided eye contact. Vico on the other hand, locked eyes with Sonny's scornfully, saying nothing but passing judgement on Sonny's presence.

"I'm Vincente." Sonny paused and looked at Vico and Enzo for a reaction, "Consentino."

Cargo sat at a table by the window facing the road and searched through his ash tray for a cigarette butt that had a little bit more to smoke.

"No shit?" he asked. "He related to you, Enzo?"

"Probably cousins or something," Enzo said, keeping his eyes fixed on the drywall across the room.

"Small world, huh?" Vico said, eyes not leaving Sonny's tapping feet.

"Want to see a picture of the guys we're after?" Cargo said, balancing a cigarette butt in his lips as he fumbled through his pockets.

"Sure." Sonny set down his suitcase by the stove and tried to ignore Vico's scowl as he looked over Cargo's shoulder.

"This is Fennuci," Cargo said pointing to the crumbled picture in his hand.

"Cargo. The guy's name isn't Fennuci. How many times I gotta tell you? It's Ferrigno." Enzo shook his head.

"Yeah, Ferrigno. Whatever." Cargo flipped the photograph, revealing another. "And this is Joe the Boss. If we see him, we gotta make the hit, or at least report his presence to someone."

Sonny looked at the picture of Masseria and recalled seeing him stuff his face while Morello and Maranzano talked business. He looked just as obese in the picture as he had in real life, although in person his suit didn't look nearly as well-tailored.

"He's a fat old bastard, isn't he?" Cargo laughed. "Gagliano calls him 'the Chinese' because of that pudgy face and those squinty eyes."

"Yeah, I've met him."

"Who, Gagliano?" Enzo sprung up from the bed.

"No, Masseria."

"Why didn't you put a bullet in his head then?" Cargo straightened, as if he suddenly felt threatened.

"It was a sit-down. Before the war. Believe me, if I could have, I would've," Sonny said. He didn't really mean it. Despite recent events, he didn't have much of a penchant for violence. He killed Morello because he thought he was his father's killer.

"Must'a been something to see that fat man shove a plate of food down his gullet," Cargo said.

"Most of it ended up on his shirt." Sonny forced a laugh, but Cargo was the only one to join him.

Cargo returned his attention to Ferrigno's photo and pointed out the window at a brick building across the road.

"That's where Ferarro works."

"*Madonna Mia*. It's Ferrigno, Cargo. You stupid?" Vico rolled his eyes.

"Ferrigno. That's where he works."

"You seen him yet?" Sonny asked.

"Not yet. But we have orders to make the hit when we see him. You got a piece?" Cargo said.

Sonny pulled back his suit and revealed his pistol. Cargo nodded approvingly, the twins gritted their teeth, and Sonny only hoped he wouldn't have to use it.

2

TURRIDRU

Palermo, Sicily—September 24, 1916

Turridru had grown bored of confession. Since he had finished seminary and moved to Palermo to work in the St. Petersburg Cathedral, he had to sit and listen to little old ladies and young boys talking about all the wrong things they had done. He comforted them in any way he could, but didn't really care. They didn't know anything about real sin.

He gave the same prescription every time—a few Hail Marys and a rosary.

He didn't enjoy much about being a priest, and sometimes he reflected fondly on his days in Castellamare del Golfo. The tradition and decorum of priesthood suited him just fine, but pretending to be some humble father to the people was agonizing. He missed the power. The look of passersby when he walked with men like Alonzo Consentino. Just thinking of the name could bring his blood to a boil though, as he remembered what happened after Don Consentino left, leading to his priesthood in the first place.

The young mother on the other side of the confession booth finished up her monologue about how much she loved God and tried to do good.

"Go and sin no more," he said, glad that she couldn't see the look of irritation on his face.

After her, he was allowed a few minutes of rest to collect his thoughts. He leaned his head back against the wall and remembered the moment when he killed the two Armetta boys. Sometimes, after spending so much time studying God's Word, he really did feel guilt. More than not, though, the thought comforted him. There was a time when he had power. All the power in the world: over life and death. He just didn't have power over the one life he wanted to save. His mother's. If he had, the last several years might have looked differently.

The confession booth opened, and the next parishioner entered.

Turridru closed his eyes and rubbed his temples, trying to mentally prepare for the pathetic sobs and pleading.

To his surprise, the voice which greeted him was firm, strong, and even. Collected. "Forgive me, Father, for I have sinned. I am a Man of Honor, and it has been two years since my last confession."

Turridru perked up. A Man of Honor? He hadn't heard the title since before he attended seminary, but he knew it well. "What are your sins, Child?" he asked, but could tell the man was older than he.

The man exhaled and shifted in the confessional chair. "I've got a list as long as your robes, Father."

"I won't blush."

"I am an important man. And I have many friends. When they need something from me, I take care of it for them. I do not ask questions. This means doing things that many others would consider sinful."

Turridru savored every word. He wished he could be on the other side of the booth. "Men of Honor are necessary in a hard place like Sicily. I am sure there are many who pray for you."

"I'm glad to hear you say so." The man seemed pleased. "I am only here because I am tired of receiving judgmental glances from my wife. She thinks if I don't seek repentance God will punish us. But she doesn't seem to mind the dresses I buy her, or the coastal villa we've raised our children in."

"Do you love your wife, Child?"

"Like Christ loves the Church," the man said sardonically, as if he expected the preachy monologue to begin.

"And your children?"

"Of course, I do."

"And you do what you do to protect them? And provide for them?"

"That's why I do everything."

"God gives certain men power so that they can protect the weak. When we live under a government that abuses its power, when we must strive just to feed our people, God gives power to the strong so that they can protect."

The man laughed. "My wife isn't going to believe this."

"He also gives power so that men like you can exact vengeance." Turridru could tell by the silence that the man was finally taking him seriously.

"The Bible says that?"

"It does. Just as David was given strength to conquer Goliath, just as Joshua was given an army to burn Jericho to the ground, just as St. Michael was given the power to cast Satan out of heaven, the Lord gives us the ability to protect ourselves, since we cannot expect to receive justice from those in power."

"I think I may start coming to confessional more." The man seemed surprised at what he was hearing.

"There are wicked men in the world, Child. There are wicked men in Sicily and in Palermo. You are God's right hand to exact vengeance on those who would step on 'the little ones.' Accept that responsibility with honor, as I'm sure you have."

When the man left, Turridru did not tell him to go and sin no more. He didn't tell him to perform a rosary or pray the Hail Mary. He wanted the Man of Honor to keep doing exactly what he was doing.

And if Turridru had anything to do with it, he would be doing the same thing soon.

Palermo, Sicily—January 6, 1917

"God bless you, Child," Turridru kissed each partitioner as they exited the cathedral following Mass. He took them by the hand and ensured that they felt loved and valued, the center of his attention, although in reality he was waiting on one man in particular.

The Man of Honor.

He wasn't hard to spot. He stood tall over the others, and

he was greeted by everyone else with the same deference the priests were greeted with. His voice carried throughout the church. Turridru identified him immediately.

When the Man of Honor exited, Turridru took his hand and held on to it for an extended moment. "Have you considered all that we talked about?" Turridru asked.

The Man of Honor looked back, perplexed, until he finally understood. His wife led their two daughters away, happy to give her husband a moment alone with the priest. "I have." He seemed slightly offended.

"Do not worry. Confession is a sacrament. I will say nothing to anyone. I have simply been thinking about you often."

"Have you?" The Man of Honor arched a brow.

"I have. It is a righteous life you are pursuing, but a difficult one. I would be honored to become more involved in your life, and that of your beautiful family." Turridru gestured to the man's wife and daughters, who were grown and as beautiful as their mother.

"Really, I couldn't hope to inconvenience a priest. I'm just a simple man." Of course false humility, but expected from someone of his stature.

"Priests are called to look out for all of God's children, and I feel called to serve your family in any way that I can."

The Man of Honor analyzed him, perplexed. Catching a glimpse of his wife's enticed eyes, he reconsidered the offer.

"Perhaps you can join us for dinner sometime. You can pray for us and share our bread."

"I would be honored," Turridru said, he nearly

released his hand but then clutched tighter, "and your name?"

The Man of Honor looked at his wife before responding. "Don Toto."

"Don Toto, I look forward to blessing you and your family in any way that I can." He released the Man of Honor's hand and watched him descend the church steps to his family's side.

A smile creased Turridru's lips. Don Toto would be the catalyst he needed. He would use him to get what he was truly called for: revenge.

3

MARIA

Westchester County, New York—November 4, 1930

Even after months of living alone, Maria Domingo still rolled over each morning to hold on to her husband. Each time she found him missing and remembered. 'Gone on business,' he said.

She rolled out of bed, groggy but even more lonely, and opened up the curtains. She watched the children running along the sidewalk and wondered what she would do today. Each day presented the same challenge: to find something meaningful to do. She was a housewife with no husband, a stay-at-home mother with no child.

The sound of the radio playing in the kitchen caught her attention. Had she left it on all night? Her ears perked up, and she jolted as she heard the clanging of kitchen utensils over Eddie Cantor's song.

She wrapped a shawl over her shoulder and unplugged the lamp from her nightstand. She took it with her, hoping she could catch the intruder off guard.

As she rounded the corner, the smell of bacon grease filled her nostrils. Cautiously peering into the kitchen, she saw her husband standing by the stove, whistling along to the music, none the wiser.

"Sebastiano Domingo!" she shouted, exasperated, setting down the lamp and letting down her guard.

"*Mia tesoro.*" He smiled when he saw her and tried to give her a hug.

She slapped his chest and pushed him away. "You foolish man! You gave me the screaming mimis!" she shouted. In relief she nearly cried but was determined to reveal only anger.

"I wanted to surprise you with breakfast. Come on, Maria!" he said, smiling as she swatted at him. He caught her hands and stepped in to give her a kiss.

She refused at first, but eventually accepted. It hurt her that she found herself so surprised to see her own husband.

"I always used to cook breakfast for you."

It was true. He had always risen with the sun, and prepared breakfast for Maria, as well as read through the newspaper and exercise before she awoke. "Well," she asked, sarcastically, "where was my breakfast yesterday?"

"Maria." Buster shook his head. "I shouldn't even be here right now."

"Then why are you?"

"The rest of the guys are still asleep. I had a few minutes . . . and I missed you." He tried to kiss her again, but this time Maria moved her face. "Sit down. Hashbrowns and sausage almost ready. Mixed up just how you like."

Buster seemed like he had been up for hours. He was dressed casually, but for Buster that meant a freshly pressed striped shirt with white collars, shined oxford's, a vest, pleated trousers, and an apron to keep it all pristine.

Maria couldn't stay angry with someone so handsome. She looked around the house, and suddenly felt ashamed at its condition. He was a perfectionist and had previously kept his home as orderly as a military barracks. Maria was not so clean, and certainly not as neat. "I didn't know you were coming. I would have tidied up," she said, watching carefully to see if he showed any signs of frustration. If he was upset, he hid it well.

"I just wanted to see my wife." He hurried a plate of food to the table, as well as a cup of coffee with sugar and cream, just how she liked it.

"You aren't going to eat?"

"No." He shrugged. "Not too hungry."

"Still watching your figure?" she asked, sarcastically, because he was still in perfect shape.

He laid his head back and let out a laugh. "I gotta look good if I want to keep you around."

Maria ran one hand through her messy hair and placed another on her belly, wondering if "looking good" was the reason she couldn't keep him around for very long.

"Hold on just a second," he said. He approached the kitchen radio and turned up the dial, listening carefully to the reports of last night's baseball game.

"You're a baseball fan now? Goodness. Things surely have changed since you up and disappeared four months ago."

"No, I wouldn't really call myself a fan," he said, turning the volume back down and returning to the table. "I just enjoy it every once in a while. Makes me think of simpler times."

He looked at her, and she noticed the pang of nostalgia in his eyes. "When? Did you used to go to games?"

He thought for a moment, and twiddled a spatula through his fingers.

"When I was a kid. We couldn't actually afford to go to the games. But my Ma would take me to the stadium in Chicago. We'd get some popcorn and listen from outside and try to catch a glimpse of the Cubs when everyone was leaving."

"That's sweet," she said.

"Yeah. My ma was—"

"Buster, what is going on?" she asked, unable to pretend things were normal any longer. "I haven't heard from you in weeks, haven't seen you in months. What is going on?" Against her will tears welled in her eyes, and she hurried to blink them away.

"It's complicated, Maria." He returned to the table and sat.

"That's what you always say. You have to give me something. I have to have *something*, Buster. I can't just keep living in the dark. What are you doing out there? Gambling? Seeing other girls? On some important business trip or involved in some top-secret state-side military unit?" She slammed her hand on the table, pleading. "You are a music tutor, Buster. There can't be that big of a demand for violinists."

"I've only ever been good at one thing, Maria. It's all I know how to do . . ." He looked up, his eyes now as wet as hers. "I want to provide for you."

"You can provide for me. You always have."

He looked around at the apartment, his eyes stopping on the window that looked out over their quaint little neighborhood.

"I can't afford this apartment with the money I bring in from music." He swept back his hair, still short on the sides and long on top like it was in his war pictures. "My savings paid for the first few month's rent, but that'll only last us so long."

"I can go back to work."

"No." He stood and turned his back to her. "I don't want you to ever have to work. You shouldn't have to. I can take care of it."

"But I want my husband back!" She begged, standing and wrapping her arms around his waist. "We can scrape enough together. We can even move back to Little Italy if we need to."

He picked at his fingernails. "You're cold a lot aren't you?" he asked. She may have been born in New York, but she had Sicilian blood. New York's climate was hard on her each winter.

"You know I am," she said, becoming more aware of the chill in her bare feet.

"I want to make enough to get to the coast. Move away from all this. Get somewhere warm, where the world moves a little slower."

She laid her head in between his shoulder blades. She had rarely seen him so tense, and it worried her.

"Let's just sit down." She returned to her breakfast. Buster had always been a better cook than her, another fact she was self-conscious about. "I'm just worried, Buster."

"I know you are, Maria." He took both of her hands in his own. "But this will be over soon. I'm going to make sure of it. And when it is, I will be back here. With you."

"My mother says she hasn't seen Sonny in months either," Maria spit out. She felt silly for mentioning it but had long wondered if there was a connection.

"Your brother is fine."

Maria scooted away from the table. "You've been with

Sonny?" Her anger reignited. Her tone sharp. "How much have you been lying to me?"

"Maria . . . Yes. But he is safe. So are Enzo and Vico. I've seen all of them, and they're doing okay."

"You just need to go," she blurted before considering it.

Mouth open, he searched for give in her eyes, but found none.

"Go." She pointed toward the door. "I just want to be alone right now."

"All right," he said, barely audible. He grabbed his coat and fedora from the coat rack by the door, before returning to kiss her. She didn't kiss back, nor did she move away.

"Finish it soon. I don't know how much longer I can do this, Buster," she said. He lowered his gaze and began to shut the door. "And keep my brothers safe."

4

BUSTER

Bronx, New York—November 4, 1930

He thought about everything Maria said as he took a cab back to the Bronx. They didn't argue much before, and she had certainly never asked him to leave. And the company he was returning to made the situation more difficult.

He wasn't a fan of Cargo, who was a dumb hood like any number of New York gangsters. His old war buddy Vico, who went by Bobby Doyle now, was there, but would probably be half-screwed by noon and got angry when he was drunk. Enzo was anxious and jittery, always thinking he heard something or saw someone suspicious. He made them all nervous. Sonny had been there quite a bit too, and Buster enjoyed his presence just fine. But Sonny wasn't one for much conversation, so Buster was sure he would be sitting in the apartment for another twelve hours watching the windows and trying to not choke on Cargo's chain-smoking.

"Thanks, pal." Buster tipped the cab driver when he

arrived, and crossed the sidewalk to the Pelham Parkway Apartments. He was no Jew, and always received suspicious looks, but he tipped his hat and tried to smile regardless.

As he stepped on the elevator, he saw two other Italian gentlemen. He wasn't one of the *campanilismo* like most of Maranzano's crew, but it was nice to see other Italians. He held the elevator door open, and they quickened their pace.

"Appreciate it, paisano," one of them said.

"What floor?" Buster asked.

"Why don't you punch yours?" the other said.

Buster stole a quick glance at them out of his peripherals. He immediately recognized them from the pictures they had received. The first was their target, Steve Ferrigno. The other, much more important than the first, was Joe the Boss himself. It was impossible not to recognize a belly like that.

He had left his violin case in the apartment, along with his two ivory-handled pistols, so as not to concern Maria. If he had them, he would have wasted them right there.

Buster punched the button for four, even though the room was on two. They pushed six.

They faced each other, backs to opposite walls, as the elevator crept up to the fourth floor. Buster tried his best to avoid eye contact but felt their gaze.

He exited onto the four floor and tipped his hat to them. As the elevator departed behind him, he broke into a dead sprint. He took the stairs back to the second floor, and hammered on their shared apartment until someone let him in.

"You make a racket like that again and one of us is liable to shoot," Enzo said as Buster entered.

Buster hurried to the window and drew the curtains.

"I just saw him."

"Who? Fennuci?" Cargo asked.

"Ferrigno. I saw him. And I saw Joe the Boss," Buster said, his heart beating out of his chest.

"Bushwa. No way you saw Joe the Boss in some shitty Jewish apartment." Cargo laughed. Vico and Sonny listened silently and seemed skeptical as well.

"Oh shit, we gotta call someone. Vico, get Gagliano on the phone. Or Old Caesar. Whoever!" Enzo started gathering his guns frantically.

"Did they see you?" Vico asked, far calmer.

"Yeah, they saw me. But they don't know who I am. I don't think I would have made it out of the elevator alive if they did."

"What if they just let you go to trail you?" Enzo asked.

"I went to the fourth floor and took the stairs down. They weren't watching," Buster said, grabbing his Tommy gun from his violin case and ensuing the drum was loaded.

"What are you doing?" Cargo asked, suddenly nervous like Enzo.

"If I see 'em across the courtyard, I'm taking the shot." Buster had developed a makeshift tripod and propped the Tommy gun on the table, facing out the window.

"Oh! You can't shoot from here," Cargo shouted.

"Why not?" Buster aimed down the sights.

"Because it'll be traced to me. This apartment is in my name! I can't go to jail again." Cargo shook his head.

"It's Joe the Boss," Buster said. He empathized with him but remembering the look on his wife's face that morning, he was ready to get the whole thing over with. "We were given orders to take the hit if we saw them."

"Not from my damn apartment!" Cargo moved in front of the gun. "This is for surveillance. We hit them in the road if we can, but not from here."

Vico stood and grabbed his *lupara* shotgun from under his pillow.

"I'll walk straight over there and blow his head off," Vico said.

"Come on Doyle, don't be smart." Enzo blocked his path to the door. "You'd be lying in chalk before sundown."

"Not before I hit my target."

"The Thief is right," Cargo said.

Buster adjusted his sights. "You'll blow our cover."

"Old Caesar wouldn't want it that way," Sonny added.

"You really think he cares *how* it gets done?" Vico said before giving up. He exhaled and returned to his seat and his glass of whiskey.

"Look here," Buster said, craning his head.

The rest gathered behind him to catch a glimpse. Italian tough guys in three-piece black suits were entering Ferrigno's room across the apartment courtyard.

"Jackpot," Vico said.

5

SONNY

Bronx, New York—November 5, 1930

They remained vigilant all night, their eyes and guns aimed at Ferrigno's door. In a sleepless craze, they all took turns believing they had seen men creeping in the shadows, but no one, in fact, had left the room. All the men who had caused their frustrations were in that room. And they all refused to go to sleep until the situation was resolved.

After Cargo's complaining peaked at about midnight on the fifth, a call was made to Gagliano, who instructed one of the gals at the Rainbow Garden to rent an apartment on the ground floor under an assumed name. They posted guards and moved to the first floor apartment, never losing sight of where their enemies might depart from.

"I wasn't gonna miss before. But now I can't miss even if I wanted to," Vico said, looking out the window. Any of the men departing would have to march right by their room to reach their vehicles in the parking lot.

Being closer to their victims only unnerved Sonny more.

One look in their direction, and Masseria's gang would be able to spot their faces. He kept his mouth shut about it, trying to focus instead on how good it would feel for this whole damned war to be over with. Enzo, on the other hand, was more vocal about his concerns.

"We better not miss. If someone gets away, they'll know we're here. They'll surround us, and we'll be the ones bottled up."

"You haven't seen me shoot, Enzo," Buster said with a sleepy grin.

"He don't miss." Vico said, testing the weight of his shotgun. "You should have seen him in the Argonne."

"With what gun?" Enzo asked.

"An Enfield."

"My kid cousin could hit somebody with one of them. And he don't think so good."

"Not across 300 yards of No Man's Land with artillery popping off all around you and bullets whistling past your ears. But Buster did. Like I said, he don't miss. And neither do I. They're already dead."

"I hope you're right," Enzo said.

"You worry more than Cargo," Vico scoffed, "Here, loosen up." He passed Enzo a flask.

Sonny reached in his coat and clutched his father's rosary, saying a prayer as Alonzo had taught him to do. It was the only thing that could calm him.

Cargo entered with a bag of food in hand, dropped off by one of Maranzano's men.

"You know the worst part about this whole war? The food. I wanna eat something real," Cargo said, balancing a cigarette in his lips as he pulled out a loaf of bread, a wedge of cheese, two onions, and some garlic. "I wanna go to

Ferrar's and get a cannoli. That's the first thing I'm gonna do when this whole thing is over."

"Hopefully you won't have to wait long if this goes down right," Enzo said.

"Wait, wait, wait," Buster said from the window. The room silenced and everyone hurried to gather round him. "The door just opened and closed. They might be about to leave. Sonny, shut off those lights, will ya?"

Sonny flipped a switch, and each member knelt to keep a low profile.

"I got eyes on one," Vico said, looking over the top of his sawed-off.

"Two of them coming," Buster said, adjusting the tripod of his tommy gun.

"Anyone know who these two guys are?"

"They're bait. Nobodies. They figure if there is a trap these guys will get knocked off and it'll alert the rest," Sonny said.

"I think he's right." Buster nodded.

"Everybody hold your fire," Vico said.

"Duck," Enzo whispered, as the two men passed, not ten yards from their window.

"They're gonna hear you pissing your trousers if you don't calm down," Vico said as the two entered a black Ford and departed.

A few moments later, two more men left.

Buster's voice was low and even. "That's Augie Pisano on the left."

"Joe Catania on the right," Vico said. "Take the shot?"

"We have bigger fish to fry," Sonny said, and no one objected.

The room became quiet enough to hear Enzo's quick, shallow breaths.

"Why don't you go stand by the door, pal?" Buster said after Pisano and Catania passed. "Gotta have somebody guarding our flank." Enzo nodded, visibly relieved.

"Cargo, I swear to God if you don't put out that cigarette I'm gonna stick it in your eye. They're gonna see the light," Vico said.

Cargo shrugged and tapped it out.

Parties of two continued to depart together from Masseria's meeting. Each time, Buster and Vico deliberated whether or not to take the shot. Each time they refrained, wanting Masseria. But as hours passed, they wondered if Masseria hadn't escaped through a back door.

"How many guys we let go by? I'm starting to think we shoulda pulled the trigger on Catania," Buster said.

"It's my fault. I should've known to do more recon. If they have a back door I'm—"

"Oh shit," Buster said. The next two appeared at the door. He ducked beneath the window seal and ensured his weapon was locked and loaded, as if it hadn't been already.

"Who is it? Is it Joe the Boss?" Cargo asked, his mouth full of bread and garlic.

"Steve Ferrigno. He's the guy we were originally here to get," Buster replied.

Cargo grabbed a photo from his coat pocket. "Yup. That's him."

"Who's he with?" Enzo asked from the front door.

"Tell me if I'm wrong . . . but isn't that Al Mineo?" Vico turned to Buster.

"Yeah, it is."

"Who is that?" Sonny asked.

"He's the boss of his own family. His crew is aligned with Masseria though, and he's been acting as advisor to the fat man since you took Morello out."

"We gotta take the shot right?" Vico asked.

"But if Joe the Boss is in there . . ." Cargo said.

Buster whispered through clenched teeth. "We don't know if he is in there."

"We gotta do it. I'm pulling the trigger," Vico said.

Sonny's breath caught in his lungs, refusing to escape until a searing pain shot through his chest. He became aware of the sweat on his palms and the cool steel of the revolver within them. Tremors developed through his extremities, and he couldn't stop blinking.

But in the midst of it all, he experienced clarity. He thought about the promise Maranzano made to him, that he wouldn't have to pull the trigger again. But he also considered how proud Maranzano would be if he did anyway.

"I'm going out there," he said.

"What?" Vico asked through gritted teeth.

"If they get away, we're all dead. I'm going around front." He didn't give them a chance to object. He grabbed his fedora and bolted out of the room. Enzo's eyes were wide and stained pink as he passed him by.

Sonny braced himself against the wall of the Pelham apartments and listened as the footsteps of the two men approached.

"We'll get that old bastard. That's not the problem. But the longer this shit continues, the more money I lose with my business in the garment district," one of men said.

"And hiding out like some rat has ruined my booze trade," the other said. "I got trucks getting highjacked, vigs not getting picked up. If this shit isn't over by Easter, I'm gonna go broke. I'll quit and get a job pumping gas or somethin'." They were getting closer.

Sonny pulled out his revolver and placed his finger inside the trigger well. His heartbeat was violent, reverberating throughout his chest. But he was present, keenly aware and alert. He heard every footstep and could somehow approximate their distance. "Excuse me," he said, stepping from the wall and into their path.

Both men looked at him, perplexed. He lifted the revolver and pulled the trigger with what felt like one swift motion. The blast sent the .45 barking back at him, his eyelids twitching in response.

The bullet ripped through Ferrigno's shoulder. Before he could recoil or reach for his own pistol, Ferrigno's head exploded.

Buster's tommy gun rattled like a piano. Shotguns barked and glass shattered.

What was left of Ferrigno hit the pavement. Mineo took one step forward.

Panic suddenly gripped Sonny's chest. He couldn't let Mineo get away. He lifted his revolver again and pulled the trigger until it reached an empty cylinder, hardly aiming. It was impossible to tell if they landed with so many of Buster's Tommy rounds ripping through Mineo's expensive threads.

Regardless, he didn't get far.

Mineo stood tall, twitching as bullets filled his face, chest, and stomach. He collapsed on top of Ferrigno, covering his associate's headless corpse.

Sonny heard Buster shouting orders in the room, and suddenly realized how vulnerable he was. If someone else exited Ferrigno's office, he would be directly in their line of fire.

Sonny tossed the Colt into nearby shrubbery as Maranzano had instructed him to do after a hit. It didn't belong to him anyway—it couldn't be traced. Vico pounced from the shattered glass window, oblivious to the cuts he sustained.

"We got about three minutes before the Bulls will have us in their sights," Sonny said in a cold voice.

Enzo paced around the side of the apartment building.

"And I ain't going up the river again!" Cargo barked, animated in a way that made him seem like a totally different person.

"I got a car staged a block east from here," Vico said, leading the way across the early morning traffic, joining the other citizens running ignoring the crosswalks to escape the Pelham apartments.

"A block?" Sonny asked, trying to remain calm and keep his voice low. He couldn't keep from looking over his shoulders though, fearing red and blue lights would be flashing any moment.

"Yeah, Buster has a car too. He and Cargo are splitting off." Vico broke into a dead sprint, crossing traffic. Enzo and Sonny followed close behind.

They jumped into the car, and Vico started it. He pulled out of the parking lot, onto the main road, passing by frightened citizens running from the sound of the gunshots.

Sonny leaned his head against the glass of the rearseat window. He was experiencing something strange. His senses were so heightened he wondered if Cargo had sprinkled some white powder on the garlic bread. But he knew it wasn't that. The color of the Fords and Oldsmobiles passing him . . . had they always been so bright? And he could smell better too, feeling certain Vico had spilled a beer in there recently. He was keenly aware of a bead of sweat clinging to the hair on the back of his calf.

But he couldn't focus on any of it for too long, his mind replaying the murders like a nickelodeon on repeat. At first he tried to stop, but then gave up. He was surprised and curious that it didn't seem to disturb him. He focused primarily on what exactly he said when he jumped from the wall and considered the verbiage he might use when recalling the tale for Maranzano and the boys.

"And that's just the beginning, boys," Vico said, to which neither brother replied.

6

BUSTER

Bronx, New York—November 5, 1930

Buster had never seen anything quite like it. Ferrigno's face had erupted. Every pellet of Vico's shot gun blast must have hit him. That would leave a message.

He hurried onto Pelham Parkway, ensuring that his fedora was pulled low over his face. The sidewalks were filling up with curious neighbors, who mumbled amongst themselves about what had happened.

Stupid people. They would be cowering inside if they really knew what happened. He thought to himself as he squeezed in between them.

"Excuse me. Sorry. Excuse me" was all he actually said. He held his violin case close to his chest so it wouldn't swing into bystanders. The last thing he needed was for someone to ask to see his instrument. They'd be surprised by the smoking barrel inside.

He escaped the majority of the crowd and quickened his pace. He prayed silently that Cargo would find his way to the car. Otherwise, he was gonna wind up dead or, worse, in shackles again.

"Hey, hold it!" someone shouted.

He turned to find two bulls charging at him, gold badges shining on their chests.

Buster stopped, but seriously considered breaking out into a sprint. He was still quick, but his limp could slow him down. If asked, he would say he got it from shrapnel in France, like he told everyone. Vico might be the only person to know different.

"What's going on?" the other asked, unassuming.

Buster calmed himself. "I think there was a shooting, officers. I heard loud noises and a lot of shouts. Everyone's got the meemies."

The two bulls looked at one another and shook their heads.

"These stupid Jews. Probably bootlegging," one of them said.

"Let's check it out," the other replied. They tipped their hats to him and hurried away.

Buster nearly collapsed from the relief, his heart pumping like a locomotive. When the bulls entered the throng of nosey gathers, Buster broke out into a dead sprint. Even his hobbled leg couldn't keep him back now. He had been close to death. Then close to arrest. Now, all he could think of was Maria.

It's almost over, baby.

7

SEBASTIANO

Benton Harbor, Michigan—October 16, 1916

The violin was the only thing that could block out the screams. He played loud to drown it out. He closed his eyes and tried to feel the music, become one with it, as his grandfather had taught him.

But the screams continued.

Glass broke in the kitchen.

A door slammed, and his father's booming voice echoed through the home, as the door was ripped back open.

"Come ere!" he shouted.

Sebastiano tried to focus on the music but was missing every note. His hands were trembling. A knot developed in his stomach, and tasted bile that always foreshadowed vomit. One would think that because his father's outbursts of violence were so common, he might be used to it, but that wasn't the case.

"Please, don't do this. Please, I'm sorry, I'm sorry!" he heard his mother's voice.

A belt snapped, and his mother moaned.

Something else shattered.

The tiny home, and Buster's thin door didn't provide any protection from the onslaught.

The door to his room opened, and he set down the violin. He would rather have all of his teeth knocked out than something happen to the instrument he had inherited from his grandfather.

When he didn't hear heavy breathing or smell stale beer, he knew it wasn't his father.

Sebastiano's little brother, Johnny, stood in the doorway. "You mind if I sleep in here tonight?" he asked.

Tall and lanky, Johnny had the pale face of a child. He was fourteen, but had the eyes and the heart of a kid about half that.

"Yeah, of course, Johnny boy." He held out an arm, and as Johnny approached he kissed him on the head. "It's gonna be all right."

Johnny nodded.

Buster had been repeating the same lie every other night for what seemed like their whole lives. Nothing ever seemed to change. Sebastiano knew that things weren't going to be all right, and Johnny probably knew it too, but somehow the words were still comforting. It somehow calmed Sebastiano's thumping heart to imagine some providence was out there that would fix everything eventually. Maybe their pa would get sober and go back to church. Maybe he would get a real job instead of searching for day labor jobs on the docks. They could be happy.

The current of pleasant thoughts evaporated as the sound of their mother's screams heightened. Something was different than usual.

Often she tried to hold in it in so as to not worry the children. She always told them they were simply arguing, as all parents do, and that she could handle it. Tonight, she belted out the screams.

Sebastiano turned to Johnny, finding him with a pillow clutched to his chest, and his tears staining it.

Something shifted in his gut. The knot that visited him each time his father was like this now burst into flames.

He stood and moved quickly for the door.

"Buster, what are you doing?" Johnny asked.

Sebastiano didn't stop to reply and yanked open the door. He navigated through the cluttered living room and opened the door to his parent's room.

His mother was on the floor, pinned in between the unmade bed and the wall. Her face, buried in the side of the mattress, was red and overflowing with streams of mascara.

Beside her, his father sat, panting and catching his breath. Belt still in hand, he took long gulps from his flask and wheezed through his smoker's lungs.

"Sebastiano, whatever you do . . . when you get married one day, find someone who treats you with respect. Someone who doesn't talk down to you, belittle you, disobey you," his father said, wiping the whiskey from his chin.

"Don't ever touch her again," Sebastiano said.

"What did you just say?" his father asked, face contorted as if he was posed with a difficult math question.

His mother struggled to her feet. She looked at Buster and shook her head. But he didn't acknowledge it. All he could see was the blood pouring from her lips, the purple swelling of her eye, and the streaks of pink across the bare flesh of her legs and arms.

"Sebastiano, I'll ask again. What did you just say to me?" his father asked, pouncing to his feet and snapping the belt.

"Buster, no," his mother cried.

As his father towered over him, Sebastiano began to second-guess himself. He was seventeen and had secretly cherished the idea of the day he would stand up to his father. He imagined that maybe his Pa would be proud of him and clap him on the back, and ultimately stop what he was doing. But he knew this wasn't true.

"I said don't you ever touch her again," he repeated, less confidently than the first time.

His father whipped the belt at Buster's face, leaving the flesh of his chin and neck partially numb and burning like fire. Buster recoiled, as he always had, but then launched forward. He rammed his shoulder into his father's gut. His father whipped the belt against his back, and at first stood firm, but after a moment he stumbled from the alcohol and crashed into the wooden floor.

Buster thrust his bodyweight on top of him, each whip of the belt strengthening him more. He sat up, now towering over his father, and began to punch.

His father caught the fists, his grip like a bull, and threw a punch of his own.

Buster's head swung around and for a moment he forgot where he was. He collected himself as he heard his mother's cries, louder than ever, and saw his frightened brother standing at the doorway.

His father held back Buster's hands, "You don't have what it takes to stand up to me. Not yet!"

Buster found himself shouting as he ripped away his

hands and thrust a flurry of punches into his father's scrunched face.

Shaken, his father tried to roll over. Buster pinned him down with his legs, punching with all his weight and not stopping even when as his knuckles cracked and his father's blood or saliva splashed against his cheek.

His father, no longer protecting himself, absorbed every blow to the cheek like it was playful.

Buster quickly stood, his adrenaline flooding through him. He grabbed a vase from his parents' dresser and shattered it over his father's head.

"Baby, no, no," his mother cried hysterically, collapsing to the floor again.

Buster kicked violently at his father's chest and gut, then to his face. He didn't stop until blood and teeth laid in a pool beneath his head.

He paused and collected himself and looked at his brother. Johnny held both hands over his mouth, his eyes wide and terrified.

A rush of emotions swept over Sebastiano. He didn't know how he felt, but he needed to vomit. His whole body seemed to vibrate. His legs felt like his mother's overcooked bucatini and he wondered if he might collapse.

"You hear me, pa? Don't ever touch my mother again. Or Johnny. You do and I'll kill you next time," Sebastiano said, his father rocking to his side, barely conscious.

He stepped back and caught a glance of himself in the mirror. Droplets of his father's blood dripped from his face and night shirt. Sebastiano moved past his brother and across the cluttered living room, back to his bedroom. He sat, picked up his violin, and continued to play.

Benton Harbor, Michigan- October 21, 1916

Sebastiano now felt like the outcast in his home. His mother avoided all eye contact with him and kept communication brief, cautious lest their interaction be seen as treachery by her husband. Johnny boy said nothing of the incident, but he no longer came to Sebastiano's room at night when he was scared.

His father said nothing. He was laid up in bed for several days, Sebastiano's mother nursing his wounds. He had lost his violent temper, but he seemed to lose something else too. He seemed soulless, drifting through the home with a distinguished limp and a battered face. He still drank a few bottles every night and took the cocaine the dentist prescribed for his chipped and missing teeth, but he simply stared at the wall. He said little to nothing, and never mentioned the incident to Sebastiano.

After a week passed, Buster almost wished to see his father return to that violent state he had grown accustomed to. He felt that a beating from his father would surely be easier than silence. But his father wouldn't even look him in the eye.

One of Sebastiano's favorite things to do growing up was chopping wood with his father and brother. When they were outside, in the cold air, thick with the smell of pine cones and white furs, they felt like men. They could laugh and make bawdy jokes, and Sebastiano didn't have to worry about the safety of his mother. Now, as they began to prepare for the 1916 winter, they gathered the wood in silence.

Sebastiano hadn't been playing music. It didn't feel right. There had been a time when his mother would play the piano, and his father would sing in Italian. Johnny boy would even cry sometimes. It was Buster's only fond memory with both of his parents. He doubted it would happen again, and his desire to learn how to play so he could join them in their symphony was now diminished.

"I'm going into town," he said to his mother one afternoon.

She continued working on the coat she was sowing. "For what?" she asked.

"I'm going to go talk to someone about the Army." He anticipated an avalanche of questions. Maybe a pleading cry for him to recant the statement and stay at home. Perhaps she would promise they could fix everything.

"Oh? What makes you want to do that?" she asked, straining her eyes to focus on the needle in her hand.

"Serve my country." He shrugged, disappointed in her response, and no longer had any desire to discuss it.

"I didn't know you were so patriotic."

"I'll be back by supper."

"I doubt it, but I'll leave something out for you. Pick up some onions while you're out, I'll need them for tomorrow's supper. I'll pay you back."

His mother had never seemed so cold. He opened the door, half in the warmth of the house, half in the Michigan cold. He lingered for a moment, wishing someone would stop him.

His father hobbled out from his bedroom and leaned up against the doorframe. For the first time since their fight, he looked Sebastiano in the eyes. But he said nothing.

8

SONNY

East Harlem, Manhattan—November 5, 1930

Sonny and his two brothers burst into Vico's apartment like a stampeding herd. Vico, not much of a host, didn't offer to show them around but searched for a bottle with a few drops of booze remaining. There wasn't much to see anyhow.

"That was close," Vico said, in good spirits for the first time since Sonny had seen him outside Maranzano's safe house.

"Close? Close? Are you kiddin' me?" Enzo threw off his coat and wiped the sweat from his forehead.

"We could have bulls on our tail now. No reason to think we got away clean," Sonny said, his eyes on the doorknob, imagining that it might start spinning. He double-checked that it was locked.

"We have a rock-solid alibi. Three brothers, back together at last," Vico said, finding a bottle beneath the kitchen sink.

"When they get here, should I tell them you are Vico Consentino or Bobby Doyle?" Sonny asked.

Vico drained the bottle of what little remained and turned to him. They locked eyes. "I've done what I had to."

"Seems like you've done a little more than that," Sonny said.

Vico shrugged and looked around the barren apartment.

Enzo paced to the window and pushed Sonny out of the way, keeping an eye on the road the way they had been watching for their enemies.

"You should have never been wrapped up in this shit, Sonny. We were going to take care of it," Vico said. He finally stopped and looked at Enzo across the room. "I was going to take care of it."

"And how would I have known that?" Sonny said, a bit of anger in his voice, something that he felt unable to express except with his family. "You guys disappeared fifteen years ago. We were surprised you showed up at the damn funeral."

Vico's anger flushed for a moment, and he moved across the room like he was approaching a target. "Papa kicked us out. We didn't want to leave." Vico put a finger in Sonny's chest.

"Yeah," Sonny said, lifting his hands in surrender.

"We should have gone back, Vico." Enzo's voice cracked. "We should have went back home, hat in hand, after I got out of Sing Sing and you got back from war. That's where we messed up. None of this should have happened."

"That's on you, 'Enzo the Thief'!" Vico roared, hurrying now to his twin. He picked him up by his shirt collar and buried his forehead in Enzo's. "You did this. You told me they didn't want to see me. You tried to get me involved with your little operation. You made damn well sure I would never go back. Didn't you? You knew I would do anything you said, right? Cause I always did."

For a moment, Sonny thought Vico might strike Enzo, but the elder twin closed his eyes and remained passive and still.

Shame in his voice, Enzo finally said, "You're right, Vico."

"But I'm not your little brother anymore, am I?" Vico said. "I don't follow your orders anymore, do I? I'm my own man." He stood and looked back at Sonny. "And I'm gonna make sure that whoever killed dad is chopped up into little bits. You hear me? I don't care if I die doing it. I will kill him myself."

It was hard for Sonny to imagine that the man before him was his mild-mannered older brother. So much had changed. "That's what I've been trying to do," Sonny said, careful to keep his voice calmer than before.

"What? You? Little college boy? What do you know about killin'?" Vico found another bottle on the couch and sat to indulge.

"You saw me shoot Ferrigno and Mineo, right? Or did you miss that? And I already got the guy I thought killed dad. Old Hook Hand," Sonny said.

Enzo shook his head. "Old Peter Morello didn't do it. That crossed my mind too. Me and Vico were both suspicious. That greaseball was a weird cat when we was growing up. But it seems like he actually vouched for dad. Took care of him."

"That's what I decided too. But only after the fact. It was Maranzano that told me it was Morello."

"That old man was a nobody back then. He might be a

pezzonovante now, but he didn't know what was going on. Smoke and mirrors," Vico said.

"I wouldn't talk like that anymore unless you want to wind up dead yourself," Enzo said.

"What? One of you two gonna rat?" he asked, analyzing his brothers. Both were silent.

"If it wasn't Morello, then who was it?" Sonny asked, trying to extinguish the guilt he felt in eliminating a man who may have been his father's friend.

"We talked to Gagliano," Enzo said, "he was on the General Assembly."

"What is that?" Sonny asked.

"Group of a lot of bosses from all over the country. Makes important decisions about who lives and dies, at least big shots. And I guess they still considered Papa a big shot from his days in Sicily, or at least because of his connection to Morello. Gagliano was there when Papa was discussed. Some fella from Sicily was the guy who wanted dad out of the picture."

"They said his name was Turridru," Vico added.

"Turridru?"

"Yeah," Vico nodded, "me and Enzo knew that Papa palled around with a guy named Turridru back in Sicily, but he was a nobody. And I don't know why he would want to see Papa whacked. I mean we called the guy 'Uncle Turridru.' It doesn't make sense."

"We need to figure out who he is then," Sonny said. He was glad to finally hear a name. If he could just find that man, maybe he could get away from this life. Move away, start over, knowing that his father could finally rest.

"Why?" Enzo walked over to them. "Why in the hell do we have to know? Everyone thinks that it was Morello who done it, and he's dead. Everyone knows it was Sonny who killed him, so they think Papa's death was repaid."

"See this?" Vico looked at Sonny and pointed at his twin, "he talks like this all the time. He wants to just let it go."

"You're right. I do." Enzo spoke with more color than he had in a while, using his hands to express what his words could not. "We just keep getting deeper and deeper and deeper. Eventually we're all gonna die chasing down this guy we don't know from a cup of applesauce. We're gonna die, or end up behind bars again. And for what? It's not gonna bring Dad back. It's not gonna put food on Ma's table. Nothing. It does nothing."

"I want to see Turridru dead, Enzo. I can't rest until then," Vico said.

"And you're willing to give up everything so's somebody else dies? Give up your freedom? Your life?"

"If that's what it takes," Vico said.

"That's not what Papa would have wanted. He wanted us to stay out of this shit," Enzo pleaded.

"He was involved too," Sonny added.

"So?" Enzo said. "He was involved so that we wouldn't have to be."

"Well, you did a standup job dragging me into this shit for someone who wants to get out," Vico said.

"You're right." Enzo knelt before his brother. "I know I did. I had it all wrong, brother. I wanted the cars, girls, respect, and some damn fun. I wanted to move into a place that didn't have bedbugs and we didn't have to wait for Mr. Testa to finish taking a hot shit before we could shower. I thought I could sell some hooch, rob some folks, have a different life. But now we gotta get out. This isn't what we signed up for. We just killed two guys we don't even know, for some war we don't know anything about."

"I did that a lot in France, remember? I got used to it." Vico looked away and took a swig of booze.

"This is different, and you know it. We have to find a way out of this life," Enzo said.

Sonny hung his head and considered it. What if Enzo was right? What if they could just leave? Maybe they could reopen the barber shop and be the men Alonzo had wanted them to be. Maranzano would understand.

"Enzo," Vico said, his voice barely audible. He lowered his head. "I need this."

"You need what?"

Vico stared off in contemplation. He lit a cigarette. "The hunt. I need something. It gives me purpose, trying to track this guy down."

"You can find something else, Vico." Enzo looked up at Sonny, his eyes wet. "We all can."

"Not me. You two, maybe. Not me. I can't just go back to boxing or working construction. This is who I am supposed to be," Vico said.

All three brothers remained silent for a moment.

"You were always a leader, Enzo. You were funny, charming. People liked you and liked being around you. Sonny, you was always too smart for your own damn good—could have been anything. You're right. You two need to get out. But this is all I've ever been good at. I'm a killer, boys, it's who I am supposed to be. At least killing Turridru will bring something good out of all the bad I've done."

"We can't let you go at it alone," Sonny said. Things would never be the same again—the life they had once lived together was severed for good—but he felt there was a bond that existed between them that was theirs to keep.

Vico looked up at Sonny and nodded.

Enzo stepped back, away from them both. He. His breathing seemed labored and his nostrils flared.

"Well, you two can go ahead then," Enzo said. His eyebrows furrowed, tears welling up again. "I can't imagine letting you do anything without me," he addressed Vico, "but I can't keep doing this. I was wrong. I can't do this, and I thought I could." He grabbed his coat and put on his fedora. "I'll take care of Ma after you two are gone and make sure you receive proper burials. Alongside Papa."

The door closed behind Enzo as he left.

Sonny sat on the couch beside Vico, who offered him the bottle of whiskey without saying anything. In silence they sat, thinking about who this Turridru might be, and whether they were actually right to try and kill him.

Upper East Side, Manhattan—November 6, 1930

Sonny was ushered into the safe house by Charlie Buffalo. Bodyguards and lookouts filled the room, but Maranzano's low voice was the only sound. The Don was hovering over a map, Bonanno and Gagliano seated on his left and right, respectively.

They stood when they saw him.

"If it isn't the war hero himself," Bonanno said, extending his arm for a hug.

Cargo stepped in front of him. "Everything went hurdy-gurdy, Mr. Maranzano. We got 'em," he said, anxious to get his share of the credit.

Charlie Buffalo, always the most annoyed with Cargo's perpetually incorrect vocabulary, popped the back of Cargo's head. "The saying is honky-dory. Or Hotsie-Totsie. Damnit, just get it right."

Everyone seemed to ignore them and looked to Sonny.

Sonny addressed Maranzano directly. "The hit went successfully. Joe Masseria never popped up again, but Ferrigno and Al Mineo are no more."

The boss kissed Sonny's cheek and held his hands within his own.

"I'm very proud of you, Vincente," he said.

Sonny nodded but lowered his head.

"Gentlemen, would you excuse me for a moment?" Maranzano asked, taking Sonny in his arms and leading him away from the war room to the kitchen. "I know that a lot has been asked of you, Vincente. And for that, I apologize." Maranzano was genuinely contrite. He locked eyes with Sonny, his brows furrowed, and his face contorted in guilt.

"Don't mention it." Sonny tried to shrug it off.

"But I have to. It was not so long ago that I met you as a businessman. Sometimes I feel guilt for having wrapped you up in all of this. I would not have done so if it wasn't because I need you,"

"Don Maranzano . . ." Sonny started but didn't know what to say.

"No, listen to me. I have been selfish. I know that you never desired this life. Like me, you are not just chasing the money, and the passing pleasures of this short life. You search for honor, as I do. In my drive for success, I have overlooked that you had other desires for how to achieve your honor."

"Everything I've done has been by my own consent. You have nothing to apologize for," Sonny said.

Maranzano patted his shoulder and nodded. “I am pleased to hear you say so. But regardless . . .”

Sonny began to think Maranzano was going to offer him a way out. He waited anxiously for the Don to continue.

“I have begun to look on you as a son. I want what is best for you,”

Sonny choked up. He nodded along with the Don but couldn’t find the right words to respond.

“This will be over soon, Sonny. I know that you have now avenged your father, and you will want to return to your regular way of life. This is chief amongst my concerns, to get you back to selling insurance and making us all money.” Maranzano smiled for the first time, and patted Sonny’s blushing cheeks.

“Well, I’m not sure that my father has been avenged, Don Maranzano,” Sonny said.

“What do you mean?” Maranzano asked, perplexed.

“Morello doesn’t seem to have been behind my father’s murder. I’ve talked to my brothers, and they’ve done some research themselves.”

Maranzano became serious. “Vincente, if I have misled you, I apologize. You must understand that that was what I heard.”

Sonny recalled how Vico had said Maranzano had been a nobody even as recently as 1928, and so he believed him. “I do not place the fault with you. I should have spent less time collaborating with the police who didn’t care about my father, and more time talking with those who knew about what happened.”

“I am grieved. Morello needed to be disposed of regardless, but it could have been someone else to do so. I wouldn’t have given this task to you if I had known.”

Sonny nodded. At times he did wish he hadn’t killed

Morello, especially if he'd truly been looking out for Alonzo's best interests. But the event taught him one thing: he had the ability to kill. And he would need that if he was to confront the true killer. "It put me one step closer to finding who really killed my father. And as you've said, my Morello needed to be disposed of."

Maranzano tried to smile, but sadness lingered in his eyes. He seemed human for the first time since Sonny had known him.

"My brother Enzo told me the man who ordered his death was named Turridru. A man who may have known my father in Sicily."

Maranzano's face hardened, then his eyes narrowed in confusion. "Turridru? They said the man who killed your father was named Turridru?"

"Called Turridru, at least. It may have been a nickname."

Maranzano tapped his forefinger against his lip and considered it. "I feel as if I've heard the name. I knew your father briefly in Sicily as well, and I may have come across this Turridru."

"Anything you can tell me about him would help," Sonny said, hoping the Don would have something for him.

"I cannot recall anything, but I will think on it. Turridru, Turridru . . ." He looked at the ground, his eyes moving rapidly as if watching a nickelodeon reel of his time in Sicily. "I will make it my chief concern to find him, Sonny. I will make things right by giving you the correct killer."

"That's the only thing I would ask of you, Don Maranzano." Sonny bowed his head.

"Joseph, can you come here?" Maranzano shouted into the living room.

Bonanno hurried to answer the call. "Yes?"

"Vincente has received the name of who killed his father. It was the nickname of a man who came from Sicily. He went by the name Turridru. I want all of our men to keep their ears pinned. If we find out who it is, I need to be alerted immediately."

Bonanno looked blank, but eventually nodded.

Maranzano kissed Sonny's cheek again and clasped the back of his neck. "The moment I know something, you will too," he said.

And Sonny believed him.

9

VICO

Argonne Forest, France—September 20, 1918

Vico's feet were soaked within his muddy boats. Lice made nests in what little hair he had left after basic training. His skin crawled with a permanent itch. His ankles were swollen, and he had a nagging suspicion he had actually broken something in his left forearm. But, when he laid still, he felt a bit better.

His helmet had worn indentions in his forehead. At first he resisted it, and took it off for a scratch whenever he found a moment outside of an officer's sight. Now, he let it sit.

He leaned the tip of his bayonet up against the brim of his helmet and sat in the dirt. Gun shots and artillery shells sounded in the distance, but they no longer worried him. They faded into his subconscious. For now he was safe, and that was all that mattered.

"Consentino, where's Buck?" Sergeant Camponello asked, his Lewis slung over his shoulder.

"On point," he said, trying again to settle into his mind. The more he tried to ignore everything happening around him, the more the movements of the doughboys to his left and right bothered him.

"Hey, you got a light, Private?" one of the other platoon's Sergeants came and plopped down beside him before receiving an answer.

Nearly all the men in the battalion were immigrants. Most of them were Irish, a few were Italian. This sergeant, Domingo, was from Castellamare del Golfo, though.

"Yeah, Sergeant." He fished it out, and resumed his restful stance, like a Buddhist priest. He didn't want to move. Any movement proved that all this was real, that he was really here. When he was still enough, he could imagine himself back at the apartment he shared with Enzo on the corner of Sixth and Grand, or better yet, he could imagine himself back in Little Italy with his entire family.

"Thanks."

Vico and Sergeant Domingo were alike in more ways than heritage. They both had an appreciation for silence and solitude.

"You ever think about Sicily?" This time, Domingo seemed set on interacting, and Vico took note.

"Sometimes, Sergeant. I was young when I left. Can only remember certain things."

"Yeah, me too," He took a long drag of his cigarette, and Vico decided to have one as well. He still had six left of his week's ration. "I would like to go back."

Sergeant Domingo was fair skinned for a Sicilian, with an oval face and pursed lips. He was slender and fit, every part the soldier, but was somehow an individual in the midst of all his men. Something about his green eyes, maybe.

"I'd go back. Move there, even."

"Really? Be a helluva lot closer to all this shit." They both smiled. Sergeant Domingo laughed at himself. "Sometimes... Sometimes I think that if I died out here, I'd like Heaven to be a place like Sicily."

"Yeah? You think it will be?"

"Golden streets wouldn't do it for me. I don't even know what a pearly gate would look like."

"Come on, up! Up!" the call came.

Vico lowered his head and exhaled. No matter how much quiet time they were given, it was never enough.

Domingo rose beside him and extended a hand to help him up. "Whenever all this is over . . . if we make it back . . . you should look me up back in the States. We'll grab a drink."

Vico was caught off guard by the cordiality.

"I'd like that, Sergeant."

"See you on the other side." Sergeant Domingo shrugged and ensured that his Springfield was clean and loaded.

Vico did the same and followed him to the line.

Argonne Forest, France- October 8, 1918

Vico's hands caressed the leather of the Army-issued New Testament in his pocket. He received it in boot-camp and hadn't read a single word since that evening, but it felt good to have it near him. He just liked to hold it, touch it. It somehow calmed him.

He rested against his pack in the foxhole he dug the day before. It was time for some much-needed rest, and the artillery fire in the distance wasn't going to keep him from it.

The shallow breaths and quiet sobs from the foxhole beside him just might, though. He pecked over the edge, to Domingo's foxhole beside him.

"Hey, Sergeant, you square?" Vico asked.

Since they arrived in the Argonne, he had seen several men cry in their foxholes, he had seen several men break under the weight of what the war did to them and asked them to do. He was surprised to find he cared very little about most of this. It was part of life in the War. When Domingo wept though, he took notice.

It wasn't only because they were friends, although they had been inseparable the past several weeks. As the men of both of their companies had received their "wooden crosses" in death, the two companies had amalgamated, and the two had stuck by each other ever since.

But that wasn't why he was concerned. He had never seen Domingo break before, and Vico didn't assume the noncommissioned officer was the kind of man to fold under pressure, despite all the things they had recently seen and done.

The sobs continued, so Vico ignored his weary bones and climbed out of his foxhole.

Domingo leaned up against the wall of dirt behind him, with one hand on a letter and the other on the helmet, pulling it over his eyes.

"Hey, Sergeant? Everything okay?"

Domingo looked away to hide the tears on his face. "Yeah, yeah. It's fine, Consentino." Vico didn't move, so the Sergeant continued, "It's word from back home. My dad killed himself."

Death had been very much a part of their life in France. They made light of it, and often made the extinguished lives of their pals into a joke. They had to. Vico couldn't think of anything to say about a death like that back home. Only crude and unhelpful jokes came to mind, so he deferred to silence.

"He had his problems. But he was my dad."

"I'm sorry to hear that," Vico said.

Finally Domingo looked up. Tears had left trails through the soot covering his face, and his eyes were strained. "I wanted something better to go back to."

Vico wanted to say something else, but instead, he hopped in the foxhole beside his Sergeant. He fished out his last two cigarettes and handed one to Domingo. He lit the Sergeant's, and then his own, before materializing a canteen. He lifted it into the air and locked eyes with Domingo.

"To the lost," Vico said, pouring some out.

Domingo began to cry again, and the two sat beside each other, smoking the cigarettes until the very end.

Argonne Forest, France—October 21, 1918

They had been on recon for almost a week. Five days and nineteen-hours, to be exact. Sergeant Domingo was tasked with the objective of taking a lone pillbox on top of a thickly wooded hill. Several Germans were held up there, but it was difficult to tell how many. Regardless of their numbers, they had weapons and ammunition, and they had been plucking off doughboys for weeks, halting their advance.

Vico was beginning to lose his senses. He assumed from the droopy, pink-rimmed eyes that his comrades were as well. They had drank very little, eaten even less. They tried to hold their piss at first, as some of them had been suspicious that the Germans might smell it, but as the days rolled on it became impossible to do so.

They were exhausted but restless. When the night would turn to morning, they would each look at Domingo, awaiting the order to attack the hill. But he was being cautious. Ever since he had received word that his father was dead, Domingo had been different. He had been promoted quickly after enlisting, based on his courage and reputation as a sharpshooter alone. But now, facing his first objective as the Noncommissioned Officer in Charge, he seemed unsure of what to do.

The morning of October 21 was like the rest, freezing cold and dark. They could never tell if the sky was covered in clouds, or if it was the canopy of trees above them that blocked the sun's rays. A little drizzle was falling, and it stung the bare flesh of Vico's face.

Domingo, who Vico hadn't seen sleeping since they had left, was looking over the dune of mud at the pillbox in the distance. They hadn't spotted the jerries in more than twenty-four hours, but every once in awhile, they thought they heard them. Given the distance between their position and that of the Germans, it was highly improbable. It was most likely a trick of deception by the forest, and their own weariness.

The reticence on Domingo's face told Buster that he was wondering whether or not the Germans had been starved out and simply left their position. If that was the case, they wouldn't have to take the hill, or sustain any casualties.

"Franklin," Domingo whispered at length, turning to the four men spread out behind him, "move forward. Post up, three hundred yards, nine o'clock. Give us a signal if you see them."

Franklin nodded and crouched. He wobbled for a moment, unaccustomed to being on his feet after five days in recon, but then hurried forward.

"Time to move up, Sergeant?" Corporal Flaherty asked, a little bit of Irish in his voice.

"Maybe, Corporal. I want to make sure they're there. I don't feel comfortable rushing in when we don't know what kind of manpower they have." Domingo stated the obvious. He was clearly not comfortable with advancing, otherwise they wouldn't have been laying in the cold for five days.

Vico tried to be patient though. He knew that Domingo had their best interests in mind, and so decided that if they must wait, it was so that more of them could make it back alive.

As Private Franklin shrunk in the distance, Domingo looked at Vico. They didn't spend as much time joking. Most of their interaction was simply in silence and the sharing of cigarettes. But regardless, the bond they had created was strong. That one glance told Vico all that he needed to know. That Domingo hoped he was doing the right thing and hoped that Vico and the rest of them would make it back all right.

Franklin's silhouette stalled in the distance. He

crouched behind a formation of rocks and laid his Springfield overtop it. He pulled out a pair of binoculars and analyzed the hill. After a moment, he turned and signaled.

"He went more than 300 yards. I can't see him." Domingo said, flustered. "Hand me some binoculars." He stretched out his hand and Corporal Flaherty hastened to do so. Domingo focused them for a moment.

Franklin stood and continued to signal.

"That's it. He's giving the hand and arm signal. Let's move," the Sergeant said. They grabbed what little they had around them and began to align in a wedge formation.

A gunshot pierced through the silent morning air and rang out across the treetops.

Franklin's head jerked, his body crumbled. Even from the distance, they could see a red mist rising over the private's corpse.

"Shit, shit," Corporal Flaherty said, his eyes alight with terror as he watched his friend tumble down the embankment like a discarded child's doll.

"They got him," Vico said, as they all hastened to find cover.

Domingo remained standing. He dropped the binoculars from his hand, and his rifle hung from the sling around his shoulder.

"Orders, Sergeant?" Corporal Flaherty asked.

Domingo turned, wide-eyed, staring through them at nothing in particular. His lips quivered and his nose flared.

"Sergeant, we need orders." Flaherty said again.

"He's shell-shocked," said the only other doughboy of equal rank, Sergeant Mckenzie.

"Just give him a second," Vico pleaded.

"They know we're here. They know he wasn't alone," Flaherty said. "Sergeant Mckenzie, you need to take command."

"Come on, he's just thinking," Vico said, but his own faith was wavering.

Domingo took off his helmet and took a knee. He put his hands in the dirt and scooped up some in his hands.

"You three, on me," Sergeant Mckenzie said, standing from his position and moving forward.

Domingo remained behind.

They hadn't crossed half the distance to where Franklin's body now lay before the gunshots rang out. They were covered by trees, but the bark exploded all around them.

"I count three guns, maybe four," Private Murdaugh said, one hand on his rifle stock and the other on his helmet.

"Four," Vico said. His heart raced but somehow his breathing slowed. This was much less agonizing than the waiting.

As the other men waited for the volley to cease, Vico took a few lunges up the hill, stopping for cover a few times along the way.

He positioned his Springfield overtop a jagged rock, and focused in on the pillbox. He waited and counted in breaths. He spotted the grey uniform of a soldier and pulled the trigger immediately.

German curses rang out from the pillbox.

"Got one," Vico said, hurrying to his feet to change his position. The others followed his example. Bullets began to fly again, the dirt springing up like a land mine explosion all around them.

Vico found a spot that suited him and set up once more. A bullet ricocheted off the ground in front of him, cutting his face with bits of broken rock. He shook the pain off and readjusted. He fired, and more curses rang out through the forest valley.

"Another down."

After a moment, more gunshots ignited, but much slower and more controlled.

"All right, let's move," Sergeant Mckenzie said, whipping the dirt from his Springfield. "Maintain your spacing."

They hurried to follow the Sergeant, but Vico kept a weary eye on the pillbox.

They moved up the hill quickly and tried to ignore the corpse of Private Franklin lying to the right of their position. The German's fired again, but behind them.

"Go!" Mckenzie shouted as the group reached due west of the pillbox, less than a hundred yards away. They all raised their rifles and shot. The Germans were protected by the cement pillbox, but at least they would let them know they were there.

"These assholes better surrender!" Murdaugh said, jolting from his rifle blast.

Vico moved around and past them. He was going to be the first man to the pillbox. He would kill them for what they did to Franklin. It was war. He didn't blame them. He didn't hate them. But the debt must be repaid. Blood for blood.

When he reached the side of the German position, he heard their frantic cries from within. Some of them were wounded. He couldn't tell by what they said, but the fear in their voices made him sure they had already won the day. He braced himself against the cold cement fortification and ensured his magazine was loaded, and his bolt was clear of any obstructions. He counted his breaths again and went through a line or two of the Hail Mary his father had taught him. Springing from the wall, he charged at the entrance.

A man appeared around the other side. He lifted his rifle, and almost shot, but quickly realized that his Sergeant Domingo had circled around from the East.

Domingo charged into the pillbox. He popped off three rounds, and when the wails of the German's reached their highest, he lunged his bayonet into a man's chest.

When Vico entered, the German's were all cold and dead, silent and harmless. Vico stood over them, breathing heavily. He turned, his face streaked with tears and splattered with blood.

The others on the patrol had ceased their volley and hurried to the entrance.

"Got a pigeon?" Vico said, placing his hands akimbo on his hips.

Private Murdaugh reached into his pack and pulled out the bird cage.

"He's weak."

"He'll make it back to camp," Vico said. "Send a message. Tell them the hill is ours."

Murdaugh hurried to scribble out the note.

Domingo looked first at the corpses, and then at Vico. As before, that glance told Vico all that he needed to know.

Argonne Forest, France—November 10, 1918

"What in the hell are we supposed to do now?" Private Murdaugh said with a sad grin.

Vico shook his head and took a sip of beer. Nothing had ever tasted better. They had passed the drinks out in crates, and cigars too, to celebrate the cessation of combat, which was rumored to be effective the next day. But Vico didn't feel like there was anything to celebrate.

Private First Class Franklin from Knoxville, Corporal Flaherty from Boston, Sergeant Mckenzie from Louisiana: they weren't celebrating. They had been good friends of Vico's, and Sergeant Domingo's too, and now they were buried in the overgrown Argonne Forest. The war never ended for them.

"I mean, seriously, what are you boys going to do?" Murdaugh asked again.

"Maybe I'll shine shoes," Vico said with a wink as he relit his cigar. "You got big plans, Sarge?" Vico nudged Domingo with his boot.

"My grandfather owns a distillery in Chicago. Maybe I'll work there. I worked in construction before the war, maybe I'll do that. I hadn't really considered it," Domingo said.

It dawned on Vico that he hadn't either. None of them had truly expected to make it out alive. The concept of death was difficult to comprehend, even for the doughboys who had seen a great deal of it, but they rather imagined that the war would continue forever. A perpetual existence of "going over the top," dodging bullets and bayoneting jerries.

"Could you really go back to that? After all of this?"

Murdaugh bit his thumb nail. His feet tapped beneath him.

"The first thing I'm gonna do, Daugh, is drink myself into oblivion. Then maybe I'll eat some pasta and take a nap. That's about as far as I plan ahead."

"You ever considered law enforcement?" Domingo patted his Springfield. "At least you'll get to keep a gun in your hand."

"Nah, all the cops in Manhattan are Irish. I'm not sure I'd fit it," Vico said. "Plus, I'm not sure how they'd feel about my arrest." He had mentioned it to Domingo before, who hadn't asked any questions or treated him differently, but it was still uncomfortable to bring up.

"I'm gonna find me a girl," Murdaugh said.

"Good luck with that, kid," Domingo said as Murdaugh kicked dirt at him.

"Come on, now, there will be dames lined up on every street in South Carolina waiting for a war hero like me to come along."

Domingo laughed, and it infected them all. "I can't tell you how many times I've laid awake in the trenches trying to remember what a woman smells like." Domingo shook his head.

"Yup."

Vico echoed. "You better believe it."

"I can hardly remember it," Domingo said.

"Oh boy, Sarge is gonna be chasing skirt like a wolf." Vico laughed and slapped Domingo on the shoulder.

"I'll leave that to you, Consentino. I'd take one good one over a thousand of the kind of broads who'd keep company with the likes of you two."

They laughed. Each soldier returned to his own thoughts, trying to answer Murdaugh's question in a way that satisfied them. They watched as the other doughboys sang songs and chugged their drinks, good cheer abounding.

The smile faded from Vico's face. It was going to be a long road home.

10

LUCIANO

Bronx, New York—December 4, 1930

"Why would you tell me? Because if you don't tell me I'll break your damn legs." Charlie Luciano cracked his knuckles.

The man sitting at the desk before Luciano was the stereotypical slummy landlord. Fat, lazy, and entitled. He came to the Pelham Parkway apartment complex to get some information, but he was beginning to hope the landlord would keep acting so arrogant so he could rough him up a bit.

"I apologize for my friend." Luciano's associate, Meyer Lansky stepped forward, and held out his hands for them both to calm down. "Do you mind if I speak to Mr. Rosenburg in Yiddish, Charlie?" he asked.

Luciano shrugged, losing interest in the entire situation. Luciano had been beaten and cut up within an inch of his life a year ago and had the scars and droopy eyelid to prove it. This helped him appear intimidating, which could be useful to be certain, but Meyer's babyface and calm demeanor could take a different tact if required.

"Why is he so rude?" the landlord said in Yiddish.

Luciano couldn't speak it, but he had picked up a great deal from spending time with his Jewish associates like Meyer and Arnold Rothstein.

"My friend is overzealous," Lansky said. The landlord locked eyes with Luciano, who shrugged and pretended he couldn't understand them.

"We need to know who rented that apartment. We would be very grateful if you would be inclined to tell us. And we are good friends to have." Lansky smiled his famous smile, and the landlord's shoulders relaxed.

"I can't do that. It's against the rules. I'm not supposed to share any of my tenants' information except with the coppers." Rosenburg shrugged, as if helpless, wishing he could do more.

"But whoever rented that apartment is no longer a tenant, are they? They used your property to murder two fine gentlemen and then fled." Lansky said.

Luciano was pleased with how his friend was handling it, but still wished he could knock the landlord out.

"That is true. But how can I expect to get more people to come and live here if I am throwing their information around so casually?" Rosenberg asked.

Meyer gestured to the apartment complex behind him. "It doesn't look like there are many people here. I'm sure business is struggling since the murders took place."

The landlord crossed his arms and attempted to look unperturbed, but eventually exhaled and consented.

"Yes. My tenants are leaving in flocks, and not a soul has dropped off an application in a month." Rosenberg threw up his hands, defeated.

Meyer reached into his coat and pulled out a crisp roll of dollar bills.

"I'm sure you could use a little help until the bad press dies down." Lansky smiled, and Luciano felt himself doing the same.

"Probably true." Rosenberg tapped his chin, and then reached to grab the cash. "I suppose it wouldn't hurt if I simply told you the girl's name?" he said, beginning to thumb through some files.

Lansky turned to look at Luciano, eyebrows raised. He seemed both proud at his successful persuasion and surprised to hear that the apartment was registered to a female.

"Ah, her name's Marsha. Marsha Wallace."

Luciano shrugged, not placing the name.

"Think you could tell us anything else?" Meyer asked, brandishing another clip of dollar bills.

Rosenberg took it and licked his thumbs to flip the page.

"Her former residence was in Greenwich Village. She works at the Rainbow Gardens."

Luciano's ears perked up at the mention of the bar. Lansky shot him a look. They were thinking the same thing.

"Gagliano's crew. The bastard," Luciano said under his breath.

"Sounds like it," Lansky said. He wrapped his knuckles against the landlord's desk and turned to leave. "Thank you for your help, sir." Lansky tipped his hat.

"Sure you don't need to know anything else?" the landlord asked.

Luciano rose a middle finger to the man as they departed.

"So it wasn't the Castellamare crew after all," Lansky

said as their dark and imposing associate Vito Genovese opened up the door for Luciano.

"Use your noodle, Meyer. They're involved. They're shacked up with Gagliano's crew. Practically paintin' it on the damn walls. We need to tell Joe the Boss. He's gonna want something done fast."

"Then let's beat him to the punch," Meyer said.

"What did we find out?" Frank Costello asked from the driver seat, as he stepped on the gas.

"Apartment was registered to some quiff from the Rainbow Gardens. What was the name?" Luciano asked.

"Marsha Wallace," Lansky said.

"Right. Marsha Wallace." Luciano clicked his tongue. "Frank, drop us off at the place. Then I want you and Genovese to do some homework. Find out who this girl is and who she saves her last dance for. I'd say that's our guy."

"Done."

Garment District, Manhattan- December 8, 1930

"Fold," Luciano said, throwing his cards onto the table. He was having shit luck. Not just in his card game, but in life.

"Hey don't worry, Lucky," Luciano's friend Costello said with a wily grin. "I'll keep taking your money all night."

"*Vaffanculo*, eh?" Luciano cursed. His friends seemed to be in good spirits, but he certainly wasn't. Luck was a bitch, he thought.

He had more guts and brains than all the bosses put

together, but it didn't matter. He had hitched his horse to the wrong wagon. He and his crew had attached themselves to Joe "the Boss" Masseria because he was the most powerful gangster in New York. He was supposed to be invincible, savvy, intelligent. Luciano hadn't found that to be the case.

Instead, Luciano had decided that the gluttonous boss was inept and had no business leading the war against men like Maranzano and Gagliano. But that was his fate, to be tied to a dumb boss.

The next hand was dealt, and he was more pleased with his cards. Two pair and a chance for a flush. He leaned back in his chair and hoped that the others couldn't identify his tell.

Hell, maybe he shouldn't be so downcast. Maybe the fat boss would die, and then he could take over as the boss of bosses and take the fight to Gagliano and Maranzano himself. In the meantime, he would have to do the groundwork to solidify his position.

The door to the backroom opened, and Genovese hurried to the table.

"Whoa, slow down, Buster Brown," Costello said. "What's eating you?"

"Sorry, Mr. Luciano," the door guard said. "I told him it was a private game, but he wouldn't listen."

"Lucky," Genovese's voice was low and serious, as it always was, "I found the guy."

"Who? Oh the guy from Pelham? Who was it?"

Genovese eyed the other members of the table cautiously.

"Don't worry about them. I vouch for them," Luciano said.

"That broad, Marsha Wallace. She saved her special

dance for one of Gagliano's guys. His name was Enzo Consentino."

"Never heard of him," Luciano said.

"I have. Enzo the Thief, they call him." Costello nodded. "Low level guy, but he's made some friends in the Gagliano crew."

Luciano leaned back in his chair and rubbed his chin.

After a moment of deliberation, he stood and scooted in his chair. "Cash me out."

"Oh, come on, Lucky! That cat can wait a few hours. I'm sure he's in no rush to die," Costello said, anxious to win more of Luciano's money.

"I'm going to see Joe the Boss," Lucky said. "I'll let him decide what to do."

Coney Island, Brooklyn—December 10, 1930

Luciano ascended the steps to the *Nuovo Villa Tammara*, an Italian restaurant in Coney Island, and tried to prepare himself. Masseria liked to test him, making little comments that got under his skin, to see if he would react. Luciano couldn't afford to do so.

"The Boss here?" Luciano asked the man standing guard by the door. After a moment he recognized Luciano and stepped aside.

The *Tammara* was empty, except for Masseria's table in the center of the room. Luciano knew the owner, Al Scarpato, and it irritated him that his acquaintance was losing out on revenue from the dinnertime rush to fill

Masseria's needs, but he was sure the Boss would pay him back in other ways.

Luciano took off his hat and approached the table. Masseria and his dinner guests were jubilant and still reeling from what must have been a good joke and didn't acknowledge him for a few moments.

Masseria, regardless of his laughter, was attacking his plate of spaghetti like a drooling mastiff. Of course he was, thought Luciano. He was becoming a caricature. Dressed in the finest clothes, but with marinara and wine stains on his pinstripe suit, Masseria didn't have the charisma to be a boss controlling as much as he did. But there were two things Luciano knew about Masseria that kept him in power.

First, he had proved over the years to be nearly invincible. Twelve men had tried to take his life, and twelve had failed. All of them disappeared shortly thereafter, only to be discovered months later filled with bullet holes and bloated from spending so long buried under water.

Second, Masseria would kill a man as easily as look at him. No matter who someone was, Masseria wouldn't hesitate to order someone's death if they so much as looked at him wrong. Luciano knew if he didn't mind his place, he was likely to end up in Masseria's meat grinder that was just large enough to dispose of a human body.

"Well, if it isn't the luckiest man in New York," Masseria said, finally looking up at Luciano, "thanks for joining us."

Luciano tried to smile and fiddled with the brim of his fedora.

"Took me awhile to find you." Luciano shrugged.

"You know me. I go where the food is," Masseria said, aware of his reputation and in no hurry to dispel it. "Best pasta in New York."

Luciano knew that probably wasn't true. Masseria was forced to dine in Coney Island because he did his business in Manhattan, and he was less likely to get shot at in the process of gorging himself.

"Take a seat, Charlie," another man at the table, Joe Catania said, pointing to one of the two empty chairs at the round table.

"That's all right. I can't stay long. I just wanted to let Mr. Masseria know something." Luciano said.

"Go ahead," Masseria said, taking a gulp of wine to wash down a mouthful of garlic bread.

"I found the guy who tried to kill you."

"Which one?" Masseria said, always anxious to remind others of his combat record. The table erupted in laughter. Masseria's bloated cheeks blushed from the effects of his wine, and his eyes reduced to narrow slits. That was why some had taken to calling him "the Chinese," but only behind his back.

"The most recent one. Pelham Parkway, the one who killed Ferrigno and Mineo." Luciano reminded himself to smile and play along affirmingly. Masseria might have been childlike in his playfulness, but he was also childish in his anger, and wouldn't hesitate to cut Luciano's balls off if given a reason to do so.

"Who was this vigilante?" Masseria asked.

"His name is Enzo. Enzo Consentino. Some call him Enzo the Thief."

Masseria looked around the table approvingly, like a tutor pleased with a pupil.

"See what a good boy he is?" he said. Then he seemed to register something. "That can't be right. Consentino. Somebody brought him up to the Assembly a few years ago. I gave the approval for that to be taken care of."

"I think that was his father, Mr. Masseria. Genovese did some looking and found out that the guy had three kids. Enzo is shacked up with Gagliano's crew. He also has two brothers though, Vico, who hasn't been heard of since he got back from the War, and Vincente, who's been seen with Maranzano, but keeps a low profile."

Masseria's face contorted with disgust at the mention of Maranzano.

"Who are these people? Who are these Consentinos who keep causing me trouble? Where are they from?"

Masseria's famous temper was beginning to flare.

"Castellamare," Luciano said.

"Of course, they are," Masseria cursed underneath his breath and shook his head.

"What do you want me to do?" Luciano asked.

"We need to keep an eye on that Vincente. He may be a problem. If he peeps his little head up, I hope that someone will shoot it off. Same goes for the war hero if he shows up again."

"What about Enzo? Want me to take care of it?" Luciano asked.

Masseria took another bite of food and considered his answer. "No, I don't think so. I want Joe to handle this." He gestured to Joe Catania. "Take this stone from my shoe."

Catania looked up at Luciano and shrugged, a smile on his face that seemed to say, "You'll get there one day, kid."

Luciano had a famous rage as well, and he did all he could to keep it hidden.

The diners returned to their plates of food when Catania stood and left to do the Boss's bidding.

"Joe," Luciano said.

The room fell silent.

Masseria went by many names. Joe the Boss, Mr.

Masseria, Mr. Giuseppe, even just "the Boss." But no one called him Joe. Masseria looked up with a mouth full of spaghetti.

"What gives? Why don't you want me to take care of this?" Luciano asked.

Masseria sat silent for a moment, as did his guests, as everyone awaited a response. Finally his expression softened.

"Charlie, my boy," he said, munching open-mouthed on his spaghetti. "It isn't personal. But who would you ask to kill this man if I gave this task to you?" He shook his head and smiled to pacify him.

"Why does it matter?"

"You would ask those Jew friends of yours to do it, wouldn't you?" Masseria said quickly.

"Maybe,"

Masseria wagged a finger at him. "I don't care how you do your business, Charlie. If you want to work with those Jews in the Garment District, then be my guest. But on family business, we work with our own people."

These old greaseballs, Luciano thought. He shouldn't have been surprised to hear such ignorance from an ol' timer like Masseria.

"My *Jew friends* wouldn't be identified. Who better to make the hit?"

Masseria laughed, forcefully enough that the others joined him.

"But I want the killers to be identified! How else can I send a message?"

"I can get Costello to do it then, or Genovese. Hell, I'll even do it myself," Luciano said.

Masseria shook his head. "My words are final, Charlie.

Who cares about this Consentino shmuck? There will be more men to kill. Keep playing your part, Charlie."

Luciano stood at the table for a few more moments, trying to think of something to say. He became painfully aware of Masseria's drunk friends staring at him. He put on his fedora and departed, but only after kissing Masseria on the cheek and showing the proper respects to his guests.

But Luciano had made too much money for Joe the Boss to be tossed aside. He had killed, been beaten within an inch of his life, and sacrificed everything to ensure that Masseria maintained the empire he had built. He wanted his due. Someday, that fat bastard would get his. And anyone else who stood in his way would too.

11

BUSTER

Upper East Side, Manhattan—December 15, 1930

"Sounds like damn wood chipper," Vico said of Cargo's snoring.

Buster laughed and dimmed the light. The clock read nearly 2:00 a.m., and he was exhausted. But they had another hour before Vico and Buster's guard shift was over.

Enzo was out like a light. Bonanno and Charlie Buffalo were bunking in the other room for more sleep since they had orders the next day. Sonny tossed and turned, probably thinking about the Irish girl he mentioned once and refused to discuss again. Antonello passed out after supper in the recliner and hadn't moved since.

"My eyes are getting heavy. I could use a smoke," Buster said, careful to keep his voice a whisper.

"Outside then. You know the boss won't want it in here." Vico stood, careless about the noise he made as he exited onto the front porch.

Buster peeked around the corner into the kitchen,

where Maranzano was seated at the table. His two ivory-handled pistols were deconstructed there, oil-stained rags resting underneath them. In his hands the boss meticulously weighed out the pellets for an empty shotgun casing.

"Hey, boss. We're gonna step out for a smoke. That all right?" Buster said.

Maranzano didn't look up. "'To me belongeth vengeance and recompense; their foot shall slide in due time: for the day of their calamity is at hand, and the things that shall come upon them make haste.'"

Buster waited but the boss said nothing else. Instead he carefully tipped his hands until the pellets and powder poured into the shell.

"Is that Revelations?"

"Deuteronomy 32:35," Maranzano said.

"We'll be on the porch if you need anything," Buster said. He turned to leave but heard the boss clear his throat. He turned to find a bottle of Canadian whiskey extended.

"The two of you need to talk," the boss said as Buster accepted the bottle. "So be thirsty, but don't be drunk either."

"You got it, boss." Buster was careful to interpret his meaning as he departed. Maranzano knew the two had served together in the war, and everyone quietly assumed Vico's peculiarities were a result of whatever happened there. Buster decided the boss was tasking him with addressing it. Buster shut the screen door quietly behind him. "Got two glasses and some brown."

"The boss won't care if we hydrate?" Vico said.

It was typically a rule that they weren't permitted to drink on guard shift, but then again this was implemented mainly because Antonello and Cargo had a habit of putting back a few too many and getting sloppy with their surveillance. Vico, despite his typical excess with the bottle, was always vigilant as a hawk when he was on shift.

"It was the boss who gave it to me."

Vico didn't offer any other objections. He lit a cigarette and held out the lighter for Buster.

The crispy smoke of a Lucky Strike filled Buster's lungs as he poured two glasses and handed one to his old buddy. He plopped down in the rocking chair beside them and silently scanned the streets for any abnormalities.

Buster considered where everything went wrong in France. It was always bad, worse than he cared to remember. But by the end things were so mixed up it was difficult to tell what was reality and what were the nightmares. Most of the time reality was worse.

He recalled Franklin's grisly death, which he and Vico witnessed together. He remembered when one of their sergeants got gangrene. They couldn't afford to remove him from the front, but he didn't have to suffer long. They got gassed the next day, and when he couldn't get his mask on quick enough, he put his Springfield under his chin and pulled the trigger. Buster remembered their last night there, and the drink he and Vico shared with Murdaugh. As soon as the thought formed in his mind he started laughing. Vico looked at him cock-eyed.

"First sip hitting you that hard, Domingo?"

He shook his head and tried to calm himself long enough to speak. "You remember that shithole we had in the Argonne?"

Vico cracked a rare smile. "Yeah, I remember."

"When we filled it in, we put those wooden crosses over top it and . . . and . . ." They were both laughing now and Buster could barely get it out. "When those Frenchies walked by, they stopped to salute it."

"And one of them was crying and singing that song," Vico added as they both struggled to silence their chuckles.

"Same shithole Murdaugh fell in a few weeks before."

"He was covered in frozen doughboy waste for the entire assault the next day!" Then they both lost it at the memory. But just as quickly as they bent over with laughter, they sobered and straightened.

Buster knew what Vico was thinking. Same thing he was thinking. That assault the next day was a bad one. Maybe the worst. He kicked himself for mentioning it.

A mine went off in No Man's Land, and they knew they only had minutes to occupy it or the Germans would and use it to bomb them.

They got there, but it was hard fighting on the way. Lost a lot of good men.

McKenzie took shrapnel to the torso and face, and his cries were loud and long as the flesh of his cheeks burned. The Sergeant Major barked for someone to put him out of his misery before their position was given up. And Vico was closest.

Vico knelt by Mckenzie and tried to quiet him, but his eye was half hanging out and his body was in shock. He was like a broken alarm clock no one could stop. The Sergeant Major screamed again, this time to Vico directly. He was in the way of anyone else taking the shot, so he'd have to be the one to do it. He resisted as long as he could. The Sergeant Major threatened him with a court martial, and there was nothing else he could do.

Buster remembered how Vico put his forehead on McKenzie's and said, "I'm here", as he placed his pistol against his buddies' chest and pulled the trigger.

They were on light and smell discipline at the time, which meant no smoking. But Vico would never forget how

Vico pulled out a damp cigarette and lit it, not bothering to wipe McKenzie's blood from his face. He locked eyes with the Sergeant Major, daring him to do something. He had every right to from a military perspective, of course, but any man with half a brain could see the rage in Vico's eyes, and the man was smart enough not to test him.

And Vico was never the same again after that day. He never laughed as much, never told as many stories. He didn't make eye contact as much, except when it was accompanied with clenched fists and flexing muscles.

For the three weeks that followed before Armistice Day, Vico's violence toward the enemy increased trifold. Whereas he once killed only when necessary and with no more force than necessary, he began to take increased pleasure in using his bayonet, in feeling the heat of his enemies' flesh as they collapsed into him with their final breath.

Buster took a long drag on his cigarette and swallowed the smoke with a sip of whiskey.

"It wasn't you that killed him, you know?" Buster said.

Vico finished his glass and held it out for another round. "How would you feel if I said the same about Franklin?"

Buster flushed. "That's different and you know it. I gave an order that got him killed. You *were* ordered," he said. "If it wasn't you, another doughboy would have put him down."

As quickly as the drink had been poured, Vico finished his second glass. He filled it up himself and topped off Buster too.

"Nothing that happened over there was really our fault, you know?" Buster said. "We were dumb kids. We were poor men in a rich man's war. Young men fighting an old man's war."

Vico turned to him, his face half-illuminated by the moonlight. "What are we doing now?"

Buster took one last hit of his cigarette and tapped it out, careful to discard of the butt properly or face the boss's displeasure.

"You know you're the only reason I made it back, right?" Buster said.

Vico pulled out his revolver and verified there were six bullets prepared, a habit he was known for. "I think you're remembering that the wrong way round," Vico said. "When we got hit with that mustard in Champagne and my mask was frozen to my belt, it was you found another and put it on me before the gas choked me out."

"Not like that," Buster said. He leaned forward in his rocker and considered how to articulate it. "You were the one who stayed up with me to smoke another cigarette when I couldn't sleep. And you could've. You were the one who helped me burn the lice off my coat every night even if they'd inevitably be back the next day." Buster managed to wrestle a smirk from Vico, which he considered a victory. "And when I got news that my old man was dead, you were the only one who made sure to check up on me. Without you, I don't think I would've made it back."

"Ehh. What other choice did I have." Vico leaned forward and spit off the porch.

"The only thing you didn't save me from was the nightmares."

Vico turned and made eye contact with Buster, and intimidation wasn't the purpose. There was something old and familiar in his brown eyes. "Yeah . . . guess that's a battle we can't fight together."

"And now we're brothers. Crazy to think about, isn't it?" Buster said.

Vico chuckled and shook his head. "One big happy family."

"It'll be over one day. You know that right?" Buster asked. "Just like the trenches, this will end."

Vico didn't reply, but the look in his eye concerned Buster. There was nothing familiar there at all. He didn't want the fight to end. He wanted to keep hurting people. People like the Sergeant Major, or whoever it was that killed his father.

The only sound was their rockers on the wooden porch and the sound of the insects in the trees between the apartments across the road. Vico took another drag on his cigarette, which was so short now it must have been singeing the hair on his fingers.

"Shifts about over. We should probably wake up Sonny and Antonello, and hit the hay," Buster said. "I'm running out with Buffalo and Bonanno." He poured the rest of his whisky into the bottle.

"Leave it." Vico pointed to the whiskey.

"You don't want to crash? I think I hear Sonny getting up."

Vico leaned back and slouched in the rocking chair. "I don't feel like fighting the battle alone tonight, Buster," he said. He pulled out a new cigarette and wet it with his lips. "You go on ahead."

As Buster pried open the screen door, Vico pulled out his revolver and rested it in his lap. Then he uncorked the bottle.

Lower East Side, Manhattan—December 14, 1930

. . .

If Buster was going to write a book, he'd probably title it *Waiting on Buffalo and Bonanno*, because that's what he did most of the time. Charlie was one hell of a driver, but he wasn't known for his punctuality.

Buster leaned up against the window of a barbershop and lit his second cigarette. He watched car after car go by, and no sign of his irresponsible friends.

Today wasn't the kind of day you wanted to be late for. Word around town was Al Capone's boys were showing up with weapons and ammunition for Masseria. Capone wasn't Sicilian and was nationally rejected by anyone who mattered in The Bad Life, and now Masseria was opening the door for him if he supported his war against the Castellamarese.

At least that was the rumor. And if it was true, they'd be in Manhattan by 1 p.m., and Maranzano wanted to give them a New York welcome: specifically the kind that includes a hailstorm of bullets and clouds of smoke.

Buster checked his watch. It was a quarter past eleven a.m. He cursed.

A little voice sounded from underneath the shade of Buster's fedora. "Hey Mister. You want a paper? All kinds of good stuff in this one, I tell ya."

The voice belonged to a Jewish kid, no older than five or six. He wore what was probably an older brother's overalls, and his ol' man's newsboy cap. He looked the part, and his gap tooth grin probably sold a lot of papers to little old ladies passing by.

"Yeah, sure." Buster dangled his Turkish cig from his lips and fished out his wallets. "Which paper is it?"

"*New York Herald Tribune*, sir! The most best paper in all New York."

"Don't have the *Times*?"

The boy furrowed his brows and shook his head.

"Herald'll do. How much did you say it is?"

"Uhh . . ." He tapped a finger on his lip like he couldn't remember. "Five cents. That's right, sir. Only five cents."

"Five cents?" Buster balked. "You told the last guy two cents."

"Yeah but . . ." He rubbed the back of his neck. "You look like you got more dough than that fella."

After a few moments Buster laughed and tossed him a nickel. "All right, bud. That's business."

Buster took the paper and the boy scurried off to find his next buyer. He flicked his cigarette to ash it and opened the paper, careful to keep an eye on the road so Bonanno and Buffalo didn't catch him unaware.

There was a big picture of Governor Franklin Roosevelt, underpinned in big bold letters proclaiming he would likely be running against incumbent President Hoover on the Democratic ticket.

A black car like Buffalo's pulled up front, but a pretty young gal got out with a mustached older gentlemen.

Buster didn't much care for politics. He had his own system of government, and it began and ended with Salvatore Maranzano. He was more curious about the crime section. Just as he suspected, there was another big section on the murders of Al Mineo and Steve Ferrigno. Everyone kept an eye on the papers, but Buster took additional interest. He knew if his name appeared in connection with the slayings, there would be Bulls coming all the way from Chicago to strap him in the electric chair. And where would that leave Maria?

He shooed away a few pigeons pecked at his feet as he scanned over the black print, searching for anything new.

The investigators confirmed the slayings were

connected to organized crime, and a few lines mentioned it might be the start of a new beer war in Manhattan. They claimed they had no definitive subjects, but they were hot on their trail. Buster took a sigh of relief, reading between the lines that they didn't know a damn thing. The Irish cops in that part of town wouldn't hesitate to throw a few dagos behind bars if they had even a shred of evidence.

He heard a loud horn blaring across the street. Buffalo and Bonanno were sitting within the car, and both wore grins from ear to ear. They were gonna get a mouthful for this one.

He threw the papers down and flicked his cigarette on top of it. He started shaking his head at them as he crossed the road. He hadn't made it past the first lane of traffic when sirens sounded from just around the corner. Then more rang out from the other side of the road, near the Brooklyn bridge.

Buster stopped like a deer in a Model T's headlights as the patrol cars spun around the corner and pulled to a stop right by Buffalo's front door.

"Oh shit. Shit, shit, shit," Buster whispered as he back-stepped across the road.

"What's the big idea?" Charlie shouted as he popped out. "You know this is exactly what I should expect from a bunch of—"

He received a shift jab to the nose. Blood dripped over his lips instantly.

Bulls swarmed the car on both sides, pistols drawn and aiming at the vehicle.

He sprinted toward a nearby phone booth. Some college boy was on, twirling the cord around his finger and blushing like he was chatting with a pretty girl.

"Hey, fella. Get out," Buster said.

"How 'bout you jump in a lake?" the boy said, sure to let whoever remained on the phone hear.

Buster pulled back his suit jacket to reveal the ivory handle of his pistols. "You got three seconds or I shove that receiver down your throat."

The young man tried to formulate a response but dropped the phone and scurried off.

Buster picked up the receiver. "He'll call back," he said and slammed the phone down to clear the line and frantically dialed the operator.

He looked over his shoulder through the glass to find Bonanno and Buffalo both laying down—face first—on the pavement. Before he turned away, Bonanno got a swift kick to the side of the head.

"Come on, come on," he whispered. His heart was beating so fast he could hear the blood pumping in his ears despite the noise. "Yeah, give me Doc Louie in the Upper East Side." He gave them the appropriate news and before he could catch his breath, Sonny was on the line.

"Give me the old man," Buster said. "Now."

Fortunately it was Sonny answered, cause he was smart enough to not ask questions. Cargo would have kept him on the line for twenty minutes before passing it off.

Maranzano's smooth and firm voice came out crisp through the receiver. "You have Caesar."

"Boss, the bulls swarmed us before we could even get to the car. They pounced out, barrels aimed right at them. I don't—"

"Please slow down." Maranzano was unperturbed. "Police arrived and are arresting Calogero and Joseph?"

"Yeah . . . they got 'em eating pavement right now." Buster took another look and cringed as Bonanno received a whip of a police baton.

"They likely don't know who they are. The policemen don't know they belong to me," Maranzano said. "Did they find the weapons and ammunition?"

"Uhh . . ." Buster looked again and saw the trunk opening and a bull pulling out a Thompson submachine gun. "Yeah. They got them."

Maranzano sighed, but otherwise revealed no distress. "I will call my associates on the force and get in touch with my attorney."

"What do you want me to do?" Buster asked.

"Remain calm. Follow them to the police precinct and find out as much information as you can. Find Sergeant Morgan if he's on shift and mention my name."

"Right." Buster exhaled. "Do I need to worry about getting arrested too?"

"Unfortunately we all do," Maranzano said. "But this is the life we've chosen to live. Calculated risks. If anything happens to you, rest assured I'll take care of it."

"I hear you."

"I always take care of it, don't I?"

"Yeah, boss."

"See it done then."

The line clicked.

Buffalo was characteristically still popping off at the mouth as the bulls cuffed him. But if Buster knew anything about how suspects got treated at the precinct, he wouldn't be talking for long.

12

SONNY

Holbrook, Long Island—December 22, 1930

For the first time since he'd known him, Sonny decided to disobey Maranzano. He imagined The Don's disappointment, and it made his stomach churn. He was even more afraid of upsetting his "family" than he was about the danger involved. Regardless, he couldn't remove his foot from the gas pedal.

He was going to see Millie. It'd been a long time since they'd last seen each other. Even longer since they last kissed, but he still thought about it every night while he was trying to fall asleep, distracting him from Cargo's incessant snoring.

He wrote a letter a few months prior and sent it to her old address in Brooklyn, hoping she was still living there. He couldn't give her the address of the safe-house—that was a rule he was unwilling to break—so instead he told her to send a reply to St. Peter's in Little Italy. The last time Sonny visited Father Sammy the letter was waiting on him. The envelope was rose scented and delicately wrapped in pink lace. It looked better than any Christmas present Sonny had ever wrapped, but he tore into it regardless.

She said she'd be visiting the Nevins and Griswold cigar factory located in the old Long Island Railroad station on December 22 to buy a Christmas gift for her father. Sonny knew this meant she wanted to see him, and he immediately decided he'd go.

The lengthy drive to Long Island presented him with many opportunities to turn around, and part of him knew he should. But he couldn't. He was afraid he'd forget the color of her eyes or the sound of her voice, and he needed that just to get by.

As he pulled to a stop outside the cigar shop, he finally pondered the one concern he'd so far refused to consider: it could be a set up. All it took was one dirty mailman who let Masseria's boys in on the meeting and Sonny would be walking into a hail of bullets.

But he was still stepping over the railroad tracks. He spotted Millie through the window. She was impossible to miss. She was quite the sight surrounded by the other guests —leisured, old, and mustached men.

Sonny stopped and watched. They were speaking with her, but more like she was a friend than an attractive girl half their age. She was handling herself well. She said something that made them laugh.

He took off his fedora and straightened the brim. He licked his thumb and tried to smooth out his eyebrows, but he already knew damn well they wouldn't cooperate.

The door opened as a cheerful gentleman exited. He held the door for Sonny, and Millie noticed him as soon as he entered.

"Hello, Sonny," she said, the emotion in her eyes unreadable.

Sonny nodded to the men around her, who all turned to leave. He wondered if she mentioned him beforehand.

"Find anything good for Patrick?" he said. He cursed himself silently. What a stupid question to ask after all this time. He didn't care about Patrick, didn't even like him. He wanted to ask how she'd been, if she was happy, if she'd found someone new. Instead, he asked about a cigar.

"Actually, Patrick passed away in October," she said, her voice a mixture of sadness and relief. "We always knew the drink would get him eventually."

Sonny didn't hear any of it at first. He couldn't take his eyes off her. She wore a blue and yellow cloche with a dress to match it, an English primrose tucked into the brim. Every hair of her strawberry blonde hair was delineated perfectly to accentuate the softness of her cheeks. Her eyes were the color of summer's first blueberry, and the brows above it were shaped like Clara Bow's lips.

Lips. He focused on those in particular. Pink and plump, he remembered clearly how they felt parting around his.

Panic set in the moment he realized he hadn't said anything.

"Oh, I'm so sorry to hear that, Millie," he stammered. "I know how close you were."

She smirked, and the dimples it created in her cheeks made his knees weak.

"You know what he was like. Probably giving St. Peter a real fit at the gates." She started walking to the counter and Sonny followed. "Do you want a cigar?"

"Yeah, sure. I'll take one. We can go somewhere else if

you want though." He rubbed the back of his neck, which despite the winter chill was burning hot.

She leaned up on the counter. "Here's just fine. You might not think it very ladylike, but I prefer a cigar to a cigarette."

"That's not so uncommon these days." Sonny lied. He'd never seen a woman smoke a cigar, but he wasn't about to say it.

"Two Romeo Y Julieta's, Harvey," she said. A wily smile crossed her face and her eyebrows danced. "That's pretty fitting isn't it, Sonny?"

His cheeks blushed but he didn't say anything.

"Coming right up, Mil," the clerk said.

Accepting two robustos, they found two red leather chairs in a quiet part of the station.

She cut and lit the cigar like a professional. She leaned back in her chair, a strange mixture of delicate and powerful.

"So with Patrick gone who is . . . uh . . . who is taking care of you?" he asked. He intended to discover if she'd found someone new. Maybe if she had he could stop daydreaming about her all the time. But what a terrible way to ask.

She placed the back of her hand on her forehead and gave her best damsel-in-distress impression. "Oh, poor little ol' me can't make it without a man to take care of me. Whatever will I do?"

Sonny conjured up a face awkwardly mixing humor and contrition. "That's not what I meant, Millie."

She shook her head. "I'm teasing you. You know Patrick never took care of me though. I took care of him." She met Sonny's eyes, the flesh of his face feeling like it just caught fire. "Now I have one less mouth to feed. Just my own now."

"We can talk about something else," Sonny said.

He knew from the start he was going to bungle this. The past year of his life was spent with nobody but his crew, and he'd developed a noticeable deficiency in talking to the fairer sex. Then again, he'd never been a Rudolph Valentino.

"I really just wanted to see how you've been doing, Sonny." She took off her cloche hat, crossed her legs, and set it down delicately in her lap.

"Oh, me? You know me." Sonny forced an unnatural smile he knew was unattractive. "Working in the financial business. Still surviving despite the Great Crash."

She chuckled and flicked the ash on the end of her cigar. "Is that what you've been doing?" she asked.

He realized he'd been preoccupied with the smoothness of her legs, so he quickly answered, "Yeah? Yes. What do you mean?"

"I've had a lot of free time on my hands. I've been reading the papers a lot."

Sonny thought intently about her meaning but knew none of his crimes had ever been linked to him.

"What's been in the papers?" he said, and squirmed in his leather chair.

"Well, not the new ones. The Public Library in Manhattan keeps an archive." One of her eyebrows raised.

Sonny gulped.

"I read what happened to your father. I wept for you. I saw where your brothers got arrested—well, I'm assuming they were your brothers."

"Really did your research, huh?" Sonny hid himself behind a puff of cigar smoke.

"I saw where your sister got married. And that's where it all got pretty interesting." She placed her cigar in a black ashtray on a small table between them and took off her white satin gloves. Leaning forward in her seat, Millie's face softened. "I saw the public listing of your new business. The man listed as your partner, Salvatore . . . M, something with an M."

"Maranzano."

"Yes, Salvatore Maranzano. He'd been in trouble with the police several times in Wappinger Falls and Poughkeepsie. They couldn't get him for long, but anyone with eyes to see could tell he was a bootlegger."

The storekeeper came and discreetly offered them both a small glass of whiskey. Sonny was quick to accept.

"Kinda scary thinking about all that information being out there." Sonny tried to laugh.

"It was easy enough to put the pieces together, especially after running into your friend during our night out on the town. I know what you are, Sonny," she said. "And I know what you're doing."

For the first time his nerves turned to frustration. So what she figured it all out? He hid it from her for a reason. But what did it matter now? What did she want from him?

"We need to get you a gun and a badge," Sonny said. "Real detective work."

She closed her eyes and licked her lips. It was innocent and without thought, but again Sonny's mind wandered from the topic at hand.

He imagined what she'd look like in the morning, with no makeup and sleep still in her eyes. Probably even more beautiful, he guessed.

"I wasn't trying to invade your privacy. I was worried about you. I would have asked you about it myself, but you weren't there, were you? Who else but a gangster disappears from his residence for months on end?"

"What do you want then, huh?" He raised his voice to her for the first time ever. "You want me to say I'll walk away? You want me to say I'll stop? What do you want, Millie? Why come all the way out here to see me if you know what I am?" He looked over his shoulder to ensure no one was paying attention.

Millie's eyes were fixed on him.

Patiently she listened, and when she spoke her voice was confident but smooth as silk. "Because I wanted to let you know I don't care about any of that."

If Sonny's heart hadn't been racing before, it certainly was now. He cleared his throat. It felt like it was filled with Georgia cotton.

"That's what you wanted to tell me?"

"You left me because you were worried. I know you wouldn't have otherwise. I know it." She swept a curled strand of hair behind her ear. "I felt what you felt that night, Sonny. You wouldn't have left unless you thought you had to."

Sonny leaned closer and ensured he whispered. "You say you don't care, but how could you know?" He lowered his voice further still. "You don't know what men like me are capable of, what we've done." He considered saying he didn't *want* to do any of it, that if she thought he was a good man she was right, and eventually he would get away from it all. But none of that matter. The facts were the facts, and he had to own the choices he'd made, and those he would likely make in the future.

She continued to meet his gaze, unperturbed. "I told you, Sonny. I've had a lot of time on my hands. I've done a lot of reading. I'm not one of those naive girls from the pictures. You'd be surprised."

"You sure seem like a naive girl from the pictures,"

Sonny said, but instantly regretted it. "You want to go with me because I'm a big shot like Al Capone? Is that it?"

She pursed her lips. "I want to go with you because you're you. I want every part of you. If that's who you are, that's what I want," she said. "Besides. I'm a good Catholic girl, so I know not to ask any questions." She stifled a smile.

"You want me? Why?"

She straightened and batted her lashes, before staring deeper into Sonny than he usually allowed. "Because you make me feel alive."

He swallowed. There was fire in her eyes, and it threatened to melt Sonny.

"Are you going to take me to a hotel or not?"

"We'll take my car." He shuffled through a wad of cash and threw a few bills down for the whiskey and hurried with Millie to the exit.

Sonny decided a regular hotel wasn't good enough, so he made for the Oheka Castle in West Hills and broke every speed limit on the way there.

Their room door was barely closed behind them before they were on each other. They knocked over every delicately arranged decorations on their way to the bedroom. They fell into each other.

Was this what love felt like?

With his college sweetheart the lines between love and lust were so blurred he could never tell the difference. But he wasn't thinking about that, or about right or wrong. He wasn't thinking about the future or what happens next. He wasn't thinking about anything. He knew what Millie meant now: this was what it felt like to be *alive*.

Her thighs warmed him. Her breath filled his lungs. Her hands traced every contour of his muscles and fixated on every scar. Sonny explored every inch of her skin, his heart beating quicker with every new discovery. He pulled her bare chest to his, but they could never be close enough.

They were halfway between the immediate present and another world too intense and beautiful to describe. But Sonny was only certain nothing outside of it mattered. There was no war, and his father's killer didn't need to be found. There was no Maranzano or Masseria, and he wasn't worried about his mother eating properly. He wasn't worried about hitmen hiding in the shadows. He felt no shame for the bad he'd done and wasn't afraid of what he'd have to do afterward. She was the only thing real to him, the penultimate truth.

Exhausted, they collapsed into a mess of sweaty blankets and both laughed. She laid her head on his chest and he smelled lilac in her hair.

"Quite a Christmas present, isn't it?" she said. And that's all she said. They didn't discuss what would happen the following morning or what the future looked like. They only closed their eyes and held each other like morning would never come.

13

ANTONELLO

Holbrook, Long Island—December 23, 1930

The way that Maranzano and his "Boys of the First Day" traveled around, Antonello felt he was part of one of those Roman Triumph the boss always talked about. He probably wasn't really considered to be part of select group, but recent absences had opened the door for Antonello.

Antonello sat in the front passenger seat of Maranzano's car. Cargo was behind the wheel, and Maranzano was behind his machine gun in the back seat. Buster and Vico were in the front vehicle.

Typically, Antonello would have been left at a safe house on a day like this, for a meeting this important. But after Charlie Buffalo and Bonanno were released a few days after their arrest, the boss granted them a few days R&R in Long Island. They'd celebrated with champaign because they both remained silent during their abusive interrogations, and because Maranzano had the power to free men from arrest on a whim. That was some real authority that could win allies in this war.

Antonello, however, was celebrating his chance to ascend in the family ranks. With Bonanno and Buffalo out on rest and Sonny calling in sick gave him his chance. One of those potential allies had called and arranged a meeting, and whether they liked it or not eventually they invited—or ordered, he could never tell—Antonello to come along.

"Be wary, gentlemen. If this is a trap, they'll find us ready," Maranzano said from the back, cautiously eyeing the cars following behind them.

Antonello was skeptical as well. The men they were meeting were former Masseria associates, under Al Mineo's authority, and they claimed they wanted to switch sides. This was the kind of set up Men of Honor had used to lure victims to their death for centuries, but Maranzano couldn't refuse the offer and Antonello couldn't refuse an opportunity to prove himself.

Besides, if they could win men in Masseria's camp, they would have a far better chance of getting Masseria. The Don had cited Julius Caesar as an example of how winning over enemies was the key to strategic victory.

They chose a neutral location, in Long Island, where neither party had any special interest. The building was an office building, owned and operated by the head of the only neutral five families, Joe Profaci.

"If you see anything strange, don't be afraid to shoot. If this comes to bloodshed, we shoot first," Maranzano said, stepping down out of the Lincoln when they arrived. "They need us more than we need them."

The air was thick, much as it had been on the day that Maranzano aligned with Gagliano. Antonello hoped that was a good sign, but knew he was grasping at straws.

A doorman greeted them at the car and led them into the building. Vico and Buster exited their vehicles and followed close behind.

"Are you armed?" the doorman said.

"Of course we are. We did not come here to kill though," Maranzano said. "They called this meeting. Not us."

"If we wanted them dead, they would be dead already," Buster said from behind him.

The doorman thought for a moment, shrugged, and led them on.

The office building was empty but for two men standing beside a fireplace. They were sipping coffee and talking quietly.

"Paisano, it is good to finally meet you," one of them said in Sicilian.

Antonello felt confident in understanding it, even if he couldn't speak it worth a lick. The man placed his coffee on a china dish and paced across the wood floor to embrace Maranzano. The Don accepted the gesture, but the remainder of his party eyed the man cautiously.

"We didn't know there would be so many of you," the other man said, more reluctantly.

"These are my men. They go everywhere with me," Maranzano said and Antonello beamed.

"Ah, well it is nice to meet you. I am Frank Scalise," the first man said, shaking each man's hand in turn. He had the wrinkles and warm smile of a grandfather, and bushy eyebrows that seemed to cover the majority of his forehead.

"I'm Joe Traina," the other man said, going down the line to kiss each man on the cheek. He was older as well, but more refined, with hair swept and combed back with copious amount of Brilliantine.

"I do not want to begin our friendship on a bad note, but I'm sure you understand I am very busy," Maranzano said, his voice soothing but commanding.

Antonello smiled. The boss got more powerful when his enemies were around. Antonello was proud to be one of his guys.

"We know this, Don Maranzano. And we do not want to take up too much of your time." Scalise bowed his head humbly.

"We are honored with your presence," Traina reiterated.

Buster narrowed his eyes. "You're both interested in making a deal?"

"Would any of you like some coffee?" Scalise asked.

"No. Again, we must make this quick," Maranzano said.

His demeanor was friendly, but Antonello figured his haste was more a result of caution than practicality.

"Yes. We would like to make a deal. We want to align ourselves with your borgata, Don Maranzano," Traina said.

"You would?" Maranzano asked rhetorically.

"Yes," Scalise said. "Don Maranzano."

Buster cocked an eyebrow. "And if you would betray your current family, what is to make us believe you would not betray us?"

"I was just thinking the same thing," Maranzano said.

"We had no love for Mineo. Or Ferrigno for that matter," Traina said.

"They were both behind the murder of our old boss, Toto D'Aquila. We've wanted to see them go since then, since they aligned with Masseria. But we wanted to avoid another war."

"So you want to join our family?" Antonello asked.

Maranzano looked over his shoulder at him. His eyes were calm, but it was clear he wasn't to speak again.

"We want to align our family with yours," Traina said. "The D'Aquila family is without leadership now. Masseria will try to put someone in charge, and assume he still has command, as he always does. We want to ensure that doesn't happen."

"And will the rest of your family stand behind you?" Maranzano asked.

Scalise stepped away from them and warmed his hands beside the fire. "Most of them feel as we do. The others can be persuaded."

Traina added, "Everyone wants this war to end. We want to get back to our booze, our gambling. We want to get back to earning."

"You can help us accelerate that process," Maranzano said.

"That is our intention."

"I believe it is best, then, that you remain formally aligned with Masseria. And inform me of his every move. Once Joe the Boss is dead, his followers will be pardoned, and we can return to peace," Maranzano said.

"We hope your amnesty speaks for Gagliano as well?" Traina asked.

"I speak for all of New York. Once Masseria is dead, the war will be over," Maranzano said.

Traina and Scalise looked at one another and nodded.

"Then we will do all we can to help you win, Don Maranzano," Scalise said, stepping away from the fire to kiss Maranzano's cheek.

"We must go. Is there anything you can tell us now to help in the war effort? To establish some trust and a feeling of good will?"

Scalise clicked his tongue and considered it. "Masseria is being careful. He doesn't want to get caught. But we've heard they are searching for someone."

"One of ours?" Buster asked.

"One of Gagliano's actually. They believe he was behind the hit of Ferrigno and Mineo. Masseria sent Joe the Baker's boys to do it."

"Joe Catania?" Maranzano asked.

"Yes, Joe Catania."

Maranzano's eyes grew dark. "Who is this man they're searching for?"

"What was his name, Joe?" Scalise asked.

"The thief. Enzo the Thief."

14

AUGIE

The Bronx, New York—December 23, 1930

"Wait up, fellas!" Augie Patterson chased after his older brother and his two friends, but the sand beneath his feet shifted and made it hard for him to run. They always liked to visit Orchard Beach in December. There wasn't a soul in sight, and they would peruse the docks to see if they could find any souvenirs to offer as Christmas presents.

"Keep up the pace, Augie," his older brother shouted, clearly irritated that the six-year-old was insistent on tagging along.

He reached their sides and tried to catch his breath. They noticed how flustered he was, and laughed.

"You might have to take that coat off if you keep sweating the way you are," his brother's friend, Ernie, said, ruffling the toboggan on his head.

"I'm fine." Augie jerked away from him.

They moved on down the beach, kicking a crushed can of soda between them as they did.

"You guys want to go to Pelham Bay Park instead?" Augie asked.

His brother, Arthur, grinned like a devil. "You aren't scared of the water are you?"

"No, I'm not scared of the water," he said. It was true. He wasn't scared of the water, although the water at night time was a different story. The tide that reached their feet was as black as the sludge in his father's old engine. Anything could have been lurking in the depths, and he didn't like that.

He didn't want to embarrass his brother anymore, so he put any notion of leaving for the park aside.

Arthur and his friends talked about girls at their school, and Ernie boasted about his first kiss a few weeks prior.

"You're full of shit, Ernie," Arthur said.

Augie's first inclination was to tell his brother that their mother didn't allow such words, but decided to keep his mouth shut.

Along the shoreline in the distance, Augie spotted a large sack washed up onto the beach. Arthur and his friends were too distracted with their tall tales to notice, so Augie shot ahead as quickly as his little legs could carry him.

"Where ya going, kid?" Ernie shouted.

"See that? It could be alcohol! Some fella would buy that and we can get momma something nice for Christmas," he shouted and kept running.

As he reached the sack, he knelt and began to untie it. A putrid stench wafted to greet him. He nearly choked. It smelled like a thousand dead fish, but he continued working on the knot, just in case something nice was inside.

Augie finally managed to open the starchy sake.

He leapt back.

He couldn't hear his own cry, but he must have been

screaming, because his brother was running to his side. Augie tried to look away but couldn't.

The eyes were staring back at him.

A dismembered man.

Legs, arms, hands, a head. All severed. Patches of a fine Italian suit still clinging on. The torso was missing.

He screamed again, and this time it was loud enough to pierce through the ringing in his ears. The empty beach echoed his cry. Arthur reached his side and tried to pull him away, but his gaze was fixed.

The eyes just kept staring back, as if the man wanted to say something. All of the wounds were fresh, the blood clotted and bloated from the sea water. There was one old wound though, and it was a scar beneath the victim's eye.

PART II

15

TURRIDRU

Palermo, Sicily—January 11, 1917

Don Toto's wife must have been some cook. The entire home was filled with the smell of spiced olive oil, baked eggplant, and marinara sauce over broiled chicken. Turridru hadn't had a meal cooked by a real Sicilian woman in several years, and it was impossible to dine like this at the Cathedral.

"I am honored to be your guest, Don Toto," Turridru said, situating himself at the table and folding a napkin across his lap.

"We are honored to have you, Father," Toto's wife, Saverina, answered for her husband.

Don Toto sat at the head of the table with each his daughters by his side.

"The meal smells amazing, Saverina," Turridru said, anxious to leave words like "child" and "father" back at the confession booth.

"Oh please, I would have made my famous bucatini

if I had known you were coming." She blushed and found her own seat.

"She is the best cook in Palermo. What do you think I married her for?" Don Toto laughed. His girls and Turridru did the same.

"I'm sure that's not the only reason. And look at the lovely daughters the two of you have created." He gestured to the girls, who blushed and batted their eyelids.

The older was the one who impressed him. The younger was chubby, submissive, and of a weaker character. The older girl, Elizabetta, had something in her eyes. A quiet strength, a rebellious spirit, that intrigued him.

"They're just as stubborn as their mother. Hopefully they'll turn out to be the same caliber of cooks if we're to find them husbands," Don Toto said.

The girls rolled their eyes and laughed.

"Father, would you like to bless the food?" Saverina asked.

Turridru looked around, as if searching for a priest. "I don't see any Father here." He smiled. "Please, when I am a guest in your home, when I am not wearing my robes, you can address me by my name. I find it refreshing."

"And what is your name?" Elizabetta asked, receiving a glance from both her parents for her forwardness.

"Cesare Clemente," Turridru said. It was a name he had assumed after leaving Castellamare years earlier, and one he much preferred to his own.

"It's a pleasure to meet you then, Cesare. Tell the Father we will see him on Sunday," Elizabetta said.

Her parent's tensed up, until Turridru laughed, and they did so as well.

"I will bless the food though," Turridru said, as they all bowed their heads. He said the proper thanks, and the food was parceled out. Turridru partook thankfully and tried to make it seem as though the meal and good conversation was the intention of his visit.

After the dinner plates were removed and coffee was brought out along with a freshly baked plate of desserts, Turridru became serious. "Don Toto, how is your work?" He leaned across the table and fixed his eyes on the head of the family.

Saverina squirmed and the girls looked away.

Don Toto shot them a look of disapproval before replying.

"It has been trying lately, Father . . . I mean, Cesare. Things have not been going well."

"Is that so? You can tell me about it, if you'd like?" Turridru asked. The women in the room became even more uncomfortable. "You should respect Don Toto." He addressed Saverina and the girls, "It is God's work he is doing."

Their eyebrows raised in silent disbelief.

"Yes. With the growing tide of fascism and the influx of corrupt officials, we need strong men to protect the common people of Sicily," Turridru said. Don Toto straightened and jutted out his chin. He was the kind of man who thrived on being puffed up, and Turridru was sure to pander to that. "Tell me more about what is troubling you, Don Toto."

"Girls, let the men discuss for awhile," Don Toto said, and they departed quickly. "There are four other cosche like mine in Palermo. In other cities, there are most often just one, perhaps two. But Palermo is so large, that most cosche desire to lead the city."

"And these other cosche are giving your trouble?" Turridru asked as if he were personally offended.

"Not all of them. We mostly exist in peace. But there is one family that is causing me quite the concern . . ." He tossed his napkin on the table and leaned back in his chair. His lips snarled as if he tasted something bad. "I have no proof of their treachery, or I would approach the other families about it. But they are stealing my cattle, disrupting my operation, and undermining my family every chance they get."

He ensured his voice was low, serious yet calming. "And who is their leader?" Turridru asked.

Don Toto looked at him for a moment and swallowed. "I can trust you? You say you are not a Father right now."

"Cesare Clemente is just as reliable as a priest." Turridru raised his right hand, as if to God.

"His name is Giuseppe Fontana. He is jealous of everything I have built and is doing everything he can to hurt me and my honor."

"And you believe Fontana is behind all of his family's actions?" Turridru asked. Don Toto abruptly stood to his feet, and for a moment Turridru thought he had upset him.

"I try to lead my family as a Father to them. He leads his family as a dictator." Toto flicked his chin. "They do as he says and only as he says. And he hates me. He has always hated me. We were playmates in our youth, and even then he was jealous of me."

"And he cannot be eliminated?" Turridru asked.

Don Toto was now pacing and using his hands to

speak for him, as Sicilians are want to do. "No. I cannot eliminate him. Without proof, I would become the enemy of the other cosche, and place a target right here." He slapped his forehead.

"So you are forced to sit and allow him to do these things to you." Turridru touched his lip and pondered.

"Yes. I must sit and allow him to destroy the things I have built. Until he shows his face or I can catch the devil in the act."

"And if this man was to, say, go missing, would the other families not have to find proof that you were behind it to place the blame on you in the same way?" Turridru asked. Don Toto froze and stared at him. After a moment he retook his seat.

"Yes. This is true."

"You have trust in Cesare Clemente and told him things you do not tell others. Now I would hope that Cesare can open up in the same way to you," Turridru said.

Toto pondered for a moment, and then nodded, pride glistening in his eyes. A man with a simple but powerful ego like Don Toto was easily won over by believing he held a place in someone's life that no one else did.

"I am planning to resign myself from the priesthood."

Toto leaned back, his simple mind trying to make sense of all he was hearing.

"Oh? Is this allowed?"

"In practice, the priesthood is meant to last for life. But God has called me to a different life. One that does not fit easily within the restrictions of priesthood.

"And what will you do?"

"What I will do is unimportant. The only thing that matters is who I will be."

Don Toto stared at him with his mouth open for a moment, and then it registered. "A Man of Honor."

"Yes. God has called me to be a Man of Honor. It has been his purpose for my life since I was but a child, and I can refuse the call no longer."

Toto leaned forward and placed his elbows on the table. He took a sip of his coffee, thinking deeply.

"Is Giuseppe Fontana a church going man?" Turridru asked.

"It's his only redeeming quality."

"Perhaps my last act in the official role as a priest would be to eliminate the man who is impeding the work God has tasked you with." Turridru narrowed his eyes, ensuring that Don Toto's simple mind could follow along.

"Perhaps . . ." Don Toto nodded. "Perhaps."

"I would be honored to serve you in this way."

"And what would you want in return, Cesare?" Don Toto asked, attempting to hide his excitement at the thought of being rid of his enemy.

It was Turridru's turn to stand and express himself with his hands. A man with Don Toto was easily captivated by a display of charisma.

"I am a simple man, Don Toto," he began, "there are only two things I would ask. First, that I be given safe passage to America. I will need to escape retribution and law enforcement. In time I may return, but for now, a trip across the seas would be necessary."

"I have powerful friends in New York," Don Toto said proudly. "I can make the connection." It was exactly what Turridru had hoped and expected he would say. "What is your second request?"

"The hand of your eldest daughter, in marriage. If I'm no longer a priest, I'll need a bride," he said bluntly.

Don Toto's jaw dropped. "My daughter is still unwed because I have found no one worthy of her."

"Perhaps the right man has come along." Turridru said.

The Don analyzed him, perceiving something different than before. "What makes you think I would do this, Cesare?"

"Because you need this man gone."

"And why my daughter?"

"During my time as a priest, I was forbidden to look upon a woman. Now that I am nearing the end of that time, I see your daughter. She is beautiful, intelligent, and possessing many of the qualities that make her father such a fine man. The journey to America will be a lonely one. I would like to have a companion."

Don Toto inhaled and exhaled heavily and thought for some time. "You ask a great deal of me, Cesare. You are a bold man."

"It's a cruel world. Your daughter deserves to be with a bold man." Turridru fixed his eyes on the Don and felt for the first time he was in total control of the situation. "Of course I would not desire to marry your daughter if she has no interest in me. Talk to her. If she objects, I will proceed regardless. Although, we both know that taking Elizabetta from the brutality of Sicily to the Promised Land of the Americas is in her best interest. Think on this. In the meantime, I will pay a visit to Fontana."

Don Toto nodded.

The two discussed the semantics for a few moments.

Don Toto told Turridru where his enemy attended Mass, and where his vulnerabilities may lie. Turridru rose from the table before sundown, and kissed the man he hoped would soon be his father-in-law.

"I will go, and I will return," he said, and departed, knowing that his true journey was about to begin.

Palermo, Sicily—January 20, 1917

Turridru had contacted the Priest at Saint Rosalia's Cathedral the day after he dined with Don Toto. He made his intentions clear that he would be visiting the Church the following Sunday and would help in any capacity he was able. They had replied that they would be happy to have him.

Wearing his priestly robes, Turridru had arrived early that morning to help consecrate the Communion and prepare for the gathering of parishioners. He discussed the weather with the other priests, and they had a lengthy discourse about the current affairs of the Catholic Church. He made sure to invoke all of his charm, without allowing his personality to outweigh his capacity as a priest.

An hour after the orange sun rose to shine through the stained glass windows, the parishioners began to arrive. He stood by the entrance and greeted each comer as he often did at his own church. They didn't seem to notice he was a stranger there. The robes often rendered a priest invisible to churchgoers.

Luckily, someone else stole all the attention away from Turridru. A Cardinal was visiting from Vatican

City, and he gave a powerful message on the root of all evil: the love of money. When offering was collected, Turridru could tell that the amount of collections was greater than usual. A useful distraction.

Turridru bided his time and stood by the Holy Water at the entrance to the chapel. He blessed each Child but made sure to take a look at each of them in turn. When Giuseppe Fontana arrived, he was unmistakable. Built like an ox, and with a bovine face, he was a powerful force. The Mass attendees seemed to gravitate around him, and he treated them with the indifference of a king before his court. He accepted their flattery as his due.

Turridru smiled. Don Fontana wouldn't find himself so lofty for much longer.

When the sacrament of communion was offered at the end of the service, everyone lined up to partake in the Lord's Feast. Fontana assumed the front of the line, others stepping aside to allow him to do so. He partook and accepted the Cardinal's blessing. Afterward, he nodded to his wife and exited as she waited for her own portion.

Turridru waited a moment and then followed him outside.

Fontana was lighting a cigar when Turridru approached.

"Something is troubling you, Child," he said.

"What? How do you figure?" Fontana seemed irritated at the disturbance.

"I can see it in your eyes. You can sense something is not right."

Fontana's eyes narrowed, and he began to size Turridru up. "I don't believe the gift of prophecy has been given to you, Father," Fontana said.

Turridru stopped in front of him and placed a hand on his shoulder.

"No, I can see it." Fontana stared at the hand on his shoulder, unused to such a gesture, but didn't step away. "Terrified," Turridru said.

Distracting Fontana with his eye contact, Turridru reached into his robes and brandished a dagger. With a swift motion he brought the blade up and severed the man's jugular.

Fontana tried to push away but was forced to clutch his throat as the warm blood spewed out in bursts. His eyes bulged out, looking on the face of his killer in righteous indignation.

"I'll see you in hell, Child," Turridru said, freeing himself from the man's grasp and walked away at an even pace.

Some of the other petitioners had begun to exit the chapel, and seeing the dying Man of Honor, began to wail. Turridru kept his pace steady.

"What has happened, Father?" a well-dressed woman came pleading. Her wide eyes fixed on the scarlet stains on Turridru's priestly robes.

"The Lord's will," he said, passing her by.

As he escaped view of the Church, he removed his robes and buried them beneath a bush off the side of the road. He knew he would never wear them again.

Palermo, Sicily—January 20, 1917

Turridru knocked on the door and bounced on his toes while he waited. No one arrived to answer it, but to his relief, he turned to see Don Toto arriving with his family.

"Father, it's good to see you. We missed you at Mass!" Don Toto's wife, Saverina, said as they approached. She looked at Turridru in a way that told him she was not informed of his deal with her husband.

Elizabetta, on the other hand, eyed him with an innocent lust that informed him that she was.

"I'm sorry I couldn't be there," he said, stepping down from the porch to shake Don Toto's hand. "I had important business to tend to."

"Oh. Priestly business?" Saverina said.

"Personal, actually. I need to speak with your husband in private, if you'd allow me to be so rude."

The women gave a curtsy and entered the home.

"Take a seat," Toto gestured to the wooden chairs on his porch.

"Don Toto," Turridru said.

"Want a cigar?" He pulled out two and extended one to Turridru.

"I don't smoke actually. We need to discuss something," he said.

Don Toto rocked in his chair, at peace. "No we don't. You have only to say 'yes' or 'no'. Has the job been done?"

"Yes," Turridru said, finally taking a seat.

"Then nothing else needs to be said. Don Toto is a man of his word. I'll uphold my end of the bargain."

He puffed on his cigar and did all he could to not portray his delight. He failed to do so.

"Both ends of the bargain?" Turridru gestured to Don Toto's home, and the eldest daughter inside.

"I've discussed the matter with her. As it turns out, she is quite enamored with you, Cesare."

"I am relieved to hear so."

"Don Toto will uphold both ends of his bargain. But you will need to remain here for a while."

"In your home?" He hoped that Don Toto wasn't suggesting he return to his church. That would certainly mean an arrest.

"Yes, you can remain here while I contact my associates in America."

"What if someone sees me here?"

"You won't be able to leave the home."

"I've gotten rather used to remaining in a building." He had spent most of his recent years within the confines of his church. Secrecy was a virtue he had learnt by necessity.

"That is good. It will give you a chance to court my daughter before you depart."

"You shouldn't tell anyone I was a priest. No one followed me here, but there were a few that saw Fontana's fate. They will likely be looking for a deserting priest."

"What should I tell them?" Don Toto let out a billow of smoke.

Turridru thought for a moment. "Tell your associates in America that I am a local cheese merchant. Friendly, humble . . . but also resourceful. Tell them I am a Man of Honor."

Don Toto looked him and nodded. "I can do that. And should I tell them your name is Cesare Clemente?"

Turridru titled his head and tapped his chin. "No. I will leave that name behind." He was becoming used to shedding identities. It wouldn't be too difficult to get used to a new name. Or to readjust to an old one. "Tell them only that I am Turridru."

"Turridru?" Don Toto asked. "An alias?"

"No, Don Toto. It was a name of affection I bore as a young man. I gave it up only when I became a priest."

"You know," Don Toto said, pausing to ensure his cigar was burning properly. "I heard of a Turridru once. From my associates in Castellamare. He had a reputation as a fierce warrior, even as a young man. He was said to have disappeared several years ago. You wouldn't have happened to know this Turridru, would you?" Don Toto turned to him and analyzed him through a haze of smoke.

"I can't recall any such thing." Turridru shook his head but made sure to leave a bit of sarcasm in his voice. It wouldn't hurt to have a mythology develop around him, as long as he could still maintain his distance.

"Turridru, the cheese merchant, husband to my daughter." Don Toto smiled and shook his head, the ridiculousness of his entire situation not lost to him. "I will see to it that you receive safe travels to America, with a bride at your side. And you will have friends anxiously awaiting your arrival."

"That is all I could ask," he said.

His journey to America, though, was simply one means to an end.

16

SONNY

Upper East Side, Manhattan—December 24, 1930

Sonny had barely left the bed the past two days, let alone the hotel room. He couldn't tell if it was all a dream, or if it was the only thing real in the world. He wondered if he was really asleep, or perhaps he was dead. Maybe this was his own personal heaven. Maybe he was in a coma, and he'd wake up in some hospital in Brooklyn whenever he walked out that door.

In his more lucid moments, Sonny realized that he would owe Maranzano and the rest of the family an explanation when he returned. He wasn't looking forward to it, but despite what repercussions he might face, he was determined to stay one more day. As crazy as it sounded, he'd decided to bring her home for Christmas dinner with his family the next day. He'd leave out all the details about the hotel, and he knew they'd fall in love with her the way he had. Even Rosa might perk up for once.

The curtains were drawn, so the room was mostly dark

except a stream pouring in from the bathroom where Millie was washing her face. It was probably noon by now, but Sonny was still getting his eyes open.

"Maybe we should get dressed and actually go out for awhile?" Millie said.

"Yeah, maybe we can do that," Sonny said. In reality, that probably wasn't a good idea. The more he was out, the more likely he'd be seen. Whether it was Masseria's boys or Sonny's own family, either way it would spell trouble for him. Instead, he'd try to lure her back to bed for kissing and pillow talk, promising he'd take her on a thousand fancy dinner dates as soon as the war was over.

He rolled over and grabbed a copy of the papers left outside their door earlier that morning. Millie must have brought them in and placed them beside a lukewarm cup of hotel lobby coffee.

He turned on the side table lamp and sat up. Sonny was more interested than usual to see if there was anything new on the Al Mineo and Steve Ferrigno killings. No names had been mentioned, but every few days there was a new article saying that the police were hot on the trail, and Sonny hadn't check in a few days. He never believed it, but it was always worth keeping an eye on.

The crime section was always easy to find. They used the same attention-grabbing headlines they used to drum up support for the war.

"Another Gangland Slaying," he read aloud, shaking his head.

He scanned over the article, assuming at first that it was nothing he didn't already know, when he read that a body had been found in a sack, washed up on a beach in the Bronx. His eyes slowed.

The victim is reportedly a bootlegger from Harlem by the name of Enzo Consentino.

Sonny froze.

"I could really go for a bowl of Hoover Stew. Cheap and tasty too. Sound good?" she said.

He didn't reply. He pulled away from the newspaper and looked around the room with darting glances. This must be a dream. Or a nightmare. A hangover or fever, induced nightmare. He must in a coma. Something.

He slapped his face to see if he could feel it. He punched his legs. He'd had nightmares this bad since his father died. That's all this was.

Maybe he misread. He returned his focus to the newspaper, and his eyes clung to his brother's name.

He fell back on the bed to keep himself from falling, choking for air, gasping like a tide was pulling him under. He crumpled the paper and omitted a low, primal moan.

"What is it?" Millie rushed into the room.

The shaking that began in his hands began to engulf his whole body, increasing in intensity, until it erupted with the roar of a wounded animal.

Little Italy, Manhattan—December 28, 1930

The Consentino's were once again back in Little Italy. Two years and a month after burying Alonzo, Sonny returned to Old Saint Patrick's to bury his brother.

Several inches of snow had accumulated over the cemetery, entombed the headstones so that the names of the deceased couldn't be read. But Sonny knew exactly where his father was buried, and Enzo was to be interred just beside him. Father and son were reunited at last.

Rosa's cries reached a new height as the coffin was lowered. She reached out to it as Maranzano and Antonello steadied her. The casket remained closed during the service to spare everyone the sight. Rosa had begged the undertakers to allow her to see her boy, to touch his hand.

But they had seen him. And they wouldn't put that on anybody else.

The tears froze on Sonny's face as Enzo's coffin found its resting place. Father Russo, who had offered to perform the rites at the burial, was speaking. All Sonny could think about was Enzo's intoxicating laugh, his simple wit, boyish charm. No matter what they had done, Sonny concluded the killers wouldn't have killed Enzo if they had known him.

Sonny supported Maria on one side while her husband did so on the other. A black veil covered her face but failed to conceal the agony in her eyes. Buster looked on with a pensive gaze, a thousand-yard stare that many of the doughboys returned with from the Great War.

Of all the Consentinos, it was Vico who was suffering the most. He stood away from the rest of them, alone. He seemed to be having trouble simply breathing and hadn't been able to utter a word to any of them. His eyes were akin to a convict on trial, penitent but accepting full blame.

When the grave diggers began to shovel dirt on top of his brother, Vico collapsed to his knees. He covered his face with his arms and rocked.

Sonny stepped away from the crowd and put his arms around the surviving twin. Vico resisted at first and tried to push him away. Sonny held him, tenderly but forcefully, until Vico's weight collapsed into him. He buried his face in Sonny's overcoat and sobbed.

"May you find the rest that eluded you the last season of your life," Father Russo said, hands outstretched to the grave.

How could any of this be true? Sonny's thoughts spiraled. He experienced it all from outside his body. The wailing of his mother reverberated in the space between his ears.

When the gravediggers finished their work, the funeral procession departed in reverential silence. Buster led Maria away, Rosa was supported by Don Maranzano himself—a great sign of respect—who showed as much remorse for the death of a boy he barely knew as any of the gatherers. Only Vico remained, and Sonny with him.

"Come on, let's go, Vico," Sonny whispered. He tried to help Vico to his feet but couldn't. Despite Vico's broken state, he was built like a Greek sculpture, and wouldn't budge.

"Wha . . . wha . . . why wasn't it me?" Vico managed to say, his voice muffled by Sonny's coat.

"That isn't for us to decide, Vico," Sonny said.

"It should have been me . . . I . . . It . . . . it's my fault."

Fresh tears ripped from Sonny's eyes, and he kissed his brother's head.

"Do not put that on yourself, Vico. Don't do it. This is hard enough as it is."

Vico stood of his own volition and approached Enzo's grave. He fell to his knees again and placed his hands on the fresh mound of earth. He churned the loose dirt through his fingers.

"I'm so . . . I'm so sorry, big brother," Vico said. Sonny covered his eyes with his gloved hand. "You didn't deserve this. I did." Vico's tears seemed to dry, but his face was still riddled with grief. "I'm going to find who did this, Enzo, I swear to you. And when this is all over, I'll be right back by your side, just like we used to be." He patted the unused lot beside Enzo's grave.

Sonny approached Vico and placed a hand on his shoulder.

"We need to check on Ma," he said after some time had passed.

"You do that. Give her a kiss for me," Vico looked at Sonny and gave him a nod. He was trembling, less from the cold than his broken heart. "Hell of a Christmas present."

Sonny glanced at the only headstone not covered in snow.

It read: *ENZO CONSENTINO 26th January 1900 - 21st December 1930. Son, Brother, Friend.*

The epitaph didn't do him justice. But there weren't any words that could fit onto a headstone that would.

Sonny turned and left Vico kneeling at the grave.

17

BUSTER

Westchester County, New York—December 28, 1930

Buster drove Maria back to their home. She sobbed the entire car ride, and he tried to comfort her.

When they pulled up in front of the apartment building, Buster put the car in park. "I'll stay here and keep the car warm," he said.

Maria was just going in to grab a few things before they left again for Little Italy to stay with her mother. "No, come on in. It will take me a minute." She exited the car and ascended the stairs to the apartment without waiting on him.

As he entered, she was sitting on the couch across from him, glaring.

Her voice was steady, but her lips continued to quiver. "You told me you would keep him safe, Buster. You told me my brothers were safe."

Buster hung his head and pulled the fedora from his head. He didn't know what else he could say. He inched towards her, hoping to find the right words. When he reached her, he declined to say anything but tried to place his arms around her.

"No." She slapped his hand and pulled away from him. "No, Buster!" He tried to kiss her and she pushed him as hard as a woman her size could. "You can't just make it go away!"

"Maria . . ."

"Never mind. I don't want to hear it. You talk and talk and talk and I eat it up like some two-bit schoolgirl. I'm done with it. So this time just keep your mouth shut." She shook her head as tears rolled to her chin. Her eyes suddenly fixed on his hands. "These hands . . . what have they done?" She looked up at him, her head cocked, her eyes filled with suspicion and disappointment.

If only she knew, she wouldn't be with me. "Everything these hands have done has been for you. If I could take it all back, if I could change everything . . . If I could bring Enzo back . . . I would. I'd give my life away to do so."

"And then I would lose you too . . . I feel like I'll lose you everyday. I feel like you're already gone." Her voice softened but she looked away from him. She would never give him the privilege of eye contact when they argued.

"Maria, look at me." She didn't comply. "Please, Maria, I'm begging you. Look at me." He leaned away from her when he realized she had no intentions of giving in. "You aren't going to lose me."

"Your words mean nothing. You told me Enzo was safe. You lied to me. You're a liar." She bit her thumb nail and dabbed at her tears with the sleeve of her dress.

"I didn't know . . ."

"I think you did." Finally, she turned to look at him. "I

think you put yourself and all my brothers in danger. I trusted you. I gave you my heart." Her voice broke.

"I . . ." A vision flashed in his mind, for just an instant. He could see, clear as glass, Private Franklin signaling in the distance. Then the gunshot and the pink mist. The body rolling down the hill like a rag doll. "I didn't want anything to happen to him," he said, his voice hoarse and barely audible even to himself. "I'd do anything to take it back." His vision shimmered through his tears.

"There is nothing you can do." She looked at him now. Anger had replaced sadness. "All you can do is find who did this, and you do to him what they did to my brother. Then you come back home to your wife."

He nodded and obeyed the order like she was a Commanding Officer.

"I will," he said. And meant it.

18

SONNY

Upper East Side, Manhattan—January 12, 1931

Maranzano ordered a curfew after Enzo's murder. They had become careless, he explained, because of their recent success. He reminded both his Family and Gagliano's that Masseria still outmanned them and had more resources to boot. They would have to be more careful if they wanted to continue to live, let alone win the war.

They worked to establish new safe houses that were further apart and more hidden than the previous locations. Word was spread that no man was to travel alone.

Sonny and Vico both kept their mouths shut about Enzo. They didn't tell anyone that Enzo was wanting out.

"That Bobby Doyle sure took things hard," Charlie Buffalo said as they gathered around to eat the meager meal they were provided. "I've never seen so someone broke up about a death."

"We did a lot of work together. They stuck together a lot," Cargo said, still none the wiser.

Sonny again kept his mouth shut.

"I bet it reminded him of the war. Some of those dough-boys didn't come back right," Charlie said, taking a bite of stale garlic bread.

Sonny bit his lip.

As if Vico had heard them, he appeared at the entrance with Buster. The two had been out receiving a fresh supply of weapons from Chicago.

The table quieted when the two entered.

"Another feast?" Buster said taking Vico's coat and hanging it up.

"Better partake while you can. We don't have much left," Valachi said with a mouthful of onion soup.

"Go ahead," Buster gestured for Vico to take a seat.

"I'm fine. Not too hungry," Vico said, shoving his hands in his pockets and looking away. The table continued to persuade him to eat, but he wasn't listening. "Hey, Sonny. Can I talk to you?"

Sonny nodded and followed him into the kitchen.

"How's ma?" he asked when they had found some privacy.

"Broken up. She's worried about you," Sonny said.

"No need for that. I'm fine." Vico lit a cigarette.

"You aren't worried? I'm worried for the both of us." Sonny tried to look his only surviving brother in the eyes, but Vico wouldn't return the gesture.

"No. I'm not worried at all."

Sonny exhaled and looked down.

"Enzo was right, Vico." Sonny said, blowing hot air into his hands. The safe houses they were installed in weren't know for being very warm this time of year.

"What're you talking about?"

"We just keep getting in deeper. How many more

people need to die while we're trying to find out who got rid of Papa?" Sonny kicked his oxfords against the kitchen floor, nervous about broaching the subject with his temperamental brother.

"Just two." Vico finally looked at Sonny's face.

"Two?"

"The guy who killed dad and the guy who killed Enzo." Vico was stone-faced. He took one last drag on his cigarette and then extinguished it on the bottom of his wingtips.

"And what if someone else dies in the process? It's starting to seem like that's par for the course," Sonny said, keeping his voice low.

"Don't try to get out, and you won't get whacked. Simple as that. Obey the rules and keep your head down. We'll take these guys out and then . . ."

"Then what? What do we do then?"

"It's like the war, Sonny. You only plan for the next day. We'll figure it out when we come to it."

"You don't want this to end do you? You just want the war to keep going and going and going. Until you get killed. Is that it?" Sonny asked. Replaying the words in his head, they didn't sound quite right. But he couldn't find better ones, either.

"My intentions aren't important, Sonny." Vico shook his head. "I have an objective. And I'm going to keep at it until I take care of it."

The two brothers hushed themselves when some of the others entered the kitchen to wash their dishes.

Vico nodded at Sonny to indicate that their conversation was concluded.

"Hey, Sonny, where's that big guy you run around with? Fella that wears half a can of Brilliantine in his hair?" Charlie Buffalo said turning on the faucet.

"Antonello?"

"Yeah, that one. He should be here doing this shit. Washing dishes is something right up his alley," Charlie said, trying to elicit a laugh. He failed to do so.

"He's out. He has some business to take care of," Sonny said.

"Getting into trouble?" Cargo said, reaching out for one of Vico's cigarettes.

"He usually is," Sonny said.

Maranzano entered the kitchen, and the men stopped what they were doing, and turned to him. He had spent much of the past few days in his room alone, cleaning his weapons and thinking about their best course of action moving forward. He looked disheveled for the first time since Sonny had met him. His eyes were pink rimmed, and for once his clothes weren't recently pressed. Enzo was the first of his men he had lost since he assumed command, and he seemed to be taking it to heart.

"What's going on, Caesar?" Cargo said. Charlie Buffalo smacked him in the back of the head. Since Gagliano's crew had amalgamated with Maranzano's, Cargo had been a regular around the Don. Charlie wanted to remind him that regardless of the face time he received with Maranzano he was still to treat him with respect. "Mr. Maranzano," he said, lowering his head like a scolded dog.

"We're going to hit them hard," Maranzano said, almost to himself.

"Who? Masseria's boys?"

"Yes. Masseria himself. I have a plan. They're not going to know what hit them," Maranzano said. "After Masseria is dead then we may yet have peace."

"We can't have peace until we find out who whacked Enzo the Thief," Vico was quick to add.

"It was Masseria's orders. The guy who followed through with it isn't important," Charlie said confidently but turned to look at Maranzano to ensure he had said the right thing.

Maranzano was silent for a moment and seemed to be in his own world. He took a step toward Vico and pulled him close by his shoulders. He ensured he had Vico's full attention before he spoke. "I swear this oath to you: the man who took Consentino's life will die. I will kill him with my own hands if required to do so. There will be no peace until his life is extinguished," Maranzano said, and then looked to Sonny to ensure he believed him. "The evil done to us will be repaid in full." He stepped back, and analyzed each man in turn, as if sizing them up to see if they contained the ingredients to do what needed to be done. "And it will be soon. I can feel it in my bones."

19

ANTONELLO

Garment District, Manhattan—January 12, 1931

Antonello was nervous.

He had grown used to carrying a briefcase full of heroin. That didn't concern him. He was still afraid of the dark though and didn't like the chosen location for the deal, a factory building rooftop two hours after sunset. The darkness played tricks on his eyes. He was never afraid of the guys who came to buy from him. He could handle himself as good as anyone in New York if a deal went south. He didn't feel as confident about whatever could be lurking in the darkness.

He tossed one cigarette and then lit another, checking his new pocket watch every few moments, wondering if they were going to show up.

Any time he could unload some of his supplies, he was happy. But tonight was more than that. Maranzano didn't like that he was a dope peddler, and it was the explanation offered for why he hadn't been brought into the family officially. Tonight, the Don said he would make an exception, and give his blessing. If he could do some fact-finding.

"What family you belong to?" a voice came from the other side of the rooftop. All Antonello could see was the glow of a few cigarettes.

"The trigger finger." He exhaled, pleased with himself that he'd remembered.

They stepped forward.

"Do you have what we need?" the man asked, squinting his eyes in search of the briefcase.

"Every bit of it." Antonello patted the briefcase and held it out for them to weigh.

Antonello could tell the two men were Jewish but spoke with the same New York street slang Antonello was known for.

"Take your time and measure it," Antonello said, trying to still his shivering from the cold. "I don't want your people coming back and saying I stiffed you."

One of them pulled out a bag and tested the weight in his hand. He unfolded it, and reached in. He licked his finger and nodded his head.

"It's good," the man said to his partner. One of them reached into his pocket and began to sift through a roll of bills. "Where do you get this?" the taster asked.

"I know a Chinese fellow. It's pure, and I buy it on discount. That's how I can get it to you so cheap. I don't want to peddle it to users. Rather work with decent fellas like you," Antonello said.

"Keep it up. My associates appreciate your product," one of them said.

"So which one of you is Meyer?" Antonello asked as he waited for his payment.

"Do you not value digression, Mr. Antonello?" the man who was counting the bills replied.

"It's a gesture of good will. You know my name, I want to know yours."

"Give me a cigarette," the other said. Antonello did so, and the man nodded with gratitude. "They call me Bugsy."

"Bugsy Siegel. I've heard of you. It's a pleasure." Antonello turned his attention to the other. "I guess that makes you Meyer Lanksy?"

"You can call me whatever you like as long as you keep bringing me powder." He handed Antonello the money and gave him a contrived smile.

Antonello accepted the payment and shoved it into his pocket without counting.

"I should offer you boys a thank you," Antonello said as they turned to leave.

"Oh?" Lansky said, turning back around.

"You work with Luciano don't you? I heard you took out that Enzo Consentino. He was my biggest competitor," Antonello said. He wasn't much of an actor, but they didn't seem to pick up on the nervousness in his voice.

"Enzo Consentino pushed H? I thought he was just known for stealing shit?" Bugsy said, confused.

"That was intentional. Everyone thinks I'm a dock worker. We all need a front in this line of work, don't we?"

"If someone wants to have a phony occupation, why would they make it something illegal?" Lansky was suspicious.

"It made things easy for him. The bulls thought he was some low-level scumbag. Didn't give him too much trouble and didn't think too much when he ran with gangsters."

Bugsy shrugged, content with the answer, but Meyer didn't seem as sure.

"You're telling me that Enzo Consentino is a dope dealer?"

"*Was* a dope dealer. Dead now, isn't he? He won't be bothering me anymore, thanks to you boys," Antonello said.

"Can't thank us," Bugsy said, "you'd have to thank Joe the Baker. He was the one who took care of your rival."

Lansky immediately shot Bugsy a look of displeasure. "We need to be going. Thank you," Lansky said, pointing to the briefcase. "We'll contact you when we need more of your product."

Antonello pulled out another bag of heroin and tossed it at Bugsy. "Give that to Joe the Baker for me. As a thank you," Antonello said.

"And thank you too, Bugsy. You stupid kike," Antonello whispered beneath his breath as the two men departed.

20

SEBASTIANO

Benton Harbor, Michigan—February 16, 1919

Sebastiano had to set his bags down to open the door. He was returning with more than he left with but didn't want most of it. He heard water running and clanging dishes in the kitchen. The wood creaked beneath his feet as loud as a symphony to announce his arrival.

"Ma, I'm home," he said from the kitchen doorway.

"Oh," his mother gasped when she saw him and placed a hand on her chest. "You should have wrote. I would have cooked more for supper."

Still in his uniform, he removed his duty cap and set it on the kitchen table. His mother looked different now. Her forearms were twice the size they were when he left. Her hands were cracked and calloused. Since his father had killed himself, she must have taken over his labor on the farm.

They looked at one another, not as mother and son, but as complete strangers. He didn't know what to say, and judging from the blank expression on her face, she didn't either. At length he stepped forward and embraced her.

"Hey, big brother," Johnny boy said from behind him. Sebastiano turned, and they analyzed each other with the same reticence. Johnny had doubled in size since he left, filled up. A man by all accounts.

"Hey, pal," Sebastiano finally said, giving his brother a hug.

"Well go on and put your things in your room. It hasn't been touched since you left. We can use some help gathering firewood. It's getting cold," his mother said.

Sebastiano nodded and left the kitchen with his military-issued bags in hand. He paused in the living room and looked around. He couldn't identify any changes, but it looked more foreign to him now than the Argonne ever had.

He stepped into his room and set down his bags. He didn't bother to go through them. He had returned with a few things from his time in combat, trophies some called them. Sebastiano thought of them more as reminders. Reminders of what he did, of what he saw, and the men he lost. He wanted to remember those things, he couldn't allow himself to let it go. What would it all be for if he simply moved on? But the memories were too clear in his mind to need reminding right now. He pushed the army-green duffle bag under his bed.

On his lapel, he took off the citation medal he had received for the valor displayed in leading his men to take the German trench. He was nominated for the award by the men alongside him, but they knew the truth. It wasn't valor that he displayed that day, but cowardice, recklessness, and rage.

Sebastiano opened his dresser drawer and lifted up a few layers of shirts. He slid the medal underneath. That was one he was comfortable forgetting forever.

"Sebastiano?" his mother called.

"Coming, Ma," he said. He took one last look at the medal. All it represented to him was the death of someone he cared about. It represented an order given and a friend slain. He was proud of nothing he did in the Argonne Forests. Watching Franklin explode in a mist, seeing Vico ordered to put down Corporal Flaherty, burying Sergeant Mckenzie with only a wooden cross to send him on his way, saying goodbye to the only ones who could possibly understand . . . He wouldn't wish it on anyone.

He closed the drawer, determined to never open it again.

Benton Harbor, Michigan—October 29, 1919

They attempted to enjoy a family meal, but it was nearly impossible.

Sebastiano's grandfather Girolamo was irate. As they passed the side dishes around the table, Girolamo's eyes were fixed on the newspaper.

"This damned country. Full of savages, ingrates." He spoke in Sicilian, only having lived in the States for a decade or two, and never bothered to learn the "barbaric" language of the Americans.

Sebastiano's grandmother Viola, looked down, blushing from her husband's language at the dinner table.

"We can find something else for you to do, Father,"

Sebastiano's mother said, placing a dollop of ziti on her father's plate.

"I don't want to. I'm too old to learn a new trade. I've distilled alcohol since I was a boy. I made my first penny stepping on grapes in Castellamare. I don't want to learn anything else."

Grandfather was referring to the front-page article, which read "U.S. Is Voted Dry!" The previous day, the U.S. Congress had passed the Volstead Act, to widespread disapproval. No one had been able to talk about anything else since the news spread, even when they attempted to eat with their families.

"I thought the whole dry thing was smoke and mirrors," Johnny said, much more involved in current affairs than before Sebastiano had left for the war. "I never thought they would actually pass it."

"It's a phase. It'll pass soon," Viola said, spreading a napkin across her lap.

"This country is in its infancy. They don't understand that you can't take away a man's right and expect him to lie down and accept it. A man works and works and works all his days, and he deserves to have something strong to drink when he returns home," Girolamo said.

"Congress thinks they are saving us from ourselves." Sebastiano attempted to play devil's advocate.

Grandfather somehow laughed and snarled at the same time. "Jesus saves. This Government can't even save itself. President Wilson even knows it. Tried to veto the act but can't even get his house in order." Grandfather shook his head.

"I hope that look of distaste is about the news, and

not my cooking," Sebastiano's mother said with a feigned grin.

"I can't taste anything. Congress just stole my way of life. Destroyed how I earn my living." Grandfather said.

Sebastiano thought of his grandfather's distillery, where he had worked throughout his childhood. Some of his finest memories were there. If the reports were correct, though, special "prohibition agents" would be visiting soon with mallets to smash the booze and dismantle the equipment.

"I'm ruined." Grandfather hung his head.

"Don't say such things in front of the boys. They have enough to worry about," she said, poorly concealing the fact that she was referring to the recent suicide of their father.

"You know, Grandfather, this doesn't have to ruin you." Johnny took a bit of ziti. He tilted his head, thinking deeply.

"Come on then," Grandfather said.

"You have a special skill. You know how to create something a fella has to have. In my opinion, that makes your trade more valuable, rather than less." Johnny leaned forward, a smile developing.

Grandfather thought for a minute, but then shook his head. "A man my age can't afford to go to jail."

"Giovanni Domingo, don't even suggest such a thing!" Mother said reaching across the table to slap his arm. "You're talking about breaking the law."

"An illegal law," Grandfather commented.

"Who would want to arrest you, Grandfather?" Johnny asked. "Half the law enforcement in Chicago wants a drink as much as the next man, and the other half will keep quiet for a little graft."

"I can't believe what I'm hearing," Viola said, placing a hand on her forehead.

"It's the way of the world now." Johnny shrugged.

Sebastiano admired his little brother. Johnny had always been the smarter of the two, but he was different now. The way his eyes fixed as he spoke, the way his head tilted to the side. Sebastiano thought his kid brother must be some sort of genius.

"What about these prohibition agents they talk about in the papers?" Grandfather asked.

"Who would tip them off if everyone is partaking?" Johnny said.

Grandfather seemed intrigued.

"Why should I obey this law? It's an attack on us foreigners, that's what it is. It's those stronzi protestants—with their fancy clothes and mansions—that don't like our drinks."

"I think so too, grandfather." Johnny leaned back, obviously pleased with himself.

"I won't be able to trust my workers, though. I don't know how they'll feel about all this."

"Me and Sebastiano will help. Won't we, brother?" he patted Sebastiano's shoulder.

"I'd be happy too," he said. In actuality, he'd be happy to do about anything that would get him off the farm for a few days.

"What about the farm? We have too much work to do around here," mother said, reading his mind.

"If we play our cards right, we'll make enough money to pay someone else to chop wood and till the soil. Better yet, we could sell this place and move somewhere in the city." Johnny said. Sebastiano almost laughed at how clever, rebellious, and forward his brother had become.

"I like the way he thinks, Viola," Girolamo said. "If I'm gonna do it, I'll need you boys though." He gestured to Sebastiano and Johnny.

Sebastiano nodded, and Johnny stood and walked around the table.

"There's no one in the world I'd rather go into business with than my grandfather and my brother." He kissed his grandfather on the cheek, who was now beaming with excitement.

"The law won't be in effect for a few more months. We need to start preparing," Sebastiano said.

Mother stood and excused herself from the table, slamming a door after she disappeared.

Grandfather reached for his glass of wine and hoisted it in the air. "Salute."

The boys joined him in a toast and drank their last sip of legal wine.

21

SONNY

Upper East Side, Manhattan—January 14, 1931

"Sonny, you got a ring," Bonanno shouted into the shared bedroom, where Sonny was still attempting to sleep.

"Yeah. Just give me a second." He stood, feeling more weary than when he had taken to the bed the night before. He had risen like clockwork, every thirty minutes or so, with a racing heart and in a cold sweat. His dreams explored the fears that his conscious mind tried to banish. "This is Sonny," he said as he picked up the receiver.

"This is Detroit," the voice on the other line said.

He had been awaiting a call from their associates in Michigan. "I'm glad to hear it,"

"We have some produce we'd like to deliver."

Sonny knew the man meant weapons and ammunition, otherwise he would have talk to someone else. "Well, we're very hungry. That would be appreciated."

"Jamaican Bay in Brooklyn. The 16th at 8:00 p.m. Have someone there."

"I'll be there myself."

"Just put it to good use. Our friend Zerilli hopes our problems can be solved soon." The voice said, referring to the new Detroit boss, Joe Zerilli, who took over after Gaspar Milazzo was murdered.

"You tell Mr. Zerilli that we will eat the produce, and thank him in our prayers. And we'll soon return the favor."

The line clicked, and silenced.

Someone entered the living room, and Sonny heard happy voices. He rose and hurried to find the source.

Antonello stood at the doorway, holding a bag of cash in his hand, as proud as a new father.

"Stupid bastards told me what I wanted to know. I didn't have to bribe them or anything," Antonello boasted, as the others clapped him on the shoulders.

"Hey, Sonny," Charlie Buffalo turned to him, "turns out this big oaf isn't as useless as he seems. He found out who took your brother for a ride."

Antonello ignored the insult and smiled proudly. "I got a name, Sonny."

Maranzano, hearing the voices, left his room and watched from the doorway. "Our plan worked?"

"Like a charm. They sent two Jews to make the deal, and they were ready to sing like canaries. Told me the guy who got Enzo was named Joe the Baker."

"Joe the Baker . . ." Maranzano said quietly. "Joseph Catania. I should have known."

"You know him?" Charlie asked.

"I know him. He has run around causing trouble for our people for some time. He's lived with impunity because of his relationship with Joe Masseria, and it didn't hurt that his uncle was one of Masseria's top men. Those days are over."

"Want me to take care of him?" Charlie said, patting the

revolver tucked into his waistband. Charlie had never been involved in any of the hits and was used primarily as Maranzano's charming driver instead, but he liked to pretend he was involved in the dirty work.

"No. Vincente should decide the fate of Joe the Baker," Maranzano said, striding into the living room and to Sonny's side. "What would you like us to do?"

Sonny looked at the faces around the room. Each seemed to hope they would be chosen, or perhaps they only seemed like they wanted to.

"I'll take the hit," Sonny said, exhaling.

"Bobby Doyle will want it. He was pretty shook up," Cargo said from the couch, having been indifferent until then.

"Enzo's my brother," Sonny said, having admitted it to them after the assassination. He didn't want Vico to be a part of it. The hit would only fuel the fire in his soul.

"The two spent a lot of time together. He's been wanting to get who done it since we found out," Cargo said.

"You'll need someone to go along with you, Vincente. Would you feel comfortable working with Doyle again?" Maranzano asked.

Sonny shook his head and was silent for a moment. He imagined his brother's wrath if he wasn't involved. "He can be my driver," Sonny said at last.

Cargo laughed. "Doyle isn't much of a driver. He'll want to pull the trigger."

Buster, who had been sleeping in the shared bedroom, appeared. "I'll go. Enzo was a pal of mine too," Buster said, looking at Sonny in such a way that said he was not to be denied.

"He is our finest sharpshooter. It might not be a bad idea," Bonanno said from Antonello's side.

"And he's got a real fine Chicago typewriter." Cargo smiled, referring to Buster's Thompson machine-gun.

"All right. Buster can go," Sonny turned to Cargo, "and so can Doyle. But if we haven't heard from him by this time tomorrow, we're gonna have to make the hit regardless. We can't wait or the Baker is going to run to his boss or his uncle for protection."

"If I hear from him, I'll let him know," Cargo said, returning to his indifference.

"It's settled then. Go, and then return." Maranzano placed a caring hand on Sonny's shoulder.

He hoped that his brother would remain in a drunken stupor, as he often did, until the following day. In his gut though, Sonny felt that Vico's fate was already written in stone.

Southern Bronx, New York City—February 3, 1931

Much to Sonny's disappointment, Vico had sobered up quickly when he heard about Enzo's killer. When he heard the news, Cargo said his eyes lit up with fire. Sonny, Buster, and Vico immediately set about tailing Catania. Unlike Enzo, his killer traveled with a crew at all times, and a formidable one at that. Maranzano had been correct when he asserted that Catania was a favorite of both Joe the Boss and his uncle Ciro Terranova. He was protected at all times.

The three men kept a low profile, anxious to remain hidden in the Bronx borough they were unfamiliar with.

Spending as much time as they had in the Belmont neighborhood, though, they had begun to be seen. They all went by assumed names, and Sonny took the lead in explaining that they were traveling life insurance salesmen. Whenever questioned, he would use big words to confuse them, which worked like a charm.

Fortunately, Joe "the Baker" was arrogant. He had grown unafraid because of the large crew around him. He didn't take precautions. Important men like Steve Ferrigno and Al Mineo were hard to find, crafty men like Morello were even more so. Catania couldn't have been more different. Everywhere he went, he left a trail of cheap cologne and loud boasts about who he was and who he was related to. It wasn't hard to find him. The only question remained was how to kill him without ending up dead themselves.

Buster had been the one to spot the Baker leaving his home with his wife on a Thursday evening. He got in touch with Vico and Sonny and told them to meet him on Crescent Street immediately. The crew was noticeably absent, for once. Catania must have believed his presence alone could spare him a night of freedom with his wife.

The three men climbed the fire escape to the roof of a triangular building across the road from a nickelodeon theater.

"Buster, don't use that Tommy gun, all right?" Sonny said, as they tried to keep warm on top of the building.

"Come on, Betsy is getting hungry," Buster said, patting the violin case in his lap.

"It will draw too much attention. And you'll hit someone else. We don't want any civilian casualties," Sonny said.

"I'm a pretty good shot though." Buster smiled. He and Vico were comfortable in situations like this. Sonny couldn't keep his heart rate down. Looking over the roof top, he wondered how he was still in situations like this. But remembering Enzo, he thrust the thoughts from his mind.

"Seriously, Buster. The guy is with his family."

"Who gives a shit. He killed our brother," Vico said, adjusting his sights and setting the barrel of a hunting rifle on the ledge of the rooftop.

"I was only playing, Sonny. We understand escalation of force. We learned it pretty well over in France," Buster said, putting the violin case aside and reaching for the two pistols he had holstered on each side of his torso, underneath his suit top.

They waited for some time. Catania must have been seeing one of the new talkies that tended to last much longer than the old silent films.

"Can I call you Vico when it's just the three of us?" Buster asked later on. Vico shrugged. "I can't believe the rest of the guys still don't know who you are."

"I don't really care if they know who I am anymore," Vico said. "As long as they know I'm killing the guy who got Dad. No matter what."

Buster held up his hands in surrender. He tried to smile, but there was sadness in his eyes. "Hey, I won't stop you. I'm here trying to help. Maria is my wife after all."

"We appreciate the help, Buster. For what that's worth." Sonny spoke for both of them.

"It's crazy to think that all of this started in the trenches. Isn't it, Vico?" Buster said, lighting a cigarette. The two of them rarely mentioned it, but it was clear to Sonny that they still had a bond that was impossible to duplicate.

"Shut up. Look." Vico nodded to the theater exit, where people were beginning to depart.

Buster was immediately up on the ledge with his weapons drawn.

Sonny fumbled for his rifle and hurried to load it.

"Take your time," Buster said, one eye closed as he looked down the center of his two pistols, a cigarette clenched between his teeth. "If we shoot without you, it doesn't mean we don't like you."

Sonny ignored them and set his rifle down on the wall. He couldn't reach for his rosary, but he could feel the cool beads dangling on his neck, and said a silent prayer that no one would be hurt except the man they had come for.

"That him?" Buster asked.

"Yeah. Can you not tell?" Vico said.

Catania strode out of the theater, his wife's arm interlocked with his own. The Stetson on his head obscured his face, but the fur coat was thicker than a Pole's in a European Winter. No one else could afford a coat like that except the nephew of Ciro Terranova, and a friend of Joe the Boss.

"Ready to take the shot?" Sonny said, trying to calm himself and minimize the swaying of his rifle.

"Let Vico start us off," Buster said.

Vico clenched one eye and rotated his head for the right angle.

"When I fire, pop off two rounds each. Then we drop the guns. We take that back exit. We'll walk, not run, but we have to walk fast."

"Got it," Buster and Sonny both said.

Catania stepped forward with his wife and signaled for his valet to pull around.

"Here," Vico said, and pulled the trigger.

The Stetson flew from Catania's head.

Sonny pulled the trigger and his shot found its mark on

Catania's right shoulder, as far away from the pretty lady on his left as Sonny could make it.

Buster fired. Quarter sized bullet holes erupted from the Baker's torso.

The crowd around him let out a collective scream and scattered like frightened sheep. Catania's wife fell away from him, her hands and face covered with his blood. She could do nothing but stare at him, slack-jawed and silent, frozen in a horrific and tragic mask.

Sonny tried to look away but couldn't. Like stepping on a spider, he couldn't help but look at the carnage. After a moment, he said, "Let's go."

"All right," Vico said.

They stood and dropped the guns. Sonny followed them down the stairs and toward the car, using the scattering crowd as cover.

They slipped into Buster's old Buick and pulled onto the road as inconspicuously as possible.

Sonny's heart raced, his breathing labored. His lungs felt frostbitten.

Vico, however, was calm. "That's for Enzo." He looked out the window, his eyes fixed and unflinching.

22

LUCIANO

Garment District, Manhattan—February 6, 1931

Luciano leaned over the table and took a bump. He leaned back and sniffed hard to clear his nose, looking around the backroom of his shop as he braced for the high. "No good." He shook his head.

"It's the best in Manhattan, Lucky," the young Jew said.

"Call him Mr. Luciano," Meyer Lansky said, standing behind Luciano at the table. "He isn't your pal."

"Mr. Luciano, I vouch for the product."

"It'll sell, sure. But our clients have become accustomed to better quality. They don't want this garbage." He gestured to the heroin on the table.

"Our suppliers are some Greek boys in Hell's Kitchen. I'm sure they'd be happy to talk with you." The young man fidgeted.

"No deal. Pack up your shit and get outta here." Luciano gestured for him to leave.

The young peddler hesitated, clearly contemplating all

the money he just lost. Bugsy Siegel grabbed him by the arm and ushered him out.

"I don't know, Charlie," Meyer said, "our clients are dope fiends. They'll take what they can get."

"I want to make sure they keep coming back," Luciano said.

"The H guarantees it," Bugsy said, returning to the room.

Frank Costello leaned back in his chair, the butt of a cigarette wedged between his fingers, a thin stream of smoke pouring through the gap in his front teeth. "Lucky knows what he's doing."

"We need to find the Neapolitan. The guy we bought from in December."

"That Antonello fella?" Bugsy asked.

"He's been silent since the beginning of the year." Meyer shrugged. "Went off the map."

"Fellas don't just quit. If he isn't dead and didn't get pinched, he's out there. We can do our homework, can't we?" The corners of Luciano's lips twitched.

Antonello's product was the best they'd acquired in years, and it sold faster than a Manhattan fire could spread.

Vito Genovese entered the backroom of their shop, a bottle of whiskey in one hand, and several crystal glasses in the other. His eyes were cold as always, but a thin smile spread across his face.

"Do we have a reason to celebrate, Vito?" Meyer asked.

Vito set the glasses on the table and carelessly distributed the liquor across them. "You better believe it," he said, handing a cup to each man.

With a hint of irritation, Meyer asked, "Plan on keeping it a secret?"

"Joe the Baker is no more."

They exchanged glances. Everyone cheered or clapped, except Luciano.

"He's gone for a ride then?" Luciano asked with a raised brow.

"Happened in the Bronx a few days ago. The funeral is set for the eighth."

They all looked to Luciano. He tapped the table, his eyes staring into the distant. Joe Catania had been a thorn in Luciano's side for years. They obviously expected to see more of a positive reaction from him.

"Well, let's have a drink to wish him on his way." Luciano stood and raised his glass.

The crystal clinked together as Bugsy said, "Burn in hell, you rat prick."

Luciano enjoyed the smooth whiskey for a moment before he said, "Hey, Meyer."

"Yes, Charlie?"

"Didn't you say that Antonello fella asked you about Joe the Baker?" Luciano turned to Meyer, who's eyes were fixed on Bugsy.

"No, not exactly. He said he appreciated us taking out Enzo the Thief. He said Enzo was his biggest competition." Meyer gulped.

"Strange, isn't it? We did a lot of research on the Thief, and didn't hear shit about junk dealing," Luciano said. The muscles in his jaw flexed. "You didn't find that strange?"

"Charlie," Bugsy spoke up, his hands out in front of him, "we didn't ask no questions. Didn't seem important. We just told him it wasn't us who done it."

"And the Baker's name never came up?"

"Charlie—"

"I want to hear it from Meyer." Luciano pounded the table.

"No. His name never came up," Meyer swallowed hard, "to my recollection."

Luciano nodded, but made it clear he didn't believe the lie. "Now we have two reasons to find this Antonello." The men all nodded. "Then what are we doing?" Luciano stood, sending his chair to the floor. "Let's do something." He could feel the veins in his neck pulsing.

The men hurried out of the room. Meyer alone remained with Lucky.

"If Joe the Boss thinks I had something to do with this," Luciano said, "what do you think he'll do to me?"

"Joe the Boss isn't known for his deductive reasoning," Meyer said.

"We need to find this guy. Now. In the meantime, I'm gonna go see Joe the Boss and make sure he doesn't think I'm a rat," Luciano said.

Meyer nodded and started to leave.

"Meyer," Luciano said, stopping his associate mid-stride.. "You better hope he doesn't kill me. Cause if he does, he's coming after you too."

23

ANTONELLO

Central Park, Manhattan, New York—February 7, 1931

Something about birds always fascinated him. Whenever he wasn't on orders from Mr. Maranzano or Mr. Gagliano, Antonello liked to stroll in Central Park with a few pieces of bread. Still feeling the effects of the heroin he sampled that afternoon, he sat on a park bench and let the pigeons flock around him.

"Here ya go, little buddy," he whispered as they pecked at crumbs around his feet. He placed a piece in his hand and held it out. A little pigeon noticed him and hopped closer, chirping. "Come on, I won't hurt you," he said, as soothing as he could. The pigeon craned its head, its beak moving as if it already tasted the bread.

Antonello smiled as the bird neared. Something spooked it. Its wings fluttered in a fury as it darted away, the rest of the birds following it.

"Damnit," Antonello said, crumpling up the bread and sitting back on the bench. He enjoyed bird watching to people watching but deferred to the latter when he was given no other choice. His vision was hazy, but his mind felt focused, his senses collected.

Families passed him by, happy couples with small children, all bundled up in warm coats. They laughed, and Antonello found himself laughing with them. He imagined himself standing up and introducing himself. He considered telling them about his past. He pictured them nodding along as he spoke, their brows furrowed in empathy, maybe a tear in their eyes. He considered telling them about the people he'd killed and all the bad things he'd done. He assumed they would pat him on the shoulder and give him a hug. They'd say he did what he had to.

In truth though, Antonello remained on the park bench, with nothing but his thoughts. He closed his eyes and rested his head on the back of the bench, allowing himself to drift into sleep.

He stirred again hours later. He couldn't tell how long, but the tip of his nose stung from the cold, and the sun was already setting over Central Park. He stood and swayed on his feet, trying to find his balance. As he took to the path before him, he bumped into a young woman walking with her sweetheart.

"Hey, watch it, lady," he said.

He swayed along the path to his car parked on W 96th Street, and smiled when he spotted it.

He was proud of his automobile. He earned it. Himself. No help from anybody. He grew up broke, with a father who liked to break him further. Now many considered him an expert in a line of work, even if it was a seedy one. He maintained connections, like any businessman. He had money and could buy anything he wanted. He didn't need anyone.

"Antonello?" a man said standing in his way. Antonello strained his eyes to make out the man's features but couldn't place the man who wore a fedora low on his brow, casting a shadow over his face.

"What's it to you, Hebrew?" Antonello said, trying to straighten himself.

"It's nothing to me. Might be to someone else," the man said.

Antonello raised his hands and started to slur out a threat.

Before he could, a bag slammed over his head with such force that his knees buckled. He tried to fight back, but several men grabbed his arms to restrain him. He received two raps to the back of the head, and he collapsed. He struggled for air as they dragged him off the path.

"You're a hard man to find, Antonello. We have a welcome party waiting to meet ya," one of the men said.

Antonello flailed at the bag and struggled to get in just one good breath. His eyes blinked shut as he slumped into the arms of his assailant.

24

LUCIANO

Chelsea, Manhattan, New York City—February 7, 1931

Luciano could hear Masseria's booming voice the moment he entered the basement of their old distillery in Chelsea. It used to be bustling with workers, gangsters, producers and consumers. Not anymore. Masseria's attention strayed from his bootlegging Empire over the past several months. He couldn't think of anything but the annihilation of the Castellamarese.

"Good evening," Luciano said, entering the fray.

Masseria paced the floor, breathing heavily, angry like a school yard bully who finally got his nose bloodied. Mr. Joe's associates Joe Adonis and Augie Pisano were seated before the Boss, listening to his rants. "Look who shows up," Masseria said, shaking his head.

"I've been busy, Mr. Joe," Luciano said, removing his fedora.

"Busy with what? Your Jew friends and your little garment rackets?" Masseria laughed.

"Lately I've been busy trying to track down who got Joe the Baker. I assumed you'd want me to."

Masseria's face contorted in frustration. A plate of spaghetti might have pacified him, Luciano thought.

"Don't ever assume again, Charlie. You'll do what I tell you." Masseria pointed at him like his finger was a lethal weapon.

Luciano nodded and pulled up a chair to sit down beside Mr. Adonis and Mr. Pisano. "What do you want me to do then?"

"I don't care who killed Catania. We all knew who is behind it." He meant Maranzano. "We have to hit them. Enough playing defense. Enough reacting to them."

Adonis and Pisano nodded.

"We, we are the kings of New York. Not them. They must be eliminated, Charlie. We need to find their top men and chop them up into little bits. I will feed them to my dog!" Spittle flew from Masseria's lips as he shouted. He spoke poorly in both Italian and English, but his anger exacerbated that fact.

"What do you want me to do, Mr. Joe? You have my hands tied. You tell me you don't like my Jew friends, even though they're reliable and loyal to you. We could take anyone in Maranzano's camp for a ride, if you'd only give the nod," Luciano said, acting the part of capitulating follower as best he could.

Masseria stepped close enough Luciano could smell the stench of garlic and onions on his hot breath.

"I don't care who you use. I want them dead. Maranzano first. Then we round up his people and take them out like Al Capone." He formed his hands into an imaginary machine gun and pretended to mow down a crowd.

"They're a secretive bunch. And they're hard to find," Luciano said.

Masseria turned to Joe Adonis and Augie Pisano. "Sounds like excuses, doesn't it?"

Both shrugged, trying to defer judgement, but eventually nodded while Masseria's eyes remained on them. "I've heard enough excuses. I want results." He pounded a fist into his open palm. "After Morello and Mineo died . . . I made you my strategist. I have given you all my support. And yet you do nothing." Masseria flicked under his chin.

"You give me your support, and yet you gave contracts to Catania," Luciano said.

Adonis and Pisano squirmed, and for a moment Masseria looked like he might reach for the pistol on his hip.

"Well, now he is dead too. And you are very much alive. For how much longer, depends on what you do now."

Luciano locked eyes with the boss and knew exactly what he meant. They seemed to be in a contest to see who would look away first, ignoring the ringing of a phone in the background.

"Hey, Charlie," Tony Bender said from the back of the room, "you got a buzz." He held out a telephone receiver.

"Be right there." Luciano stood.

"I don't like you receiving your personal phone calls here," Masseria said, his bottom lip drooping.

"Nothing about it is personal," Luciano said walking to phone. "Strictly business."

Tony Bender handed him the receiver.

"Yeah, it's Lucky," Luciano said.

"We got him." The voice said on the other line.

Luciano recognized the voice of Vito Genovese.

"Who?"

"You know who."

"Not too difficult after all, huh?" Luciano said.

The line clicked.

Luciano turned to Joe the Boss,. "I gotta run, Mr. Joe," Luciano said, pretending to ignore the veins bulging on Masseria's forehead and neck.

"To where?"

"To go on the offense. Following orders." Luciano placed his fedora back on his head and tipped the brim to Joe the Boss.

One day he would be boss, Luciano told himself, climbing the stairs to the old distillery. And when he was, there wouldn't be a place for old greaseballs like Masseria. Or Maranzano either.

25

SEBASTIANO

Rogers Park, Chicago—August 9, 1926

Sebastiano saw Franklin's head explode. This time it happened differently. He was much closer. Close enough even to taste the iron of the blood rising like a mist.

He sprung out of bed like a shotgun blast, searching frantically for his rifle.

"Sebastiano, you're having a dream again," Johnny said from the doorway, rubbing his eyes.

He tried to slow his breathing and tried to collect his senses. His night shirt was soaked in sweat, but he shivered.

"What time is it?" Sebastiano asked, trying to forget the lingering image of tonight's war dream.

"About 5:30. I don't know, I didn't check," Johnny boy said, "Go back to sleep."

Sebastiano sat on the foot of his bed and slipped on a pair of trousers.

"No use. I'm just gonna get up."

"I'll stay up with you then," Johnny said.

"You don't have to do that."

"Yeah I do. I'll start some coffee on the percolator."

Sebastiano stumbled to get dressed in the darkness and made well on his promise to not open the top drawer of his dresser.

"What do we have on the calendar for the day?" Sebastiano said, entering the kitchen. Their kitchen in Benton Harbor was a third of the size of this one. After the start of Prohibition, their little team quickly made enough money to relocate to Chicago, where they purchased a two story home in Rogers Park.

"Hymie is wanting to meet with us later. He wants two trucks full of our product. Grandpa should have it ready but we need to test it."

"Hymie?" Sebastiano asked.

Hymie was one of the leaders of the outfit the Domingo crew fell under. But as a Pole, he generally worked with the Polish. Bugs Moran worked with the French and Irish, and Vincent Drucci handled the Italians. They all worked as one little outfit, but the Domingo's generally worked with Drucci.

"Yeah. Drucci is picking up some Canadian rot gut from the Gold Coast."

"Alright. We got some Joe ready?" Sebastiano asked. His eyelids were heavy and his body weak. He was always exhausted except for when in bed, where his mind decided to be especially active. A cup of coffee, or two, always helped.

Johnny boy slid him a cup. "You betcha."

"Was I loud tonight?" Sebastiano asked after a

moment of blowing on his coffee. His night terrors always embarrassed him.

"Not too bad."

"Did I wake the girls?" Sebastiano asked.

"Don't worry about it, Sebastiano," Johnny boy said, shrugging.

"I'm sorry," Sebastiano said.

"Don't mention it. Want to get a head start on the day, since we're already up? I'm sure grandpa has already been at it for hours," Johnny boy said, always anxious to change the subject. A look in his eye said he sympathized with his brother, but he hadn't been there in the Argonne. He couldn't understand. Easier to just avoid it. Plus, they had a lot to handle in the present without thinking about the past.

"Let me grab my guns and I'm ready to go."

"Better put your best threads on. We'll want to look good in front of Mr. Weiss."

Sebastiano laughed. "Hymie Weiss doesn't give a damn what we wear as long as we pay." Regardless, he returned to his room and slipped on the best coat he owned and selected the favorite of his new fedoras.

It took Johnny just seconds to get his car started. The Buick both brothers previously used for their means of transportation could take half an hour on a bad day.

"Headed to River North?" Sebastiano said when the car turned South onto the highway.

"Yeah. Little Hell. Grandpa said he'd be there this morning and load up a few trucks for us," Johnny boy said, taking a sip of the coffee he brought with them.

The Domingo's turned out to be the perfect team. With Johnny's cunning and business savvy, with Sebastiano serving as the muscle and "face" of their little operation, and their grandfather's expertise, they instantly found a place for themselves in Chicago.

"Is Mr. Weiss meeting us there?" Sebastiano asked.

It hadn't taken long for other, larger organizations to reach out to the Domingos. Chicago was just too big and too dangerous for people to be operating on their own. Grandfather was old and set in his ways. He didn't want anyone to interfere with his work. Sebastiano distrusted outsiders after his experience in the Argonne. Johnny, in the end, struck the deal. In hindsight, it proved to be a good one.

"No. We're meeting him at Schofield's. He's gonna stay on the second floor and look at the trucks through the window. Bugs Moran or one of the other boys will probably come and check everything out."

"Better make sure everything is in good shape. Everyone is on edge lately," Sebastiano said.

"Especially you. Last Tuesday when we were making that delivery I thought you were going to pass out," Johnny said, eyes fixed on the road ahead.

"I wasn't about to pass out I was about to piss myself." Sebastiano pulled out a cigarette and lit it. Nothing accentuated coffee better than a cigarette. "We should be on edge though. Capone is gunning for us and dying to make more paper headlines."

Their gang forced their rival faction leader, Johnny

Torrio, into an early retirement with a bullet through the throat. But they had no idea the hell they would unleash in his replacement, Al "Scarface" Capone. He was brutal enough to have any one of them killed, and some said charming enough to turn your best friend into a traitor.

"Capone's a two-bit gangster. He's all flash. We'll find him before he finds us. He walks around in the spotlight of photography flashes. Shouldn't be too hard."

"He's got about a dozen armed guards on him too. Maybe we'll get him when he's sloppy, but that doesn't mean he won't take us out first."

"Wait, is this it?" Johnny asked, straining to read the street signs.

"No, no, that's a one way, dumbass. It's up ahead." Sebastiano pointed as Johnny adjusted the car back onto the path, receiving a few errant horns as he did.

"Too many damn distilleries. I can't remember where they all are," Johnny said, his face flushing.

Johnny boy led the way into the Chestnut Street barber shop. He nodded at the barbers, who knew the drill, and took the narrow staircase to the basement. Sebastiano pulled the string to turn on the light, and they crept through the dusty basement to the bookshelf on the wall. Johnny pushed it open, and the two stepped through, like entering another world. The distillery bustled all around them.

"Rise and shine," Johnny said, tapping on a sleeping worker. The man jolted up, eyes fixed on the vat in front of him. "You fall asleep on the job again, and you'll be out of a job. Worse yet, I'll tell my grandfather, and he can take care of you himself." The worker finally looked at Johnny and nodded like a penitent child. Falling asleep on the job led to a lot of explosions and a lot of deaths. Johnny wasn't just being cruel.

Sebastiano winked at the man as reassurance, as the two brothers walked to the back of the distillery to the cramped office where their grandfather spent most of his days.

"Morning," grandfather said, looking up over his bifocals. Paperwork and mugs of cold coffee covered his desk.

"Do we have everything ready?"

"You have my cut from the last haul?" grandfather asked.

Johnny pulled an envelope from his suit top and tossed it on the table. It was a strange family dynamic to operate this way, but it worked for them thus far. Sometimes Sebastiano wished his father could have been part of it. Most of the time he didn't.

"Angelo has six barrels ready, and two milk trucks out front," grandfather said, but decided to show them himself. He led the way to the back of the distillery and opened up the garage door, where the barrels and their disguised vehicles were staged.

Johnny and Sebastiano both removed the lids and tasted a bit of the alcohol within.

"This'll do," Johnny said. Grandfather huffed, but Johnny was proud of his work. The North Side gang received most of its booze from the coast, Canadian whiskey smuggled over the boarder by boat. Still, they liked to have a bit of locally brewed booze, with a touch of Chicago in it. Grandfather could do that better than anyone.

"Thanks," Sebastiano said, shaking his grandfather's

hand more as a business partner than family member. The two brothers took to the wheel of the milk trucks and pulled out onto the road.

A thick smog rested over the street rather than a morning mist. Even when the sun shined bright, darkness shrouded the sky above River North. The railroads and docks transporting coal ensured it. Sebastiano strained to make out his brother's truck in front of him. They crossed town through heavy traffic to the corner of West Chicago Ave and North State Street, where their gang headquarters was located.

Johnny boy jumped out of his truck and signaled their arrival.

"Can I bum a smoke?" Johnny asked while they waited. Sebastiano offered him one and lit one himself.

"Good morning, gentlemen," a man said exiting the flower shop before them. Both brothers straightened when they recognized Hymie Weiss.

He was below average height, and slender enough to stand in the shower and not get wet. Regardless, his presence was seven feet tall. He wore a weathered black suit and vest and a newsboy cap to match. He would've fit right in at a funeral if it wasn't for the red bowtie.

"Good morning, Mr. Weiss," they replied in unison.

"Let's take a look at what you have," Hymie said, stepping to the back of the milk truck and opening the doors.

Sebastiano shot Johnny a look, both wondering why

the boss himself was handling the inspection. Capone's hitmen were everywhere, but Mr. Weiss didn't hide from anyone, despite the instruction of his partners Drucci and Bugs Moran.

"Just wanting to get some fresh air, Mr. Weiss?" Sebastiano asked as the boss hopped onto the truck and analyzed the barrels of booze.

"There isn't any fresh air in Chicago, boyo," he said.

After Hymie completed his inspection, Johnny said, "Does it pass the test, Mr. Weiss?"

"It does. Looks good. You have three more in the other truck?"

"Yes, sir," Sebastiano said.

"Good. You haven't been sampling it this morning, have you?" Hymie said with a wild grin.

Sebastiano found Hymie intimidating even when he was being friendly. There was a reason some said Mr. Weiss was the only man Al Capone ever feared.

"No, Mr. Weiss. Not at all. We leave sampling to the weekends," Johnny said, trying to laugh.

"Good. Since you're sober, you'll be coming with me to Mass."

Sebastiano and Johnny shot each other a look. The people to see and money to make. But when the boss gave an order, it wasn't to be denied.

"Yeah, absolutely," Sebastiano said for both.

"Hey, Bugs," Hymie shouted to his second-in-command, as the Frenchmen exited the flower shop, "move these trucks around back. Call McCarthy and Nails Morton and tell them to distribute."

"Got it," Bugs said, a wooden tobacco pipe clenched between his teeth.

"Come on, boys," Mr. Weiss said hopping from the truck.

Sebastiano and Johnny boy followed behind, both anxiously wondering why he desired to spend time with them.

"You want to take a car?" Johnny boy asked. "I can drive."

"Don't worry about it. Holy Name is just down the street here." He pointed to the Cathedral in the distance.

Sebastiano kept his eyes on the cars passing by, analyzing his surroundings as he learned to do in the Argonne.

"Vincent tells me you boys have been doing good work," Mr. Weiss said.

"We do our best. Mr. Drucci has been good to us," Johnny boy said, always taking the lead in situations like this. He was the charmer of the two.

"You've begun to make a name for yourselves. You make your deliveries on time, haven't run when the South Side gang made their threats, and kept quiet when the bulls and prohis came knocking. I can't ask any more."

Sebastiano and Johnny both stood a little taller.

"We're just trying to do right by you and Mr. Drucci," Johnny said.

"Stop," Hymie said in a stern voice. "Give yourself some credit. When someone tries to give you a compliment, accept it and say thank you. I don't waste my breath to puff you up."

"Thank you, Mr. Weiss," Sebastiano and Johnny said together.

"I've talked with Bugs and Vincent. Both think you

boys have earned a larger role in our organization. Do you think you're prepared?"

"What about our grandfather?" Sebastiano said without thinking.

"He can continue to make Chicago's finest brew. You can see him as much as you like on your time off. But you two are more useful to us than just delivery boys." Hymie began crossing the street.

The Domingo's were inclined to pick up the pace, but Hymie strolled through the traffic unperturbed by the car horns.

"We're prepared for whatever you have in mind."

Hymie stopped when they arrived on the other side of the street and stood under the shadow of the Holy Name Cathedral.

"I'm not sure you are. We're going to make a push. I'm tired of staying in the North corner of Chicago while Capone runs around like a Hollywood starlet. You boys stood by when they got Mr. O'Banion. You've got guts. But do you have the guts to kill?"

Sebastiano and Johnny looked at each other. Johnny was the brains of the organization, more suited for ledgers and handshakes than to pulling triggers.

"I've killed in combat. I don't see prohibition any different," Sebastiano said.

Hymie nodded. "Good. I'll need that kind of—"

Glass shattered and two machine guns started rattling. Sebastiano dove to the pavement, covering his head while the concrete erupted with bullets around him. He reached for the pistol in his waistband and popped off a few errant rounds in the direction of the gunshots.

His entire body tensed. A wet burning sensation

enveloped his leg. He looked down and realized he'd been shot in the thigh. Blood loss made his head spin, but he didn't stop shooting until he emptied his clip. He rolled to his belly and crawled a few steps to a street sign advertising 10c haircuts. He stared at the sky. And remembered his brother and Hymie.

"Johnny!" Sebastiano shouted, or at least thought he did, but couldn't hear himself over the gunshots.

Johnny lay on the ground too, blood seeping through his hands as he clutched his stomach.

Hymie Weiss stood, his torso riddled with bullet holes. He wobbled, his pistol pinched between two fingers. He glared at the shooters behind the broken glass windows of the third story across the street. Then he fell back like a tower collapsing. He landed flat on his back, his newsboy cap merciful drooping to cover his bloody face.

Sebastiano closed his eyes. The sound of artillery fire, over-the-top whistles, and bayonet charges filled his ears.

Then the lights went out.

Near North Side, Chicago—August 22, 1926

The fever dreams always took him back to the war. He saw Franklin's head explode, Mckenzie and Flaherty as they were lowered into ditches. He saw himself being shot and engulfed by German bayonets.

When he first woke up, he thought he was still in

France, the medics patching him up before returning him to the trenches. After a few moments, recent events flooded back to him. There were hand-picked dandelions withering in a vase of water on the nightstand beside his hospital bed. A picture of their family the previous Easter leaned up against it.

"Good morning," a nurse said beside the bed.

She startled him at first, but he calmed as he saw the innocent look in her eyes. His voice hoarse, he said, "Good morning."

The nurse checked his vitals, as he attempted to recall how he ended up there.

He traced back the memories and tried to sift through mostly fever dreams. Then it flooded back. Standing outside of the Holy Name church with Hymie Weiss and Johnny boy. The black car and the volley of bullets.

The pain in his leg reminded him of the shot that sent him to the concrete. He remembered Hymie Weiss standing on wobbly legs with a chest full of bullet holes, and his brother Johnny on the ground clutching a wound in his belly.

"Nurse, nurse," he said, panicking.

"What is it?" She leaned closer to him.

"My brother. My brother, is he okay? Where is he?"

"The man they brought you in here with?" she asked. She was young, barely old enough to drive.

"Yeah, maybe. I was with two fellas."

Her face saddened, and she placed a hand on his chest.

"One of them died before we could get him to the hospital. His name was Henry Earl... something, something Polish. I couldn't pronounce it."

"Yeah, yeah, what about the other guy?"

"They transported him to a special surgeon."

"So, he's alive." Sebastiano laid his head back on the pillow and sighed.

"And you'll recover too."

"What do you mean?"

"The doctors think you'll be able to walk again."

"There's a chance I might not walk again?" Sebastiano sprung up in bed. The irony of surviving unscathed through numerous firefights in France, only to be paralyzed trying to attend Mass in Chicago was palpable.

"Like I said, the doctors think you'll be able to. That bullet shattered your femur though. It was awful." She shook her head. "We have the best surgeons in Chicago. They did a great job of removing the bullet and repaired your leg as best they could."

"The surgeons are good enough for me, but not for my brother?"

She looked down and frowned. "He needed a someone who specialized in repairing stomach tissue and intestinal lining. They sent him all the way to Vanderbilt, in Tennessee."

She meant to sound encouraging, but it didn't work. As he remained silent, she leaned in closer. She batted her eye lids and pursed her lips.

"The newspapers said you all work for Al Capone. Is that true?" she asked.

Just another innocent, foolish girl. "Something like that," he said, and rolled over to make it clear he didn't want to talk anymore. He ignored the pain in his left leg as he did so. Then his eyes rested again on the dandelions and the picture frame. "Nurse, who brought these?"

"Oh, you've had a whole crew here to see you. Your

mother for one, and a pretty gal who said she was your sister-in-law. She had the cutest little girl I've ever seen attached to her hip."

"They coming back around?" Sebastiano asked.

"I would imagine. They've been here nearly every day."

"Wake me up when they're here," Sebastiano said, placing a pillow over his head.

He waited for a few hours, unable to sleep and feeling restless. When he tired of trying, he swung his legs to the side of the bed, grimacing from the pain radiating from his thigh. He could have used a bit more morphine, but he peeled away the tape and removed the tubes from his arms.

The door to his room opened. He looked up, hoping to see the beautiful smile of his little niece, but instead he was greeted by two ugly men—one a uniformed office with a spit-shinned gold star on his chest and a pistol on his hip and the other a "fly dick," a detective in plain clothes.

"Sebastiano Domingo," the detective said, approaching his bed.

"Who's asking?"

"I am." The detective brandished his badge and flashed it for just a moment.

"In a hurry to get somewhere?" The uniformed officer asked, tapping his fingers against his pistol.

"Just tired of laying in this damned bed."

"Why don't you remain seated?" the detective said, pulling up the nurse's bedside chair and plopping down beside Sebastiano.

"We have some questions, and you have answers," the officer said, looking at Sebastiano.

"I'm not sure what I could tell you." Sebastiano shrugged. "But you can ask anything."

"Our business is in relation to the shooting you were involved in. The one that killed your employer 'Hymie' Weiss, and your brother John Domingo."

"My brother isn't dead," Sebastiano said, swallowing.

"Probably will be soon enough. If you don't tell us what we want to know, he'll show up back in Chicago and end up dead sooner or later, anyways," the officer said with a shrug.

"I don't know what you want me to say," Sebastiano said, a tremor developing in his limbs and traveling to his core. "I was going to Mass with my brother and a friend. Some men pulled up outside and shot us while we were trying to go in. I didn't recognize them."

Sebastiano wished Johnny boy was there. He could've talked them out of this.

"You think we're stupid, you dumb hood? Hymie Weiss wasn't your friend. He was your employer. And Dean O'Banion was before him." The officer towered over him. The detective held out his arm to stay him.

"Yeah, you are stupid if you think I work for Hymie Weiss," Sebastiano said, confident of the detective's protection. He actually wasn't lying, exactly. He worked for Vincent Drucci, who worked alongside Hymie Weiss, but not for Mr. Weiss himself. Sebastiano simply forgot to mention that.

"We need you to help identify the men who shot at

you. They were sent by Al Capone, were they not?" the fly dick asked.

"How should I know? I'm a nice guy, and don't have many enemies," he said.

"But your boss did. You better start talking," the officer said, pulling out his billy club and raising it above his head.

"I'd talk if I had something to say. But I don't," Sebastiano said, shaking his head and shrugging his shoulders.

The detective looked down and sighed. The officer looked for a nod to commence a beating, but the door behind them opened again. Sebastiano's mother, sister-in-law, and niece stood at the doorway, their eyes alight with fear.

"Sebastiano Domingo." The detective pulled out a notepad and wrote something. "A war hero. Two citations for valor in the Great War and a campaign medal of victory. Shame you ended up like this." The detective shook his head.

"Yeah? Where were you? You go to France?" The detective and uniformed officer stepped away when Sebastiano's family stepped closer.

The officer pushed past them, stepping directly to the bed, and over Sebastiano.

"My name is Dan Healy." He extended a hand. Sebastiano eventually accepted a handshake. "I figure it's only right if you know my name. Since I know yours, Sebastiano. I'm keeping two eyes open for you and your damned brother," the officer said, breathing hard through his nostrils. Sebastiano tried to seem unperturbed. "If he lives, that is."

The detective waved for Healy to follow him, and the two departed.

"What was that about, Uncle Sebastiano?" his five-year-old niece said, hopping down from her mother's hip and hurrying to hug him.

"Just some men trying to do their job and protect us. Don't worry about it." He combed back her frizzy hair with the back of his hand and kissed her head.

"How bad does it hurt?" his mother asked, her eyes wet as she reached out for a kiss.

"Oh this?" he gestured to the leg bundled up in bandages and a cast, "just a scratch."

"Hardly," his sister-in-law said, a sad grin on her face. She wrapped her arms around his neck and kissed his cheek, but Sebastiano could tell she wished it was her husband returning to her, rather than his brother.

"Who do I talk to about getting out of this damn place?" he said.

His niece gasped. "Momma says that's a bad word."

Sebastiano laughed and mocked shame. "She's right. Don't use words like that. It isn't nice. How do I get out of this normal, fine, happy place?" he said.

"Are you sure you're ready?" his mother asked.

"Yeah, ma, I'm fine. Promise. I just need some fresh air."

It took the girls some time to persuade the nurses Sebastiano was ready to leave. He made it clear he wasn't going to be persuaded, and he wouldn't pay another cent as long as they kept him there. A few hours before dinner, a nurse brought a wheelchair, and Sebastiano's mother helped him into it. She wheeled him out, a bag of his belongings in hand. The police took his bloody clothes as "evidence", but he didn't care because his dog tags were present. He didn't like his medals, but he felt naked when his identification tags weren't hanging for his neck.

Sebastiano and his family took the elevator down to the first floor and approached the front desk to make their payment and sign out.

"Your grandfather brought Johnny's car and left it here. We can drive it home, if you'd like," Mother said as Sebastiano signed his name on the clipboard the nurse handed him.

"Sure, but I don't think I'll be doing any driving." He patted his left leg. "Who's going to drive it? One of you?" He smiled.

"I've been practicing, I'll have you know. I'm getting good." Mother slapped his shoulder.

"Momma, can I go start the car?" Sebastiano's niece asked. "It's been sitting there for so long and it will be hot! I'll roll down the windows."

Sebastiano's sister-in-law exhaled and finally handed her the keys.

"Be careful, now, okay? Watch for other cars!" she shouted after her daughter as she hurried to the exit.

"Thanks for your help, ma'am." Sebastiano nodded to the charge nurse who signed him out.

Mother spun the wheelchair round, and they headed for the exit.

"Take me somewhere I can get a beer," Sebastiano said when they reached the glass doors.

His mother was replying when an explosion erupted like a mortar shell.

Sebastiano jolted to his feet and fell to the ground. The heat of a fire engulfed them. He looked out over the parking lot and found Johnny's Lincoln. Flames poured from it and dark smoked rolled overhead, the silhouette of his motionless niece clearly visible in the driver's seat.

26

SONNY

Bronx, New York City—February 7, 1931

Cargo talked the entire ride. About his girl Mae, about his older brother who was in a looney bin in upstate New York, about fond memories of his first heist in his youth. Sonny nodded along and would say a few words ever so often, but he wasn't listening. As Cargo rambled on, Sonny's thoughts turned to his own past. He remembered the smile on his father's face when they would play cards. Alonzo would never let him win but would "accidentally" show his cards when he didn't have anything good.

He recalled a summer evening when the entire Consentino clan walked down to Grand Street to get some cannolis at Ferara's, and how his ice cream melted in the summer heat before he could eat it. His father wiped his tears and picked him up, holding him tight in arms like tree trunks. He fumbled through his pockets until he found enough change to buy Sonny another treat.

Memories of rushing to make it to Mass on time. Rosa

crying when she burnt the *Zuppa di Pesce* at Christmas. When Alonzo searched all over Manhattan for the perfect Christmas tree, and how they decorated it with whatever things they could find around the house. How he and his brothers would jump onto Alonzo's back, only to be overpowered and find themselves in the powerful vice grip of a tickle fight.

On summer nights, when the Consentino's apartment was too hot to sleep in, and they would climb to the top of the apartment and lay out blankets, sleep under the stars. "This city will be yours one day," his father had said that night. "I'll love you, always and forever."

Sonny had slept with his father's chest as a pillow. Enzo and Vico competed to see who could spit farther from the rooftop. Maria cried until Rosa bounced her back to sleep.

Cargo interrupted Sonny's thoughts, saying, "And I told him, 'You better find somewhere else to park that piece of shit.'"

After a moment of anticipation Sonny realized he just heard a punchline .

"That is really funny," he said, his forehead against the glass of Cargo's car, watching the city lights pass by.

"Eh, you didn't hear it right," Cargo said, holding out a pack. "Want a cigarette?"

"I'm fine," Sonny said, anxious to catch the trail of memories before they faded.

"Why'd you want to come with me to the Rainbow Gardens anyways? You Brooklyn fellas don't usually make it up this far," Cargo asked.

"Just wanted to get a little fresh air. And a drink," Sonny said.

"And a broad?" Cargo slapped Sonny's shoulder, but Sonny didn't engage. He didn't come for a broad. Or fresh air. Or a drink. He made the decision to travel with Cargo to the Rainbow Gardens for one thing and one thing only: answers. It lay behind all his decisions. He could think of nothing else but that name . . . Turridru. It haunted him. It lingered behind all his thoughts, it infested his dreams. Maranzano had been searching, but so far had come up short. How could he really gain any intel while stuck in one safe house or another? With the same people?

Gagliano might know though. There might just be one piece of information that could open up a floodgate. The hope of answers was the only thing making the ride with Cargo bearable.

"Here she is," Cargo pulled into the parking lot, underneath a neon sign. "A lot of stuff has changed lately, but the old Rainbow Gardens is always the same. Your brother Enzo used to really enjoy coming down here."

The name still caused Sonny's chest to tighten. When he heard "Enzo," he saw it etched in the cold headstone.

He followed Cargo into the bar. Sonny felt strange in the place, like he didn't belong. Cargo acted two feet taller, like he was walking into a welcome party. Men came to greet him.

"'The Gap', it's been too long." Cargo kissed the cheek of the first man.

"Yeah, cause you've been running around with those Castellamarese for too long." Other men kissed Cargo's cheek.

"Just following orders." Cargo held his hands up in mock capitulation.

Sonny stood alone. After a moment he approached the bar.

"What do you want?" the bartender asked. They were remarkably loose with their sale of alcohol. Looking around the room at the horde of Gagliano's men, it made sense. There wasn't a bull in New York who would want to test the place without an entire squadron at his back. Probably the same reason Gagliano continued to hang around the same place without fear of Masseria's men.

"Something brown," Sonny said, placing his money on the table.

"Want to start a tab?"

"No. I shouldn't be here long," Sonny said. He much preferred drinking the wine his father brewed back in Little Italy, but he needed something to calm his nerves.

"Hey, daddy. Want a dance? I'll take you to our back room." One of the Rainbow Gardens' girls came and placed an arm around his shoulder. "A quarter can buy you the best ten minutes of your life." She wore a top low enough to command attention, high enough her patrons would desire more.

"I'm not interested," he said, ruder than he meant it. He simply wasn't going to be distracted. He wasn't interested in a girl like her. He wanted a girl like Millie. Someone who could give him a family like the one he was raised in. But he wasn't a man like his father, and he couldn't have a woman like Millie.

Thrusting the thoughts aside, Sonny drained the whiskey and slammed the shot glass on the counter. He stood and moved towards the boss's table before he could talk himself out of it.

"Mr. Gagliano?" Sonny said approaching the table, "I have a few questions I've been wanting to ask you." He blurted it out as quick as he could. He knew he would stutter through it if he didn't.

Only then did Sonny realize he interrupted the boss.

Gagliano's face scrunched in indignation and looked at

one of the two men seated across from him. "Tommy, who the hell is this guy?" Gagliano said.

"I'm not sure, but he seems to think he is an old pal," the man said, and Sonny recognized him as Tommy Lucchese.

"I am Enzo Consentino's brother."

The table let out a collective exhale. Gagliano still looked irritated, but Lucchese and the other man at the table nodded their heads.

"Enzo the thief?"

"That's what you all called him. But to me he was just an older brother."

Gagliano snorted, but his eyes softened.

"Take a seat, kid," Gagliano kicked an empty chair from under the table.

Sonny sat, realizing he had only gotten this far in his mind. He didn't know how to approach the subject now.

"You said you wanted to ask a question, paisano. So ask it," the third man said, seemingly the most compassionate of the three. As soon as he spoke, Sonny recognized him as "The Gap Petrelli" he'd heard the other guys talk about. The cavern between his two front teeth was unmistakable.

"I want to know more about what happened to my father . . . to Enzo's father," Sonny said. He could feel his heartbeat throughout his entire chest and in his throat. But he wasn't going to walk away.

Gagliano rolled his eyes and exhaled. "I should have known it was this shit again. Look, kid, I told your brother everything I knew."

"Now my brother is dead. I want to hear it for myself."

"I told that Bobby Doyle too."

"I don't know him very well anymore."

Gagliano waved for the bartender's attention.

"Bring this man another drink." He pointed to Sonny. "Actually, bring another round for the whole table."

The bartender hurried.

"Your father got whacked. By One of Us," he said.

Sonny jaw went slack and he gripped the arms of his chair.

Gagliano shook his head. "Not, one of us." He pointed to the table. "Someone in our line of work."

"What was his name?" Sonny already knew, but he wanted to hear it again.

"Called himself Turridru. I don't figure that was his real name. It's what he went by. He did all his communication through couriers. He couldn't speak a word of English. He was some 'mustache Pete' from Sicily, and I didn't figure he'd be around for long. We would've told him to go push papers, but some fellas from Brooklyn vouched for him. We figured he was up the river in Sing Sing or something. We never saw him."

"But the council gave him clearance?"

"Not at first," Lucchese said, but then deferred to Gagliano to continue.

"We told him no. There was a man who had been on the council since the turn of the damn century who said your old man wasn't to be touched."

"Giuseppe Morello."

"Yeah. We called him Peter Morello. Sure. Morello didn't want your father harmed."

"But he was in prison," Sonny said.

Gagliano slammed back a shot and threw the glass behind him. "You want to tell the damn story, junior, or you want me to?"

"I'm sorry, Mr. Gagliano. Go on."

"Morello had been locked up for a while. He hadn't

been earning. We weren't even sure the guy was gonna keep his mouth shut with the lawyers and bulls always trying to squeeze information out of him. Turridru was persistent, said your father wronged him in Sicily. He said your father killed his mother."

Sonny shook his head. "Not possible. My father would never hurt a woman."

"Do I look like some kind of gypsy? We didn't have a crystal ball. I'm just telling you what he said."

"I understand." Sonny finally took his drink.

Gagliano exhaled. "Even after he said that, some of the older guys on the board weren't having it. Masseria didn't give a shit. Said it made no difference to him. But some of the old guys who probably knew your old man in Sicily said he couldn't kill a protected guy without some kind of proof."

Gagliano sipped his whiskey, and for a moment Sonny feared this might be all the man would say. But he continued, "He couldn't prove it either. Didn't have records or nothing. But he did have proof of another insult. He said he lent money to your father, a large sum, up front. And he missed a few vigs."

Sonny's face went blank as he thought about all the men like his father he'd threatened when their vigs were late.

"Payments on a loan from One of Us," The Gap explained in case he didn't understand.

"He said your father doubly insulted him. In Sicily, and then again in the States. He claimed to have ledgers to prove the transaction. We didn't have a a choice. So we gave the nod."

"That's when he killed my father?" Sonny's throat tightened.

"Actually, no. That old hook hand Morello got out of prison about that time, and he returned in a big way. As soon as he heard the news, he said he would kill the bastard if he tried to kill your father."

"What happened next?"

Gagliano threw up his hands. "That's all I know. I don't have proof it was that rat prick. It didn't seem so newsworthy at the time, paisano. That was the last I heard. And then the barber ended up dead within a few months, so I figured this 'Turridru' was behind it."

"No one tried to do anything afterward? Morello didn't try to find him?"

"No proof." Gagliano shook his head. "But yeah, Morello was a tough old bat, so I'm sure he tried. But whoever it was kind of disappeared. I never heard the name again."

Sonny exhaled and looked down at the table. He finished his glass of whiskey and stood. "I appreciate your time, Mr. Gagliano." He extended a hand and waited a moment for it to be accepted.

"I'm not sure why you're looking here. You're with the Castellamarese right?"

"Yeah." Sonny said.

"That Turridru was one of Cola Shiro's boys. He was in your family."

The color flushed from Sonny's face. His legs numbed beneath him.

"I'm not sure what good it's gonna do you to find him. Even if he is alive, you aren't going to be able to touch him. But if you're determined to keep searching, look to your own people," Gagliano said and turned away.

Sonny, lost again in a swift river of thoughts, walked toward the exit.

"Hey, Sonny boy, where ya going?" Cargo shouted, his girl Mae kissing his neck.

Sonny stopped and turned. "I'm gonna find my own way home." He pushed through the double doors and into the cold night air.

South of Houston Street, Manhattan—February 8, 1931

Sonny hid his face behind a menu until he saw Father Sammy enter the restaurant. Surely, he'd be safe with a priest, right?

He watched Sammy take off his coat and hand it to the greeter, making sure to shake hands and meet the eye of everyone who passed.

"Hey, Sammy. Thanks for meeting me outside of the church." Sonny stood and kissed him on either cheek.

"Hey, you kiddin'? I didn't just pick this place cause it shares your name. Vincent's has the best ziti in Manhattan, almost as good as my great-grandmother's in Milazzo." He licked his lips.

"Not too hungry, actually," Sonny said. "Maybe I'll try some next time."

Sammy met his eyes and sized him up. "No worries. I'm just happy to hear your wanted to meet."

"Yeah . . ." Sonny waited for the Father to say something, but he allowed Sonny to sit with his thoughts. "Sorry, it's been a while since I've tried to make small talk. Don't really know how to start."

Sammy shrugged. "Who cares for small talk anyway? Let's talk about what you want to talk about."

Sonny exhaled. "The only thing I've talked about for as

long as I can remember is how my life is falling apart. Doesn't make for pleasant conversation." Sonny met the Father's eyes and tried to convey what he hid was of a criminal nature.

Sammy nodded when he understood. He pulled out his white priest's collar and sat it on the table between them. "Go ahead. I bet you can't make me blush."

Sonny laughed and shook his head. "You don't know that."

A fair skinned girl with brown curls approached their table. "What'll it be? Padre's first."

Sammy deferred to Sonny, who said, "I'm not too hungry. Two pieces of burnt toast. Some butter."

"I'll take a cup of coffee," Sammy said.

"Actually, that sounds nice. I'll take a cup too."

Sammy met the waitresses eyes and smiled. "Why don't we make it a whole pot?"

She grinned and scribbled down the order. "You got it. Coming right up."

Sammy made himself comfortable in the booth, leaning to the edge and kicking his feet up. The only thing different from him and the guys Sonny hung around was the Father didn't turn around and watch the waitress while she walked away.

"I don't think you can make me blush, Sonny," Sammy said with a charming smile.

"Oh yeah? How do you figure?"

"I grew up on Houston. I know about this stuff. I ran with a group of other stupid kids, and we called ourselves the 'Sixth Avenue Boys'." Sammy accepted his cup of coffee and smiled at the memory.

"From gangster to priest. You should write a book," Sonny said, stirring in his sugar and milk.

Sammy shook his head. "Slow down, Buster Brown. I said I was a kid. A two-bit hood who liked looking for trouble and making enough money to buy my mom a rose for Mother's Day. That's about the extent of my criminal enterprise." He leaned forward and placed his elbows on the table, his face straightening. "We weren't much older than teenagers when we started running for a few big names. We just carried envelopes from place to place most of the time, probably cash but we didn't risk looking inside."

"A nice way to earn a little dough for a kid," Sonny said.

Sammy blew on his coffee and took a timid sip. "It was about that time I watched them smash the head in of a kid who talked to somebody's sister." He shook his head. "I figured there had to be a better way to get people to do the right thing. My Ma was always pestering me to attend Mass, so I decided to take it a bit more seriously."

Sammy leaned back. He didn't want to talk about it anymore.

"All right, we'll talk," Sonny said, "But put that collar back on so I know I can trust you won't say anything."

"Glad to, starting to feel naked without it." Sammy smiled. "Go ahead."

Sonny peered over his shoulder. "I'm worried about the acoustics."

"Look around," the Father said. "Think anyone here is listening?"

College sweethearts. Two old veterans not saying a word. Young parents with a fussy baby.

"I think I told you before Enzo's funeral that my father got killed not long ago." Sonny said and Sammy nodded. "We got involved in all this looking for the guy who did it. We wanted—"

"Justice?"

"Revenge," Sonny said. He sighed. Felt good to utter the word aloud. He lowered his voice. "We got the guy we thought did it. Well, I did. Then I learn yesterday for sure it wasn't him. Actually, this fella stuck his neck out for my old man. And we . . . took care of him."

Sammy sucked in breath, closed his eyes, and exhaled. Sonny waited to be reprimanded, but the Father nodded and opened his eyes. "You did what you thought you had to. But my question is why you thought this guy did it?"

"It's what I heard. People I trust told me this guy was behind it all."

"You're a smart cat, Sonny. I'm wondering why you didn't dig a little further before you pulled the trigger. Metaphorically speaking, of course."

Sonny sipped his cooling coffee. "I don't know. I think I worried about the answers I'd find out. Figured I might learn about my old man than I wanted to." Suddenly he couldn't maintain eye contact with the Father. "I had an image in my head about who he was and . . . I wasn't ready to give that up."

"So you took care of the wrong guy. And the right guy is still out there," Sammy said.

"Unless he's gone of his own accord. Or someone else's. But we haven't found him."

"You still looking?" Sammy raised an eyebrow.

Sonny nodded. "Still looking. And we got caught up in a . . . a damn war in the process. Probably read about it in the papers."

Sammy acknowledged he understood but didn't want Sonny to go into further detail. He fumbled through his pockets and pulled out two cigarettes, one for the both of them.

"You don't want to be in this conflict?" Sammy asked.

Sonny accepted the cigarette and lit it. "It's complicated. You ever find sometimes people sin and they hate it . . . but they want to keep doing it anyway?"

"Usually how it goes, unfortunately, Sonny boy."

Sonny's heart skipped a beat hearing the name his Father always called him. He wasn't sure why, so he kept talking instead of considering it further. "That's where I'm at. I'm close with the folks I'm with. I care about them. Their safety, obviously. But I want them to win too. The big fella more than anyone else."

Sammy nodded. "Does he ask you to do these things?"

"No." Sonny was quick to answer. "Sometimes he even says I don't have to."

"But you usually do anyway?" Sammy's eyes narrowed.

"Yeah, I do. I go with the other boys. Sometimes my other brother Vico."

"So all three brothers decided to follow this path?" The Father's eyes glossed over as he built a picture in his mind.

"All three of us. Although, I didn't even know they were doing the same thing I was for a long time. We, uh . . . lost touch for awhile."

Sammy stared at Sonny intently and took a long, slow drag on his Turkish royal. "Why?"

"Why did we lose touch?"

"No, why did you all decide you needed to find who did that to your old man?" Sammy clarified.

"I went to the coppers first. Tried my luck with them. They gave it a week or two to cover their bases but were quick to say it was just another wop who got wacked in the booze wars. We were the only ones to do it."

"Yeah, Sonny, I get that." Sammy leaned forward and placed his elbows on the table. "But *why*?" the Father said. A glazed look covered Sonny's face. "This isn't Sicily—

blood feuds don't solve anything. You aren't doing it for tradition, doesn't seem like it at least. If you believed in the old ways, I'd see the Consentino boys celebrating the feast days of the saints more often. So *why* are you doing all this? What's the motive? I'm sure it's different for each of you."

The waitress provided them with an ashtray and Sammy tapped out his cigarette while he waited on a response.

"I don't know. Enzo just wanted to matter. He wanted to be somebody," Sonny said. "Always did. He thought running with big shots would make him matter—give him purpose. He ran a locksmith's shop and wanted to make a career in petty burglary. He didn't want a war. I don't even think he wanted to hurt anybody." Sonny stopped and rubbed the back of his neck. "He just wanted to sit around playing poker, drinking with the fellas."

"Vico," the Father said. "Was it the same for him?"

"Not even close." Sonny shook his head. "Other than Buster, our brother-in-law, I don't think he likes any of the boys we run with. He looks at them like prey. Like he only tolerates their existence because of the shared goal. He'd bury them as soon as shake their hands otherwise."

"What's in it for him then?"

"It isn't the fun." Sonny chuckled, mystified. He hadn't thought about it much before. "He doesn't like cards. And he drinks to get drunk, not to socialize."

"What's his motive then, Sonny." The Father topped off both their coffees.

"I think Vico just needs a war." Sonny sighed.

"Doughboy?"

"Yeah. Served in the Fighting Sixty-Ninth. Why?"

"Just know the type. Go on." Sammy nodded.

Sonny continued, "He needs something to hunt.

Someone to hurt. His anger controls him, I think. When he sees red, it's like he's somebody I've never met before. You can't reason with him." All kinds of images of his brother's face flashed before his eyes. He couldn't connect most of them with the kid he grew up idolizing.

"I feel bad for him." Sammy lowered his gaze for the first time.

"He decided he wants to get the guy who killed Dad, and he's going to no matter what anyone else says. When it's over, he'll find another war to fight."

"What about you then, Sonny? You need a war?"

Sonny shook his head.

"You like kickin' back with the boys? Does your organization make you feel important?" Sammy was seeking to understand, but he still didn't.

"No. None of that."

"What is it then?" Sammy said.

"I don't know. I really don't . . ." Sonny started and stopped speaking several times. He couldn't find the right words, and he wanted to be careful about how he responded, feeling like his answer would give meaning to everything he'd done or invalidate it all. "I guess I just want to be a good man. My biggest fear—and it haunts me—is being a bad man. Or a weak one. I just want to be good." He kept rambling on to find something meaningful to say, but shook his head in frustration. The right words weren't there.

"Good and evil can be relative," Sammy said. The waitress set down the burnt toast with butter and smiled at them both. They waited for her to depart before continuing. "You want to be good. But by who's standards?"

"I don't know." Sonny grimaced. He didn't really like the question.

"God's?"

"Obviously that's the right answer," Sonny said.

"There isn't a right answer." Sammy shook his head. "Your heart knows the truth. You want to be a good man by who's standards? This new 'big fella' of yours?"

Sonny took a deep breath. "My dad's probably."

"You really think this is what your dad would want?" the Father asked.

Sonny clenched his jaw. Sammy's disposition was understanding and amicable, but Sonny felt uncomfortable regardless.

He started to answer, but Sammy thrust out another cigarette. "Take a smoke and consider it."

Sonny took his time. He wet the tip with his lips and balanced it in the middle. He took a silver lighter from his pocket and lit it himself this time. "I don't know," Sonny said, smoke rolling out of his mouth as he spoke. "Not sure I ever really knew who he was. Or what he wanted from us. But it doesn't matter."

"It doesn't matter?" The Father's eyebrows raised.

"No. It doesn't. He left me. He left me without a father. I found a new father who helped me when I was totally alone. And he's proud of me." Sonny leaned back, crossed his arms, and smiled. "So yeah, maybe by his standards."

His eyes wide, Sammy puffed out his cheeks and shook his head. "Boy, he sounds like a shitty father to me." Sonny's jaw dropped but Sammy answered before he could say anything. "He used the worst tragedy of your life to indoctrinate you. To get you to do his bidding. To expose you to a world you don't belong in."

Sonny slammed his cigarette into the uneaten toast, rage coursing through his veins in a sudden burst he wasn't used to. He felt himself stretch out a pointed finger at the priest.

"You went too far this time, Father." Sonny breath was heavy through his nostrils. He felt like a triggered bull. "Maranzano has never asked me to do a damn thing. In fact, he's kept me out of the worst parts. All he did was give me a place to belong."

The Father lowered his gaze and raised his hands in surrender. "Sonny, I didn't mean any—"

"He was there for me when no one else was. Where was the church? I don't remember my mother getting any flowers from St. Patrick's." Sonny stood and towered over the Father. "Maranzano brought me in when I had nothing of value to offer him, and when no one else was there for me."

"Sonny, I'm sorry. I spoke out of turn." Sammy met his eyes, and his contrition seemed genuine. "You're right. I don't know the guy. I'm just worried about you. That's all."

Sonny shook his head and exhaled out the rest of his anger. He pulled out a wad of dollar bills and threw several down on the table.

"I got places to be," Sonny said.

"I told you I would get it, Sonny," the Father shouted after him.

"Put it in the offering then." Sonny hurried from the diner, blinking rapidly to clear the tears from his eyes.

PART III

27

TURRIDRU

Wappinger Falls, New York—July 23, 1917

Most of the passengers on the boat brought with them less than $10 cash, and no more than two suitcases. Turridru and his new bride Elizabetta brought eight pieces of luggage between the two of them, one of which contained all the money Don Toto had given to them as a dowery. Turridru certainly backed the right horse. His future never been brighter.

He made the decision to avoid going to Ellis Island. The formalities of citizenship could come later. Men like him don't get deported. The United States only deported the uneducated and troublemaking lower class. Instead, Turridru decided to sail to Canada, and make his way south. As always, Elizabetta complied without a fuss.

After spending a few days in a Canadian hotel—making love like horses in heat—they took a tram south. When they reached the border, a carriage waited to transport them to New York City where his new associates would be waiting. It would be a long journey, but Turridru didn't mind. He had been waiting for this moment for several years. A few days on the road wouldn't dissuade him.

"My cousin Margareta says Brooklyn is a good place to settle down," Elizabetta said after waking from a short nap.

The engulfing heat and the clip-clop of the horses' hooves had a sleep-inducing effect.

"Really? Manhattan is said to be the Rome of America, where everything happens," Turridru said, putting down the book he had brought for the journey. A tale of the Ancient Sicilians. He loved learning, but he enjoyed talking with his beautiful wife even more.

"Too much noise, too much clutter," she shook her head. "There are a lot of Sicilians in Brooklyn, she said. We could fit right in."

"I'll go where you want to go, my love." He leaned across the seat and kissed her on the forehead. She smiled bashfully and laid her head on his chest. He inhaled deeply the aroma of her hair.

A few more hours passed before the driver tightened the reigns and slowed the horses to a halt.

"We've arrived, sir," the driver said in English.

Of all the languages Turridru learned in Seminary, English was his least favorite. He had no intentions of speaking it. "Thank you," Turridru replied in Sicilian and slipped the man a few dollars.

The driver understood the language of money though and nodded.

Turridru leapt from the carriage and lent a hand to help his bride down. The driver hurried to gather their luggage, probably looking for another generous tip. Turridru stopped and looked around. What a strange country America was. Untamed. Everywhere Turridru looked were trees, overgrown shrubs, and dirt paths. He hoped New York City wouldn't look like this.

A car sat parked off the main road before them, and a man stepped out. He had a finely trimmed mustache and wore a dark suit with grey pinstripes. A jovial smile creased his face while he approached.

"Welcome to America, Paisano," the man said, stretching out a hand.

Turridru accepted it and gave a smile to match his new acquaintances. "I am happy to be here," and introduced himself.

"We know who you are, and we are happy to welcome you here." Turridru looked over the man's shoulder to see two other men waited by the car. He was given quite the kingly welcome.

"This is mia tesora, Elizabetta." Turridru said, gesturing to his wife. She curtseyed, and the man kissed her hand.

"My name is Vito Bonventre. Our mutual friend in Palermo told me wonderful things about you. I believe we have a place for you in New York City."

"That is all I could ask for."

"Would you like to live in Brooklyn?" He turned to Elizabetta.

She glanced at Turridru and batted her eyes.

Her voice smooth and soothing amongst the gruff American who addressed her, she said, "We were just talking about Brooklyn. I have a cousin there."

"Perfect. Your father has already arranged payment. If you aren't too tired from your journey, a dinner has been organized to welcome you."

"How could we refuse such a kind offer?" Turridru asked.

His wife smiled. Her eyes said she was weary, but again she complied without a complaint.

"Right this way." Bonventre gestured to the car. The two other men put away their bags and opened the back door.

Turridru helped his wife step inside the vehicle and followed behind her. A few more hours and he would be in New York City, where the only man left in the world he wanted to see dead was currently residing.

Williamsburg, Brooklyn, New York City—July 27, 1917

"Is the wine any good?" Nicola Schiro asked from across the dinner table.

"Quite good, I assure you," Turridru said.

He had arrived in America to a grand feast. With more "friends" in America than since he was a boy. But that mattered little. Turridru knew by now power and security came from the top, so he requested a private audience with Don Schiro, and was granted his wish.

"As good as the wine in Sicily?" Schiro asked, kissing his fingers. "Oh, how I miss Sicilian wine."

"It's better than anything we had on the boat, isn't it, dear?" Elizabetta, beside him at the table, asked.

She played the part of dutiful wife perfectly. Schiro's wife, on the other hand, didn't put on any airs, and fussed at her husband about his table manners, consistently emasculating him. But it was just as well. Schiro wasn't a real man. He was old and leisured. He made powerful friends in his youth and rode these alliances to the top. He didn't have the real ingredients for leadership.

"Well, I hope we can keep you from becoming homesick, as long as you're in our little corner of Brooklyn," Schiro said, his teeth stained purple.

"Ladies," Turridru began, "would you mind giving me and Don Schiro a moment to talk? Just men's issues."

Mrs. Shiro rolled her eyes, but Elizabetta stood without hesitation.

"We should have expected," Schiro's wife said, standing. "Come on. Let's visit the powder room."

Elizabetta followed after kissing Turridru's cheek.

"What do you wish to talk about?" Schiro said.

"I wanted to thank you again for the kindness you've shown me," he said.

Schiro leaned back in his chair and nodded like a benevolent king. "Any friend of Don Toto's is a friend of mine. Any son of Don Toto is a son to me also."

"I'm sure a man of your position values discretion?"

Schiro nodded. "Of course."

"For the time being, I want to keep a low profile. I'm sure there are some people looking for me right now, so I hope you don't mind if I use an alias for now."

"Turridru isn't your real name?"

"It is not. A boyhood nickname, nothing more."

"Men looking for you, eh?" Don Schiro reveled in anything ominous. It made him feel important.

"In time, I will feel more secure, and I hope to stand tall amongst your associates and contribute in any way that I can. For now, I simply want to fade into the shadows and learn from a great man such as yourself."

Don Schiro was no different than Don Toto. A little bit of flattery and he was won over.

"Of course. I will teach you all that I know."

"That is all I can ask of you, Father." Turridru stretched out his hand and accepted Schiro's, which he kissed.

"Have you wrapped up?" Schiro's wife said, entering the private room Schiro had reserved for the guests.

"Of course, dear. We wouldn't want to make you wait for long." Don Schiro looked to Turridru and whispered under his breath, "You'll understand in time."

Turridru didn't engage. He found Cola Schiro to be as unpleasant as the peasants he traveled across the sea with. The only difference is they knew they were entitled to nothing. Schiro felt he was king of the world, but even after a few hours at dinner, Turridru could tell he didn't have the gumption to take it.

"A toast." Turridru lifted his glass of wine. The table followed his example. "To new friends and a bright future in America."

Their crystal clanked together.

Schiro might not have had the guts to take the world by storm, but Turridru did. A little flattery and bad dinner company was the least of what he was willing to do. He might be a shadow in New York now, but eventually he would be king.

28

ANTONELLO

Garment District, Manhattan, New York City—February 10, 1931

He was blinded by the light of a single incandescent bulb when they ripped off the blindfold. Before he could gain his senses, he received a punch to the nose. Then a man removed the cloth gag. "Ah, you're a bunch of assholes, ya know that?" Antonello said, spitting a gob of blood on the ground.

He was stripped down to nothing but his winter long johns. His feet were tied to the chair he was sitting in, and his hands were bound behind him. If they weren't, Antonello could have taken them all single-handedly.

"And you're a bum," one of them said, punching his rib cage.

For what felt like weeks, he'd been locked in that cellar. He was given water a few times, but never any food. He received a beating a few times, but nothing he couldn't take. So far, he hadn't even been asked a damn question.

"What the hell do you boys want with me, huh? Just like to tie up a big man so youse can feel tough?" He glared at them all but could barely make out their features as the light was still burning in his eyes.

"I don't want shit from you. If it was up to me, you'd be dead."

Another blow to the ribs. "Do it then, tough guy," Antonello said, stifling a grimace. "Pull the trigger if you're so macho."

"We were told to keep you alive for now," another voice said, followed by some Yiddish that seemed like an insult to Antonello.

The room silenced and seemed to straighten as someone else descended the stairs to the basement. The only sound was of the man's wingtips on the concrete floor.

"You Antonello Balducci?" the man said, a thousand-dollar fur coat draped over his shoulders.

"You betcha." Antonello smirked.

"How long have you been here?"

"Why don't you ask your goons?" Antonello spit more blood at the ground.

"Gentlemen, we aren't savages. Remove the man's restraints," the leader said.

Antonello stifled a grin. If these bastards cut him loose, he would kill them all.

"Wait, wait." The man stopped his companions. "Put a gun to his head first. Make sure he doesn't try anything brave."

The cold nickel of a revolver was placed against his temple as the twine binding his wrists were cut.

"Want a cigarette?"

Antonello contemplated it for a moment. He wanted to be defiant, but he also wanted a cigarette. "Fine." He held out his hand and accepted one, his fingers rushing with blood for the first time in God knows how long.

"My name is Charlie Luciano. Most people call me Lucky." He pulled up a chair and set it adjacent to Antonello.

The man before him was of average height with a wiry frame, but contained a deep, raspy voice that seemed bigger than him. He had a pockmarked and scarred face and a head of close cropped hair as black as coal. He didn't seem so tough. But there was something in his eyes that was cold enough to keep Antonello from swinging, even if the revolver wasn't at his forehead.

"My name is Antonello Balducci. And most people call me their worst nightmare."

Luciano chuckled and his companions followed his example. "Yeah, you look terrifying. I bet if we freed your feet you'd stand up and fall flat on your face."

Antonello leaned closer, as far as the restraints around his feet would allow him. "Why don't you try it then?"

"How about you shut your mouth and enjoy the cigarette?" Luciano said, lighting his own first.

Antonello didn't want to comply, but as the cigarette smoke filled his lungs, he felt a little better. "What now, boss? Why do you have me here? Why you keeping me alive?" Antonello, eyes now adjusted, looked around the room. He recognized Mr. Lansky and Bugsy from the drug deal in December. "Hey there, fellas." He gave them a mocking grin. "If you have me cause you're worried about me pushing dope on your territory, you don't have anything to worry about. Those days are behind me." Antonello held up his hands in surrender.

"That's not why you're here at all," Luciano said,

leaning back in his chair and taking long, even drags of his cigarette.

"What, are we gonna play twenty questions?"

"You're here because I'm gonna kill you," Luciano said as carelessly as he said anything else so far. "But first I want to hear you talk."

"Wow. My father was right. You Sicilians are stupid. Why would I talk if I know you're gonna kill me?" Antonello shook his head at their poor tactics, but his breathing quickened.

"Because I'm gonna make you talk. And then I'm gonna make you beg me to kill you before it's all over."

A few men stepped forward with Louisville sluggers in hand.

"Wait, wait, now hold on," Antonello said. He was reminded of being in the barn with Sonny and Francesco Siragusa. From the other side of the equation, he knew the man would talk before he did. Antonello didn't want the same thing to happen to him. "I'm a reasonable fella. Why don't you tell me what you want to hear, and I'll see if I can help you out?"

Luciano gave the men a glance, and they they backed off.

"You mentioned your father. But from what I can tell, you were raised by someone else. Alonzo Consentino. That name ring a bell?"

"I wasn't really raised by anyone. I lived on the streets and ate out of the damn gutter. But, sure, I stayed with Mr. Consentino a few times. He only lived a block away from me."

Luciano shrugged. "If you're gonna lie to me, I'm just gonna go ahead and kill you."

The man with the gun pulled back the hammer.

"Oh!" Antonello said, holding out his hands in a plea, "you said *Alonzo* Consentino? Oh yeah, that man nearly raised me. I lived in his house for years."

The triggerman released the hammer, and Antonello nearly wet himself but maintained his honor.

"That's funny. Isn't he funny, Meyer?" Luciano lit another cigarette. "Because you told my boys you were thankful Joe the Baker killed his son. Enzo. That right? You happy that my associate Joe the Baker killed your childhood pal?"

"Yeah, yeah, I shouldn't have said that." Antonello knew he was caught and started to squirm.

"Another thing that I find funny . . . you said Enzo was selling dope? Doesn't seem like it to me."

"Did I? Did I say that? I must of been thinking about someone else," Antonello said, the corners of his lips beginning to tremble.

"Did you have something to do with Joe the Baker's death? Huh? Did you kill him?" Luciano finally stood, shoulders back and menacing.

Antonello's hands started shaking like they did when his father came home drunk. "No, no, I didn't have nothing to do with that," Antonello said, eyes wide.

Luciano gave the triggerman another nod. He cocked the hammer back.

"Now wait. Wait! Wait just a minute!" Antonello shouted.

Luciano leaned in and blew cigarette smoke in his face. "Keep your damn voice down. I have workers upstarts. And the Chinamen startle easily. Don't upset them. Now, go on."

"Why do you care what happened to Joe the Baker?

Huh? You moved up right? Lucky Luciano moved up after Joe the Baker went out."

"We're both in Masseria's crew." Luciano straightened.

"Sure, but—"

"So you did kill him?"

"No, no. I didn't. I swear! I just told some pals of mine who did it. I was just popping off at the mouth, just like your pals here did." Antonello gestured to Lansky and Bugsy, who looked away from Luciano. "I didn't know nothing would come of it."

"*Grazie, Dio*." Luciano turned to his associates. "Can you imagine how happy Joe the Boss is going to be when I bring him the head of the guy who killed Catania?"

Luciano's henchmen dropped their bats. They had heard everything they needed to hear. The pistol at his forehead shoved deeper against his temple.

"Please, God, please, don't kill me," Antonello wept. He never realized how much he valued his life until that moment.

"Why shouldn't I? You're a rat prick. Ain't good for nothing," Luciano said, half turning away from him.

"Because I can broker a deal!" Antonello said. When he noticed they were listening, he continued, "Yeah, yeah, I'll make a deal with Maranzano! You all thought I was just some scumbag. But I'm in with the big guy. We call him Old Caesar. I can make a deal."

Everyone in the room looked to Luciano.

"What makes you think I would want to do that?" Luciano said.

"Come on. You're Lucky Luciano! Everyone knows you're the smartest guy in Manhattan. You know that Masseria's ship is sinking. And why should you go down with that fat bastard? What good did he ever do you?"

Antonello was speaking out of his ass but hoped that something was ringing true. "Maranzano is winning the war. Plain and simple. Don't you want to be on his side?"

"Lucky, want me to waste this asshole?" the triggerman asked.

"What makes you think you can broker out a deal? Those Castellamarese are stubborn," Luciano said.

"But he likes me. He trusts me real good," Antonello said. "He doesn't have a problem with you, he just wants Masseria! If we can come to an agreement, we can all be friends."

Again, all eyes turned to Luciano. A few of the men arched an eyebrow.

"You think you can do that?"

"Yeah, sure I can do it. I can talk to him within a few hours, and he'll hear me out. He just wants Masseria."

Luciano thought for a moment, and then audibly exhaled. "Cut him loose," he said, crossing his arms.

"Lucky . . ." one of his associates said.

"Did you hear me?" Luciano said again, fire in his voice. "I said cut him loose."

As the twine around his ankles was severed, Antonello fell from the chair to the ground.

"Go talk to your *Old Caesar*," Luciano said, and then crouched beside him. He picked Antonello up by the chin and forced him to look in his eyes. "And if you're playing me, I'll know about it. It won't be too long until you get doped up and stumble around another park. When you do, I'll find you."

Antonello vehemently nodded his head. Luciano stepped back and allowed Antonello a path to the exit. He was ashamed, but very much alive.

29

SEBASTIANO

Roger's Park, Chicago—August 29, 1926

"How's he doing?"

"Not well. He hasn't talked since we got him home." His mother addressed someone from the doorway.

"It's a real shame what happened."

"I think it triggered something. From the war."

They spoke as if he wasn't there. Sebastiano was seated on the couch, a wool blanket wrapped around his shoulders. He hadn't moved in days, save to the bathroom.

And it was true that he hadn't talked. He would've, but couldn't find the right words. His niece was rushed into the hospital just as he was leaving it, but she died on impact. The doctors tried to resuscitate her, but to no avail. Johnny boy's daughter was dead. And Sebastiano felt responsible.

"You think I can see him?"

"Sure. Maybe you can cheer him up."

Sebastiano kept his eyes forward as footsteps approached. His boss, Vincent Drucci, came into view.

He took off his fedora, and he played nervously with the brim. "I'm sorry about what happened," Drucci said.

For a moment Sebastiano remained in his place, but eventually stood. "Thank you for coming." Remembering his manners, he stepped forward and kissed his boss on the cheek.

"Come on, don't hurt your leg. Just sit down. Sit down." Drucci helped him back to the couch and took a seat beside him.

There was sympathy, pain even, in the boss's eyes. His face, generally a mask of emotionlessness, was ridden with guilt as well.

"It's a shame what happened, Domingo. Civilians should never get caught up in this," he said.

A rare sight, Drucci caring about others. Generally, the only time when life could be seen in his eyes was when he peeped out the firm backside of a broad. Sebastiano took notice, and it did make him feel better. "Yeah. I feel like it was my fault."

"No." Drucci took his hand and squeezed it. "Don't do that to yourself. This was Capone's doing. He wanted to make another headline. He wanted to get you, and he got the little girl."

"Why would Capone want me? I'm a nobody."

"Well, he did. He wanted you and your brother. I think the drive-by was as much about you two as it was about Hymie. He wants to get to me, and he figured going after my top guys was the best way to do it."

Drucci was not one for compliments, or friendliness for that matter, so Sebastiano didn't take the compliment lightly. "What happens now?"

"First we bury that little girl," Drucci said, bowing his head in reverence.

"Funeral is tomorrow at 3:00. Ascension Parish on Illinois Street."

"I'll be there."

It was strange to imagine Drucci in a church. His affiliation with religion extended no further than dressing up as a priest for Halloween. "Thank you, Mr. Drucci," Sebastiano said, shaking his hand.

"We called for a ceasefire."

Sebastiano looked at Drucci's face and his mouth dropped. "After what they did? Ceasefire?"

"Look, look, it ain't that simple." Drucci held out his hands to explain himself. He'd never explained himself before. "We need to recoup. Recover our losses. We just lost the boss. Hymie is dead, and we got some work to do to pick up the slack. You following? It isn't good."

"Then why did the South Side agree to a ceasefire?"

Drucci smirked. "Another fuck up like that one and the people that love Capone now will be howling for his head. They need to lay low for a while."

Sebastiano looked down. "I can't . . . I got to do something. If Johnny boy was here right now, he would want to avenge his daughter . . . his little girl . . ." Sebastiano lowered his head and tried not to cry in front of his boss.

To his surprise, Drucci put a hand on his shoulder. "Look here, Domingo. Those assholes can kill me a thousand times over, they can knock off all my men . . . and we could still come back from it. But kill a little girl? Those bastards will pay. We just gotta find the right time."

Sebastiano nodded, but still had a difficult time

perceiving how he could stay his hand if he came across any of those South Side bastards.

"Bugs wanted to kill them all right then and there. I had to persuade him to accept the ceasefire. We all want to get back to war. And we will. Right now, we just gotta get back to making and selling booze. And making money. Then, we use that money to buy a damn arsenal. And we hit 'em like we hit those Jerries in France. Capisce?" Drucci was in the Navy during the Great War. It was one reason Sebastiano had been anxious to work with him.

"I hear you."

Drucci stood and assumed his generally gregarious manner. "Take all the time you need. Recover. Mourn that little girl. And when you're ready, we'll get 'em back." Drucci placed his hat back on his head, and kissed Sebastiano's mother on the way out.

Sebastiano looked down at his bum leg. It was getting stronger every day. It would take awhile, but when he healed up there would be hell to pay. He would burn down all of Chicago if he had to.

Chicago, Illinois—November 11, 1926

As soon as Sebastiano walked into the beer hall, he felt more at home than he had since he left France on the USS George Washington. The smell was of foaming beer and a hundred burning Lucky Strikes, all at once. The sound was of coarse jokes and gut-busting laughter. The room was dim, and filled with a great deal of men adorned in their old uniforms. A veterans' rally was the last thing Sebastiano had intended on visiting, but something had called him there when he saw an errant flier on a street post in Roger's Park.

He hobbled into the room, his left leg dragging behind. For once no one looked up or shot him looks of pity. They were all just as maimed as him. Some had missing limbs, the faces of others were marred with burns, some wore eyepatches. Others wore meritorious patches, telling of the victories they won. But no one seemed to act any different. Both scars and medals were markers of service.

Sebastiano approached the bar.

"You want a drink?" the bartender asked.

Sebastiano hesitated. He hadn't touched a drop since the bombing at the hospital. He wanted to remain alert in case Drucci visited with news that the culprits had been identified.

"Don't worry about the Volstead, son. Half the men in here are police. No one would break up a Veteran's rally on the anniversary of Armistice Day."

"Yeah, sure. Scotch, neat."

The bartender slid him the drink. Sebastiano turned and looked around the room. Some of the men present were his own age, having served in the Great War. Others wore dusty old uniforms from the "splendid little war," or the conflict in the Philippines. Sebastiano could deduct that some present had served in the border conflicts with Mexico. A few of the men —so old they appeared like ghosts of Gettysburg— wore the blue jackets of a Union soldier of the Civil War.

All of them had a certain look in their eyes though, like Sebastiano knew he had. It was a mixture of pride and shame. They had memories of a Private Franklin too. He was sure they replayed it in their minds just as often, no matter how long ago it might have been.

"Where'd you serve?" a man asked sitting beside Sebastiano at the bar.

"France," he said.

"Doughboy, huh?" the man's accent was noticeably Irish.

"That's right," Sebastiano said, finally looking at his fellow veteran. His uniform was old and stretched from years of putting on weight.

"I was Fourth Artillery—Puerto Rico." The man received his drink and took a gulp. "'Splendid little war' my arse," he said with a burp.

Sebastiano forced a smile and nodded.

"Was the Great War as bad as they say? You boys came back looking like you've got the screamin' meemies. I've wondered if it's just your generation. We took our lickings and kept our mouth shut." Sebastiano felt himself become irritated, but tried to quench it. The man didn't mean to be rude. Soldiers were blunt, no matter the war. It was in their nature.

"It wasn't all that bad." He lied.

"The haze in your eyes says otherwise," the man said. He looked Sebastiano up and down. "That leg tells me otherwise too."

He must have noticed Sebastiano was putting his weight on his one good leg. Sebastiano only nodded. Then shrugged.

"Give the doughboy another drink," he said.

"No, that's all right," Sebastiano tried to stop the bartender, who was already pouring.

"It's on me. Don't worry about it." The old veteran slapped a quarter on the bar.

Sebastiano exhaled and chuckled. "I don't even know why I'm here."

The old vet's face scrunched in thought, and he fiddled with the tips of his bushy mustache. "I think you do."

"Why do you think I'm here? Why are you here?" Sebastiano asked.

The man thought for a moment, seeming more intelligent and contemplative than he had originally. "Maybe you wanted to see some of your old mates." He looked at Sebastiano's face and must have noticed that didn't strike a chord.

"I haven't talked to any of them since I got home. I've wanted to write. I had a pal who lives in New York . . . he wrote me once and gave me his address. But I can't bring myself to write back."

"Maybe you wanted to remind yourself you're not the only one," the old man said, more confidently. He nodded along with Sebastiano when he noticed the change in his eyes. "We all come back different. Different than the others, but just the same as one another." He gestured around the room. "You're not the only one."

The young and old—veterans of recent wars and those of the distant past—they all shared something.

The veteran continued, "It's funny, isn't it? When I was gone, I'd lay awake and think of nothing but falling asleep holding on to my wife. When I got back, we were divorced within the year and I fall asleep holding a bottle of rotgut. It's like I've been trying to kill myself since the moment I realized the war wouldn't do it for me."

Sebastiano met the man's eyes for the first time and nodded. He understood every word he was saying. It wasn't comforting to hear of the man's agony, but he was glad to hear he wasn't the only one."Does it ever get any better?" He immediately regretted it and wasn't prepared for the wrong answer.

The veteran thought for some time. "No. It doesn't get any better."

Sebastiano looked down and nodded, already knowing the truth in his heart.

"But, you learn how to live with it better." The veteran continued. "You have to leave it there, boyo. The dreams, the nightmares, the things you did and the things you saw . . . you just leave it over there. Leave it in the trenches. You got to understand you're back here now. The rules are different. Then, once a year, you gather with a bunch of other old vets and drink until you piss yourself." He raised a glass and waited for Sebastiano to tap his against it. "Then, when you're older, you can tell some young, foolish soldier about how he can come back." He stood and slapped Sebastiano on the back rather forcefully, as only a soldier could and get away with it. "Best of luck to you, boyo."

He wanted to believe him. He wanted to trust he could come back sometime. That he could help others come back too. But he didn't know if he could. He killed jerries because he was told to. How could he not kill, the same way, those that took the life of his little niece?

He wanted to believe he could come home. But he wasn't sure he could. And ultimately, he wasn't sure he wanted to.

30

SONNY

Bensonhurst, Brooklyn, New York City—February 17, 1931

"I fold," Cargo threw his cards on the table and leaned back in his chair with an exhale.

"You gonna play cards or pout?" Charlie Buffalo said, noticeably irritated. "Worst person in the world to play cards with, this guy. Folds anytime he doesn't have a pair in the hand."

Sonny upped the bet, and everyone else folded, including Charlie. He swept the pot to his side but wasn't really in much of a mood for cards. Ever since he, Vico, and Buster took out Catania, the tide of war had shifted in Maranzano's favor. There was talk of peace in the air, and they felt they generally had less to fear. It made Sonny restless to still be locked up in these safe houses, but Maranzano made it clear he wasn't planning on losing one of his men at the end of a successful war just because they became sloppy.

"They're here," Antonello said, like a child spotting Santa at the beginning of Christmas. He had kept his eyes glued out of the window all day, and no one knew why except Maranzano himself.

He had bruises and cuts across his face and neck, poorly disguised by some broad's makeup. They gave him a hard time about it, and for once Antonello didn't have any witty comebacks. He was anxious to prove to everyone why he had sustained the injuries. He hurried to the door and opened it. "Pleasure to see you again, boys," he said as two men walked onto the porch. The door guard looked at him like he was crazy. "It's all right. I vouch for them."

"You gave the address to these guys?" the guard said.

The two men stepped inside but didn't remove their hats or coats.

"Afternoon, gentlemen," one of them said.

"Go and tell Don Maranzano his guests are here," Antonello ordered anyone in the room who would listen, as if he were in the position to do so.

After a moment of hesitation Charlie Buffalo stood, huffing and puffing as he went to fetch the Don.

The two guests were juxtaposed in every way. The man in front was gaunt and short, a face that made him look far older than he really was. Scarred and pockmarked, he was a fright just to look at. But he had an air of intelligence about him, and power too. The tall man behind him looked around the room like an avian predator looks at prey.

Everyone in the room kept their eyes on the intruders.

Maranzano entered the room and greeted the guests.

"Good to meet you." The man in the front extended a hand. Maranzano accepted it but kept his distance.

"Mr. Maranzano, this is Lucky Luciano," said Antonello. "And his friend here is Vito Genovese. They—"

"I know who they are," Maranzano said. "But thank you."

"We appreciate the invitation," Luciano said, still distant and removed like a visitor at a funeral.

"Let's sit down." Maranzano led the way into the dining area and gestured to all the men present to follow him. Sonny, Buster, and Bonnano stood at the back of the room, as the two guests sat down with Maranzano. Their role was to keep an eye on the proceedings. Charlie Buffalo, Antonello, and Cargo remained at the door, figuring that the invitation wasn't meant for them.

"Would you like something to drink?" Bonanno asked.

"No. Thank you. We won't be staying long."

"Do you know why you are here?" Maranzano asked, accepting a cup of espresso from Bonnano.

"Yes."

Bonanno turned up the radio, so no one not invited to their little meeting would be able to hear.

"So I don't need to tell you what needs to be done?"

"No," Luciano said.

Maranzano spoke in Italian, and Luciano replied in English, but he seemed to understand the primary form of Sicilian communication—silence.

"What day is it, Joseph?" Maranzano asked.

Bonanno calculated. "The seventeenth of February."

"I hope I can have a happy Easter, then," Maranzano said.

"And my people . . . are they safe?" Luciano asked.

"I accept any friend who offers me the same courtesy."

"Then we understand each other." Luciano stood.

"Wait," Maranzano said, and Luciano and Genovese both returned to their seats. "You have to accept full responsibility of what needs to be done. I'll hold you accountable, not your associates."

The room silenced. Luciano and Maranzano maintained eye contact and seemed to be speaking their own silent language.

"I understand. I would like an insurance policy."

"How do you mean?"

"One of your people. So I know you aren't going to turn around and do the same to me."

Anger flashed over Maranzano's face. He was known as a man capable of humor and goodwill, but his anger was becoming famous. The Castellamare twitched like they were being bit by fleas.

"I am a man of my word."

"It's not personal. Strictly business," Luciano said. He pulled out a gold case from his pocket and lit a cigarette.

Sonny cringed. Maranzano wasn't a fan of smoking.

"You can take him." He pointed to Buster. "He's the finest I have." His reaction was indiscernible. "He's my finest gunman. He's been my go-to since he arrived in my employ."

"Him? Why not this fella?" Luciano nodded to Sonny.

His skin crawled when Luciano looked at him.

"He's not available," Maranzano said, to Sonny's relief.

"I hear he has a way with insurance," Luciano said.

Sonny didn't want to imagine how Luciano uncovered information about his past.

"You ever heard the name Enzo Consentino?" Maranzano's anger steeped like tea on a stove. "That's why he isn't available. I think you can understand why."

Luciano shrugged. "Then, Buster." Luciano stood. "Buster from Chicago." He moved toward the war vet and extended a hand. Buster met his eyes as he accepted it. "I'll look forward to working together then."

Buster maintained a fixed stare with the face of a statue.

"We'll be in touch," Genovese said, leaning across the table to shake Maranzano's hand. Luciano returned to The Don and kissed him on either cheek.

"Luciano," Maranzano said as the two men reached the exit. "I make this gesture of friendship only once. If you disregard it, it will not be offered again."

Luciano tipped his hat and left.

The room was silent for a moment. The two guests had only been there a few moments, but the entire landscape of the war had just changed.

Antonello stood from the card table, anxious for a compliment. "How'd it go?" he asked.

"The grownups are talking," Charlie said, tugging Antonello's shirt sleeve.

"You think we can trust them?" Bonanno asked The Don.

Maranzano took his time replying and exhaled deeply. "No. But we have to try. Caesar said the easiest way to win a war was to forgive your enemies and make them friends. If they can deliver Masseria to us, it will be worth it."

"I don't like to look in that fellas eyes," Buster said.

"They're smarter than they look. Otherwise, they wouldn't have come. They might make good associates in the end. Just as Caesar forgave his enemies, I am willing to forgive mine."

"Didn't they end up killing Caesar?" Charlie Buffalo asked.

Maranzano didn't look at him or reply but grabbed two pistols from beneath his jacket. He placed them quietly on the card table beside him.

"Unlike Caesar, I never go to the Senate House without my weapons."

31

LUCIANO

Bensonhurst, Brooklyn, New York City—February 17, 1931

Luciano and Genovese took their time departing. Maranzano was the kind of man who liked having the last word. He didn't want to meet the man again, so gave him a chance to chase them down for another empty threat. None came.

Genovese opened the front door, and Luciano slid in.

"How'd it go?" Frank Costello said from the driver seat, removing the parking brake.

"Like we expected," Genovese said slipping into the backseat.

Luciano remained quiet and contemplative. He turned over Maranzano's words in his head, trying to make sure he had everything right.

"So are we really gonna do it? Take care of the boss?" Costello said, pulling out onto the road.

"Hey, Frank," Luciano said, taking his time finishing the

rest of his cigarette. "When we get back, I want you to send word to Masseria."

Frank looked back at Vito, confused by the situation.

"All right. What do you want me to say?"

"Tell him we found the guy who clipped Joe Catania. Tell him we have a chance to take care of Maranzano."

Garment District, Manhattan, New York City—February 21, 1931

Luciano paced the floor of his workshop, smoking cigarettes like a Navy Street freight train. "He said he would call me?" Luciano asked, for the hundredth time.

"Yeah. He said he was gonna call you." Costello said.

"He said he was gonna call me here?"

"Yeah. He said he was gonna call you here."

"Today? He said the twenty-first?"

"Yeah, Lucky, he said he was going to call on the twenty-first," Costello said.

Luciano's heart rate was uncharacteristically high. He didn't know what to think. What if Masseria was suspicious? He had often thought about how stupid Joe the Boss was, but he had been crafty enough to last this long. What if his braindead attitude was an act? What if Masseria's spies spotted them heading to Brooklyn? What if word reached the Boss that Luciano and his associates visited Maranzano's crew?

He scanned the faces of the three men and wondered if one of them was a rat. He'd trusted these men for years. He grew up on the streets with Meyer Lansky, Bugsy Siegal, and Frank Costello. Vito Genovese suffered through a bunch of shit with Luciano the past decade. He didn't want to think any of them would sell him out, but Masseria's cash could be pretty enticing.

Out of caution, he made certain no one knew what he was thinking. Not even his closest associates. In reality, he didn't even know what his plan was. Masseria, for as long as he could remember, had been taller than a New York skyscraper and as untouchable as a Catholic Nun. The tide was shifting to favor Maranzano's camp, and Luciano fancied himself a forward-thinking man. But if Joe the Boss escaped again, and Luciano was behind the betrayal, he would spare no expenses ensuring that Luciano and all of his pals would suffer.

His eyes stopped on Bugsy, who was pouring himself a glass of bootlegged whiskey. They had a rule against partaking of their own product, but Luciano made an exception. He needed something to calm his nerves.

"Pour me some." He nodded to Bugsy, who hurried to do so. Luciano took the glass and pounded the liquor. The phone began to ring. All eyes in the room fixed on it.

"Want me to answer?" Meyer asked. He was generally the first on the phone because of his calm and endearing manner of communication. Luciano was rougher around the edges and had a famously short temper, especially over the phone.

"No. I'll get it this time." Luciano struggled to swallow. He took his time moving across the room to the phone on the center table. He half hoped that the ringing would stop before he arrived, but it didn't. He picked up the phone. "Hello, you got Lucky."

"Charlie, my boy," Masseria, his voice jovial.

"How we doing, Mr. Masseria?"

"Better after receiving word from your associate." Masseria said.

"I'm glad to hear it."

"You think you actually have a way to get to him? He's been hiding like a mole rat for months."

"I'm certain. We got one of his guys."

"The dope peddler? From what I hear, the Castellamerese isn't a fan of selling narcotics."

"Maybe he isn't. But the guy is in his circle. If that's true, it means he has more to gain from us winning than his own boss."

"I see, I see."

"He's a Neapolitan too. The Castellamarese won't bring him in. He knows we'd give him a chance."

"Once a traitor, always a traitor," Masseria said.

His voice was as sharp as a knife, and Luciano's stomach dropped. "Yeah. We'll take him for a ride after Maranzano gets his."

"Good. That's the only thing we can do with rats." Luciano shut his eyes and tried to compose himself.

"Yeah," Luciano said. Masseria's voice was so even and cold that it chilled Luciano's bones. Did he know?

"Let's meet and discuss how we can take care of Maranzano."

"Just tell me when."

"Sometime in April."

"April? That's a ways off, isn't it?"

"It is. It should give you plenty of time to consider your course of action."

Luciano tried to interpret any hidden meanings. "I'll do that."

"I'll call you and tell you where. No reason to take any risks."

"Understood," Luciano said.

The phone clicked.

"What'd he say?" Costello asked.

"Says we're gonna meet in April to talk about how to get Maranzano."

"Maranzano said he wanted us to get him before Easter," Genovese said.

"I know what he said, Vito, I was there." Luciano turned to his associates, his temper flaring. He softened after a moment, realizing Genovese wasn't the target of his aggression. "We'll play the cards we're dealt. Alright?" he said.

Everyone nodded. Each man seemed as anxious as he was. After talking with Masseria, he knew they should be.

32

SONNY

Bensonhurst, Brooklyn—March 28, 1931

Time crept by slowly, as the Castellamare waited on Luciano's answer. Tensions were high. There was news of a pending repeal on the Volstead act, and they were all anxious to get back to bootlegging and making money before the oasis dried up. It'd been over a year since they had "gone to the mattresses," and just as the end of the war was in sight, everything seemed to freeze. Sonny began to feel in his gut that their conflict with Masseria would never end, and that he would be forced to remain in their cramped safe-houses with men like Cargo and Charlie Buffalo for the rest of his life.

Even Maranzano was no longer a reprieve for Sonny. His demeanor was cold. He stuck to himself most often, and everyone stopped talking when he entered the room. He seemed always on the edge of an outburst. They could all see fury in his eyes when the name Luciano was mentioned. They made a deal, and since then hadn't heard a word from anyone in their camp. Everyone was beginning to believe the wiry little snake betrayed them.

"I'm going to run out and see Mae. Anyone need anything?" Cargo asked, gathering his keys.

"No, you need to stay here," Maranzano shouted from his back room.

Cargo threw his arms up in frustration since Maranzano couldn't see him. "All right, never mind then."

"What do you need to see that broad for anyways?" Charlie Buffalo asked. "I've seen her. A piece of cooze not worth the time."

Cargo pointed at him. "Keep your mouth shut, Charlie."

Bonanno reached across the couch and slapped Charlie on the arm.

"What? I'm just saying."

Cargo sighed. "She's scarier than Joe the Boss when she's pissed. And I haven't gone to see her lately." He took off his jacket and plopped down in a recliner.

Bonanno set down the book he was reading. He was the only member present on who seemed undisturbed. He was cut out for this kind of thing, Sonny decided.

"I've got a woman waiting on me as well, Cargo. If she loves you, she'll wait for you."

"Who said anything about love? She just wants a new dress." Cargo shrugged.

"If you're just feeling lonely, Charlie here is kind of pretty if you look at him just right," Buster said, as Charlie Buffalo gestured for him to go screw himself.

The phone rang.

"Better be Marty with news about some food. That pasta yesterday wasn't fit for my dogs," Charlie said, kicking his feet up and making it clear he wasn't interested in answering.

Sonny stood when no one else did and hustled to the phone. If there was even a sliver of information to be found on the phone call, he was anxious to hear it. He wanted to leave that damned house. "You've got Sonny," he said as he picked up.

"Put Buster on the phone," the voice said.

"Who do I tell him is calling?"

"Just give him the phone."

Sonny sighed and handed off the phone.

"Who is it?" Buster asked, suddenly worried. "Is it Maria?" He had given her the number only in case of emergencies.

"If it is her voice got a lot deeper."

"Yeah, what is it?" Buster said. His eyes shuffled around the room as he listened. He gestured fervently for something to write on and write with.

Bonanno handed him the hardback he was reading and a pen in his pocket.

"April 15? You fellas move about as fast as pond water," Buster said, hastily taking notes. "Yeah, I hear you. You know Mr. Maranzano isn't very pleased with how long this is taking. This better be the real deal." He pulled the phone away from his ear, looked at it, then sat it down. "That Luciano is an arrogant prick. Hung up on me."

"What did he say?" Sonny asked, as the others perked up their ears.

"Nuova Villa Tamara in Coney Island. Ever heard of it?"

Blank stares.

"Some pasta joint Joe the Boss feels comfortable in

because there are lots of greasy foods and the owner covers his tab."

"He said April 15?" Charlie Buffalo asked.

"That's what he said."

"Damn. They're making us sweat it out, aren't they?" Cargo shook his head.

"He said Masseria is being cautious. Doesn't trust him or nobody. That's the earliest we can make it happen."

"If he's talking to him, that means he knows where he is right? Why don't we just go find him and blow his brains out?" Cargo laid his head back and exhaled.

"Go for it, tough guy." Buster tossed a newspaper at him, hitting him square in the chest. "I don't really care when it is, as long as it's done clean, and this whole thing gets over with."

"You gonna take that typewriter of yours?" Charlie gestured to the violin case between Buster's legs, and more directly to the gun inside.

"I wish I could. Betsy will have to wait though. She's too big and beautiful, and I can't take her in there or someone would see." He picked up the case and cradled it like a babe. Setting it back down, he pulled out his two ivory-handled pistols. "These should do the trick."

33

TURRIDRU

Little Italy, Manhattan, New York City- January 29, 1919

"Where you headed?" The taxi driver asked, as Turridru slipped inside.

"To Brooklyn. Williamsburg," he said.

"You got it. I like your hat," the driver said, analyzing him in the rear view.

Turridru picked up on enough English since he arrived in the States to engage with the man, but he had no intentions of doing so. He was teeming with anger.

That kid was going to ruin everything.

He kept his ear pinned back for months, and after finally realizing the man he once knew as "Don Consentino" was now a barber in Little Italy. He made up his mind to go see the man. He looked at him with a mixture of pity and glee. He had won. Alonzo seemed old, his eyes lined with worry and his hair disappearing from what was once a jet black and perfectly delineated.

"Every year we get more cars, and every year the

traffic gets worse. It's a madhouse 'round here." The driver said.

Turridru avoided eye contact with the rearview. He had wanted to see Alonzo. Let him know he was here, that he'd overcome the hell the Consentino's imposed on his family when they left in the middle of a war. He wanted Alonzo to know he could find him. Turridru wanted to shake his hand, feel the fear in his eyes. Because, ultimately, he wanted to kill him.

But that kid. He couldn't kill him with that little kid around.

Alonzo introduced the little boy as Sonny, the third of his brood. He had looked at Turridru with admiration. It was easy to tell Sonny was the apple of his father's eye.

Turridru had killed many men, but he never looked into the eyes of their children before doing so.

"Are you new to the States? You don't talk much."

"A year or so," Turridru finally said, staring out the window.

"Come over with a family?"

"A wife."

"No little ones?"

Turridru exhaled. "We're expecting one," he said.

Elizabetta came to him just a few months prior with tears in her eyes and told him the good news. They wept together, and he kissed her. He loved her before, but in a different way. He had loved her for what she could bring him, for what she gave him, for the passion they experienced when coupled together and the way she played her role of dutiful wife in front of others. Now, he loved her for being the mother of his firstborn. It changed everything. But he hadn't felt right since. He was softening, and it scared him. Looking at Sonny, and remembering his own offspring was on the way, it softened him.

"Congratulations! Don't worry, the first is always the toughest. Everything falls into place before long," the driver said.

Turridru simply nodded.

Alonzo was pitiful now, after all. Maybe fate already claimed Turridru's vengeance. Maybe mercy could prevail after all. Alonzo fell from the Father of an important Sicilian Cosce to a barber with a plain wife and kids he clearly struggled to provide for. Turridru expected to find him a powerful man, with influence and friends in high places. Friends like Nicola Schiro or Vito Bonventre. It was now clear his closet companions were his own litter and a few other barbers who barely knew the mother tongue.

Maybe he could live. Maybe Turridru could come out of the shadows, and let the past evaporate behind him.

"You come back this way much? To Little Italy? I know a lot of good places around here. I grew up on the Bowery."

"No. I don't plan on coming back," Turridru said. He wouldn't be back anytime soon, he told himself. And not unless he absolutely must.

Williamsburg, Brooklyn, New York City—June 15, 1925

Turridru leaned back in his office chair and closed his eyes. He was still a nameless face amongst New York's finest, but king in his own home. The past several years had been a transition period for Turridru. He had come to America partly for vengeance, partly for power.

Having now arrived at his destination, with revenge in the palm of his hand, he had strayed from his path. At times he was disappointed with this, but most of the time he kicked himself for his foolishness. What more could he want?

He spent his dowery money to open up a business in Manhattan and used his excess capital to purchase a few stills across New York for some supplemental income. He was as rich as a Sicilian immigrant could hope to be, had the most beautiful wife in Brooklyn, and two healthy children.

"What else could you possibly want?" he asked himself as he rested at his desk. He had too many blessings to count, but still remained unfulfilled. He often dwelled on what it felt like to kill. The look in a man's eyes as he held the power of life and death over them. That was power in its rawest form, the kind of strength that could have saved his mother if he acted before it was too late. No matter how much money he accumulated, or how well he maintained his household, nothing gave him the same sensation of power.

"Dear." Elizabetta appeared at the doorway to his office.

She generally didn't enter the office without some important message to deliver. "What is it, mio tesoro?"

"You have a guest. Should I send him in?"

"Who is it?" he said, rubbing his forefingers against his temples. He imagined it was probably one of his agents, or some pesky client. He just needed some time to himself, to think.

"I'm not sure," she lowered her voice, "he said he was a friend of yours in Sicily."

Turridru straightened and his senses all heightened. "He said that? Send him in."

As Elizabetta left, Turridru opened his desk drawer to ensure his revolver was loaded. He slipped it into the back of his waist band.

The man who arrived was barely recognizable. Turridru was able to place him only because he had spent so much time conjuring the man's face in his mind. "Don Consentino, what a surprise," he said, stepping away from his desk.

The old man stood with a stooped back and a weathered fedora in hand. His head was bowed and he kept his eyes on the hardwood beneath his feet. "Please, just call me Alonzo," he said, reluctantly accepting an embrace, and returned it with a kiss on the cheek.

"To what do I owe this pleasure?" Turridru said, returning to his desk and offering a seat to Alonzo.

"I come asking a favor."

Turridru felt his face flush.

"A favor? You want a favor from me?" Turridru said.

Alonzo swallowed and then nodded. He was clearly embarrassed, and nervous also. That was the only thing that made Turridru willing to continue listening, and feigning cordiality.

"What could I give you that you do not already have?" Turridru asked. Seeing the quality of the barber shop, he guessed there was probably a great deal.

"I need a loan." Alonzo hung his head even further.

"A loan? You want money from me?" Turridru tried to stay his anger, checking the doorway to ensure his boys weren't looking in.

"My son, the youngest, Sonny. I want him to go to

university. I just simply can't afford it. I don't know how else to do it."

Turridru stared at his old mentor for a moment and imagined how he might explain it to his wife if a gunshot rang out and Alonzo's body lay dead on his office floor.

"I was under the impression that you were cared for by Piddu. Or Giuseppe Morello as he's known now."

"I am . . . or I was . . . he is in prison. He has been away for several years now and won't be home for a few more years. I don't want my boy to wait."

Turridru leaned back in his chair. Alonzo was a shadow of the man he once was. His youthful bravado had faded into weariness and persistent fear, as so often happens to low class immigrants.

"So you come to me as a last resort?"

"No, no." Alonzo held his hands out in front of him, pleading Turridru to think no ill of him. "Piddu insisted on supporting me. I actually asked him to leave me alone. And more than once too . . . I've heard stories about the kind of man he has become . . . he is not the little boy we once knew in Sicily."

"Neither is Turridru," Turridru replied, locking eyes with Alonzo for the first time, and forcing him by sheer will to do the same.

"I know that . . . I can see that. Your beautiful wife introduced me to your boys on the way in. You have such a lovely home. You've made something wonderful of yourself, despite the circumstances you were given."

"You mean when you abandoned my family in the middle of a war?" Turridru blurted, forgetting the cadence he'd practiced for years.

Alonzo hung his head again, and for a moment it appeared he might weep. "There hasn't been a day go by that I haven't thought of it. I've worried and prayed for you, your father, your mother . . ."

"Thank you for your prayers."

"How are they? Your parents, I mean, are they well?"

"My mother is dead," Turridru said, emotionlessly. The only bit of joy in Alonzo's eyes faded. "And if I was a betting man, I would place all my money on my father being dead too. I haven't talked to him in years."

Alonzo covered his mouth, and his eyes softened. "I am sorry to hear that, Turridru. From the bottom of my heart. Your mother was such a lovely woman."

Turridru's knuckles whitened as he gripped the arm rests of his chair.

When he remained silent, Alonzo returned to his purpose of visiting. "I come to you not because of your position or authority. I don't seek you out as a Man of Honor, but as a friend. We were friends once, weren't we?" Alonzo asked, but the look on his face was more like begging.

"You tell me."

"I thought we were. I cared for you, as a little brother, in some ways. And I am so proud of how you've grown, the man you've become."

The breath caught in Turridru's chest, and his grip softened, but his anger didn't dissipate. If anything, he became angrier as he realized the hold his old mentor still maintained over him. "And so now you come to me in need, when Piddu isn't there to help you? You have not visited me once since my arrival in the States."

"I would have, Turridru, I would have. But I have lived with the guilt of leaving Sicily every day since I set foot on that boat. I couldn't bring myself to see you."

"And what has changed?"

"Nothing . . . I'm still sick with myself. But, my old friend, I would not come to you if I didn't feel I must. I want my boy to have a better life than I have had, and I want it more than I want to maintain my honor. More than I want to keep the breath in my lungs. I must receive the money from someone, and you are the only man in New York I feel comfortable being indebted too."

"Not Piddu?"

"Piddu is . . . he's a monster, Turridru. I've seen clippings in the papers . . . Bodies in barrels."

"How much do you need?" Turridru asked. He knew that if the conversation lasted much longer, blood would soon be splattered across his bookshelves.

"Three thousand dollars. That should cover four years of room and board. I know it's a lot, I know it's . . ." Alonzo stopped explaining himself as Turridru reached into his desk and began counting a stack of cash.

He tossed it across the desk in front of Alonzo, who swept the money into his hand."I thank you, with all my heart, Don—"

"It is not a favor. Nor are we friends, Don Consentino." Turridru said.

Alonzo's gaze dropped. "I will repay you."

Turridru slammed his fist on his desk. "You will repay me?"

Alonzo's mouth hung open like a trout, but he could find no words.

"Not only do you ask for the money I've earned by the sweat of my brow, but now you insult me. You have not come to me as a friend, so I will give you nothing as a friend. I will expect to be repaid. Monthly. I'll send a man to collect it."

"I understand," Alonzo said. He lingered as if there

was more to be said. When Turridru said nothing, he stood and stretched out a hand to shake, but Turridru ignored it. Alonzo stepped away from the desk, his forehead covered in sweat and his eyes full of remorse.

"Consentino," Turridru shouted out. "Don't let me see you again. Do you understand?"

Alonzo looked back for a moment. Like a puppy who'd been kicked. He nodded and stepped away.

If Alonzo came to him because he wasn't as ruthless as Morello, he was sorely mistaken. Don Turridru was more capable of vengeance than the Hook Hand had ever been. He simply had to decide if he wanted it.

34

BUSTER

Westchester County, New York—April 9, 1931

Buster knocked on the door. As he waited, he picked at the flowers in his hand to ensure they were perfectly delineated. The sleepy eyed, crazy haired girl who greeted him was the most beautiful thing he had ever seen.

He stepped in and swept her into his arms without waiting for an invitation. She tried to remain distant but the smirk on her lips gave her away. After a moment of hesitation, she buried her face in his neck.

"What are you doing here, Buster?" she slapped playfully at his shoulders.

"I just had to come see you." He pecked kisses at her like a hungry chicken.

"Come on then, shut the door. It's still cold out there,"

He hurried into the kitchen to get a vase for the flowers. They weren't much, but he refused to show up with anything less. "How's my girl? Did I wake you?" he said.

"You did. But I was dreaming about you anyways."

"That's what I like to hear." He smiled at her over his shoulder.

Neither forgot their last encounter. It hadn't been easy, and Maria had asked him to leave. But they were both too happy to see one another to bring it up now. She told him to avenge her brother Enzo, and that happened whether she knew it or not.

She smiled at him, with the soft focus of someone trying to capture everything in a memory. But there was a look in her green eyes that worried him.

"Maria?" he asked, setting the flowers down at the center of the kitchen table that had been unused for months.

"Yeah?"

"Everything all right?"

"Come here and sit down."

He hated moments like this. He wanted the answers, and quickly. But for once in over a year she had his full attention, and she was determined to milk it for all it was worth.

"What is it?"

"Sit down." She took one of his hands between both of her own, stroking it like a palm reader. He watched her eyes, trying to find a hint. She bit her lip and tapped her foot.

"Come on, Maria, you're scaring me," he said as kindly as he could manage.

"I'm pregnant, Buster."

His hand dropped from hers and his jaw did the same. A thousand thoughts flew through his mind. "Is it mine?" he asked.

"Sebastiano Domingo!" she shouted. "Pregnant or not, I'm gonna hit you for that. Of course, it's yours!"

His eyes darted around the room, trying to find something to prove this was all real. For a moment he thought he was back in a trench in France, where he dreamed so many times about moments like this.

When he was satisfied, he stood and swept her up into his arms.

"A baby?"

"Yes, a baby. A baby," she said.

He held the back of her neck in his hands and kissed her. "A baby?"

"A little you," she laughed.

"No, a little *you*. Oh my God . . . we're gonna have a kid?" he started laughing with her, at himself, at the situation, out of sheer terror.

"Yeah, Buster. We're gonna have a little baby."

"God, I have so many questions . . . so much to learn." He pulled a handkerchief from his pocket and dabbed at his eyes, then laughed at himself.

"We'll learn it together, Buster." She crawled onto his lap and latched her arms around his shoulder.

For a moment, he forgot himself in her embrace. He kissed her neck, smelled her hair, ran his fingers along the smoothness of her skin. He asked questions, appearing stupid even to himself. But he wanted to know everything. A family was all he'd ever wanted. To be a better father than his own.

Then he recalled what was wanted of him. Luciano's grim voice spoke to him, reminding him what he would need to do the following day. The thought of it made his fingertips go numb. He held onto her tighter, afraid he might faint. "Sweetie," he said, his voice just above a whisper.

"Yes?" she said, still not perceiving the shift in his demeanor.

"I need to make a call."

"To who?"

"It'll only take a minute."

"You have to call now?"

Buster sat her down gently on the couch. He took his time marching to the phone, considering what he might say. He picked up the receiver and dialed the operator a few times and hung up before he gathered up the courage. He finally told the operator how to direct his call.

"Yeah?" the voice on the other end answered.

"It's Buster. Can you put on Don Maranzano?"

"What? No, he can't come to the phone. What is it?"

Buster could tell after a moment it was Charlie Buffalo on the other end.

"Put on Bonanno then."

"They're busy, Buster. What do you need?"

He silenced for a moment. He looked at the phone, and then at Maria who waited for him patiently. He swallowed. "I'm out. Tell them I'm out."

"What—"

"I'm sorry." Buster hung up the phone before any rebuttal. He returned to Maria, who stretched out her arms to receive him. "All right, that's out of the way." He fell into her embrace. "I'm not going anywhere. I'm not leaving you again."

"I should have gotten pregnant a long time ago then!" She smiled.

He patted her leg. "I think it came at just the right time."

35

SONNY

Bensonhurst, Brooklyn, New York City—April 9, 1931

"The hell was that? You look like you saw a ghost," Vico said as Charlie Buffalo set down the phone.

"Buster." He stared at the ground, perplexed, trying to make sense of whatever he heard.

"Spit it out, Charlie. Jesus," Cargo said.

"He says he's out."

"What? For good?" Sonny asked.

"I don't know. He didn't say."

"No way. I know Buster. He doesn't want out." Vico shook his head.

Bonanno peaked around the corner from the kitchen. "You think Masseria's crew got to him?"

"It's possible," Charlie Buffalo said.

"It could be a setup then. He knows its gonna be a trap," Cargo said, stiffening.

"No way. If Masseria's boys contacted him, he would have told us first. Then he would've killed 'em one by one,"

Vico said. Noticing the look of concern around the room, he continued, "I've seen that man wipe out entire trenches with nothing but balls and bullets. Give him some credit."

Sonny didn't know what to think. On some level, he was happy to receive the news. He hoped Buster would get out. He didn't like to think of his baby sister married into a life of crime. On the other hand, this was a major loss to the Castellamarese war effort. He was their best shooter, save maybe Vico. And the hit on Masseria was tantamount to the war ending or continuing.

"He means on the hit. He doesn't want to be in on the hit tomorrow," Vico said.

"How do you know?" Cargo asked.

"Spend nine months in the forest with a fella starving, freezing, and getting shot at. You'll figure him out pretty good."

"Look around you, Doyle." Charlie gestured to the safehouse around them. "What the hell is different?"

"It's different."

"Did I hear correctly?" Maranzano entered, a cup of espresso in hand.

Everyone fell silent.

"Yeah, Buster wants out," Cargo said when no one else did.

"That grieves me. Deeply grieves me," Maranzano said. "A day away from the end of the war, and he wants out." He shook his head.

"Luciano wants one of us. I'll go," Vico clenched his jaw.

"He didn't ask for you, Doyle," Charlie blurted.

"Shut up, Charlie. He don't care which one of us goes," Vico replied.

"He's right." Maranzano sipped his espresso. "He just

wants one of us. Someone he can threaten, maim, or kill if we don't keep up our end of the deal. Doyle, you will go tomorrow."

Vico nodded.

Sonny stood. "Doyle doesn't go if I don't go." He looked at his brother, who returned the look but kept his emotions indiscernible.

"We've already talked about this, Vincente." Maranzano shook his head. "It's too dangerous."

"I thought you wanted to keep your hands out of the bloody stuff, Sonny?" Bonanno added.

It was something Sonny had shared with Bonanno and Don Maranzano in confidence, but it didn't matter now.

"If Doyle goes, I go," Sonny said.

"I'll go then, damnit. I don't care." Charlie threw up his hands.

"And do what? You can't hit the broad side of a barn," Cargo said.

Charlie threw an empty cup across the room at him.

"Doyle goes. Vincente, if you want to go, you go on your own volition. I won't stop you," Don Maranzano said, looking at Sonny. There was a glimmer in his eye, one of pride, but also fear for someone who was like a son to him.

"I'm going. Me and Doyle will make sure this thing ends tomorrow."

"Luciano's boys are probably sloppy. Best to take two of our guys anyway," Vico added. "I just don't think it should be Sonny." He glared at his brother.

"I made up my mind." Sonny averted his gaze.

"It's settled then," Maranzano said, setting his espresso down on a small china dish in his hand. He started to return to the kitchen but stopped. "Calogero," he said. Charlie

Buffalo stood and turned to the boss to be addressed. "If Buster calls again, tell him I wish to speak."

"You got it, Don Maranzano."

Coney Island, Brooklyn—April 10, 1931

Vico and Sonny were silent most of the way to Coney Island. They both had a lot on their minds. Sonny thought about saying a few words, something about hoping they made it out safe. Each time he looked at his brother, the words caught in his throat. Vico only drove and stared ahead with the determination of a soldier who just received his final objective.

When they reached Coney Island, neon lights glared through the windows. They passed by billboard advertisements for Lucky Strike cigarettes, Coca-Cola, Barbasol shaving cream, and at least a dozen signs pointing visitors to various vacation destinations. People walked along the streets with their families, enjoying the Island and all its many pleasures, probably with what little they earned from their tax returns. They had no idea what was about to happen. After tonight, Coney Island would no longer be a simple tourist destination. It would be known as the resting place of Joe the Boss.

There were people out there who anticipated the next Al Capone headline with the same relish others awaited the next big nickelodeon to be released. They'd probably make pilgrimages to that Coney Island restaurant, just to sit in the seat where the famed Boss of Bosses met his death.

Sonny imagined the headlines: RACKET CHIEF SLAIN BY GANG'S GUNFIRE, POLICE MYSTIFIED IN SLAYING OF BOOTLEGGING KINGPIN, OR SUPPOSED BOSS OF BOSSES SLAIN IN NEW YORK. People would eat it up like Masseria ate spaghetti. But they wouldn't have any idea of all that led up to it, or the lives lost in the process.

"One last ride," Vico said. "One last ride and then all of this is over."

"And then what?" Sonny asked. "Then what do we do?"

"Maybe we can reopen dad's barbershop."

"You think we really could?" Sonny said without hope in his voice.

Vico narrowed his eyes and thought about it. "Do you?"

Sonny was silent for a moment and sighed. "I never wanted to be a barber like dad. I didn't want to be a regular guy. I wanted the cars, the nice threads, the expensive hats. I wanted to feel important. He told us we could run New York one day . . . but I don't think this is what he meant. He thought we could be doctors or lawyers or something."

Vico laughed. "He thought *you* could be a 'doctor or lawyer or something'. He never had any hope for me and Enzo. He gave up on us the day the Nuns told him we got caught selling cigarettes in class."

"He wanted all of us to avoid this life."

"Now we know why," Vico said, craning his head as he switched lanes. Sonny hoped they weren't close. He still didn't feel prepared.

"I'm glad it'll all be over soon," Sonny said.

"You know I'm not going to stop until we find Turridru, right?" Vico said, finally looking at his little brother in the passenger seat.

"Yeah, I know."

"The war ends tonight. And then my focus will be on finding that guy. I'll kill everybody in New York if I have to," Vico said, and Sonny knew he meant it.

"Well, I've already told you. If you go, I go to. You're the only brother I got left."

Vico didn't reply, but he didn't have to. Vico checked the address for a third time, to make sure he had it, and then pulled off into a parking lot.

He put the car in park and cut it off.

"Got your piece ready?"

"Yeah," Sonny pulled back his suit to reveal his pistol.

Vico demonstrated. "Take your time making the shot. Aim, remember your breathing, and don't jerk the trigger. Just even. Controlled."

"I got it, big brother," Sonny said.

Vico opened his door after slapping Sonny on the shoulder. "You've been here before. We'll both be fine."

They crossed the parking lot, careful to avoid the streetlights. It didn't take them long to find the other men huddled in the darkness.

"You Buster?" the man said when Vico approached and frowned when he looked past Vico and noticed Sonny. "There was only supposed to be one of youse."

"Yeah, well we got two. Buster isn't coming."

The man sighed and shook his head.

After his eyes adjusted to the dark, Sonny recognized the man as Vito Genovese.

"Luciano doesn't like surprises," Genovese said.

"He don't need to know until after the boss is dead," Vico said, meeting the man's eyes. "Won't matter by then."

"Feels like a setup."

"Likewise," Vico said, "but we both have to trust each other, don't we?"

Vito Genovese looked over his shoulder at the other two men with him. They shrugged.

"Don't quit shooting until Masseria is on the ground and as frozen as a block of ice. Capeesh? He's lived through this before, and if he does again, we're all dead."

36

LUCIANO

Coney Island, Brooklyn—April 10, 1931

It was only natural for Luciano to allow Masseria to finish his dinner before discussing important things with him. He was much easier to pacify with a full stomach. He asked Masseria to dismiss the associates after the meal concluded. Everyone departed, save two door guards who'd already been bribed with a few bucks and a case of Canadian whiskey.

Masseria insisted they play a game of cards, even if it was just the two of them.

Luciano dealt.

"I am proud of you, Charles," Masseria said as he received his cards.

"Yeah? How's that?"

"If it's true, you found a way to take the stone from my shoe. I'd like you to tell me how you plan to do that now," Masseria said.

He seemed suspicious, but Luciano hoped the fat man's desire to have Maranzano's head on a platter blinded him.

"Like I said, I got to one of his guys. Balducci. I had him in a cellar for a few days, roughed him up, and he eventually talked."

"Where has the Castellamare rat been hiding?" Masseria asked, looking at the five cards in his hand.

Luciano smiled. Masseria was no poker player, and it was easy to tell he had good cards. "Hiding spots all over the city. Right now they got a place in Brooklyn."

"Brooklyn?" Masseria threw out his first bet.

"Yeah. Bensonhurst."

"Balducci told you that?"

"Yeah he told me." Luciano didn't mention he'd gone there personally.

"And did you kill this man?"

"Not yet." Luciano checked his pocket watch, then matched Masseria's bet.

"Why not?"

"We need him until Maranzano is dealt with. How many cards you want?"

"Two. And what makes you think he can be trusted?"

Luciano dealt the cards, and then considered if he should say what he was about to. "He thinks I'm interested in cutting a deal with Maranzano."

"He does?" Masseria said, with mock surprise.

He seemed less disturbed than Luciano expected. It unnerved him. "Yeah. He says he's going to arrange a meeting. When we go, I'm going to go in guns blazing."

"Maranzano will expect this." Masseria tossed a few more chips into the pile.

"He's getting arrogant. I'll have Costello and Genovese with me. It's been arranged." Luciano matched the bet.

"And Charlie?"

"Yeah?"

"Why didn't you take the deal?" Masseria finally looked up from his cards.

His dead-fish eyes sized Luciano up. The look made him think henchmen would be strangling him any moment. Luciano swallowed and clenched his jaw. He was nervous, and he knew he looked it. "It was never on the table. I know who the real Boss is. Maranzano is a pretender."

"It would have been a good deal." Masseria shrugged. "I couldn't have blamed you."

"You can't trust those Castellamarese. How many cards?"

"One. No, you cannot," Masseria said. "No matter what deal you made with them, you'd always be an outsider to them."

Luciano dealt the cards and checked his watch again.

"Ah." Masseria leaned back in his chair and seemed to be deep in reflection.

It had to be contrived. Masseria wasn't a thoughtful man.

"I remember when you first came to me, as a boy. No more than ten years old. You were a rat, a nuisance, a stone in my shoe, a beggar boy—but as arrogant as a prince. I should have probably killed you then, for all the trouble you caused me," Masseria said, with a cold laugh.

"I'm glad you didn't." Luciano tried to smile.

"I am too," Masseria said. "You turned out to be a good boy. If I hadn't gotten ahold of you, you would be dead. But I turned you into a fine young man."

Luciano clenched his jaw again. "Thanks for saying so." He checked his watch. "What's your bet?"

Masseria threw in a few more chips. "Why do you keep

checking your watch, Charles? Am I not interesting company to you?"

Masseria's eyes were piercing when Luciano met them. "I'm meeting a broad in Yonkers. She'll have my balls if I'm late." There was no give in Masseria's gaze, only suspicion. "But she can wait." He tucked his pocket watch away, ensuring the boss saw.

"I see it in your eyes, Charlie. You envy me, but you see what's happened to the empire I've created. You didn't take the deal with Maranzano because you didn't want to serve under another man like me. You want to be the boss yourself. Eh? Am I right? Boss of bosses maybe." Masseria smirked.

"I just want to make money."

"Lie to yourself if you want, Charlie, but not to me." Masseria wagged his finger.

Luciano called Masseria's bet, directing their attention back to the poker game. "All right, what do you got?"

They laid their cards out and studied them. A two-pair for Masseria, Kings and 3s; three-of-a-kind for Luciano.

Luciano swept the pot to his side.

"You want to be the boss," Masseria said, pretending he wasn't upset he lost the hand.

"I thought you wanted to discuss how we can take out Maranzano?" Luciano said, stacking the chips.

Masseria shrugged. "You're going to take him out anyways. There's a 'plan' right? You don't need me for that. You want him dead, and you think if it's just you and me left, you'll take over and you can 'right the ship.' You think you can lead this family better than I can." Masseria's lips formed a snarl as he nodded.

"Mr. Joe—"

"You always were an arrogant boy, Charlie." Masseria

shook his head, as if disappointed in a child. Masseria spit as much fire when he spoke Luciano's name as he did Maranzano's. "You think you can do better than I have. But there will always be a 'Maranzano' to tear down what you've built. There will always be a 'Lucky Luciano' who wants what you have."

Luciano attempted a smile and shrugged. "Well as long as you're around, boss, Luciano will be your go-to-guy." He dealt the next round of cards, then resisted the urge to check his watch.

"I'll wager you won't last as long on the top as I have," Masseria said, jutting out his chin.

Luciano threw in two chips to start the betting.

"You might be a better poker player than me, Charlie, but that is a wager I would win," Masseria said, answering the bet.

"I wouldn't want to be on top as long as you. I don't know how you do it. Too much trouble. I just want to earn," Luciano said.

Masseria narrowed his eyes, smiled, and shook his head.

Luciano unwittingly pulled out his watch again.

"She must be one impatient dame," Masseria said.

"I actually like this one."

"Ah, your two weaknesses: women and power."

"I got to take a leak." Luciano stood.

Masseria eyed him suspiciously. "Do what you have to."

"Don't look at my cards."

"I don't have to. I can see it in your eyes."

"We'll see when I get back."

Luciano entered the bathroom and headed straight to the sink. He gasped, his composure finally ebbing away. He looked at himself in the mirror and started the faucet. He ran his fingers under the freezing water and splashed it on his face.

He checked his watched again.

He leaned across the sink and tried to stabilize his legs.

A gunshot rang out.

Another.

Then a volley.

Luciano looked up. His heartbeat slowed. He met the eyes of the man in the reflection. The boss was gone. The old was over. Time for something new.

37

SONNY

Coney Island, Brooklyn—April 10, 1931

Sonny's pistol was still smoking when he stepped over Joe the Boss.

"He dead?" somebody asked.

"Yeah. He isn't breathing," Sonny said.

Masseria's face was frozen in a tragic mask, with bulging eyes and an open mouth. A napkin was still tucked into his shirt collar from his previous meal, but it was now covered in blood and bullet holes. Blood leaked from his eyes, ears, nose, and over his lips. Scarlet blood—darker than the rest—rushed out like a flood from the back of his head. It ran along the linoleum floor, pooling beneath his heavy arm.

"Come on, let's get out," Genovese said.

"Sonny, let's move," Vico said, moving toward the doorway.

In the broken face before him, he saw the end of the war they'd been waging for over a year.

He couldn't look away. He noticed on the floor the

playing cards previously clutched in Masseria's pudgy, bejeweled hands before the shooting began.

"Let's go, damnit," Genovese said.

Sonny spotted an Ace of Spades, and placed it back in Masseria's cold, dead hand. Only fitting. He was killed because he thought he was at the top. The same arrogance that allowed him to kill Enzo as someone bats away a fly.

Sonny finally pried his eyes away from Masseria's face. He hurried along with the rest of the killers as the scream of sirens materialized in the distance.

Joe the Boss was dead.

The war was over.

38

SEBASTIANO

Roger's Park, Chicago—April 3, 1927

Sebastiano reread the words he scribbled down a thousand times but couldn't seem to find the right words. What was he supposed to say to his brother? Still held up in some rehabilitation center, half the country away, with his daughter dead because of Sebastiano. He leaned back on the living room couch and rubbed his weary eyes.

Sebastiano would never be able to look him in the eye again.

The medical reports from the staff at Vanderbilt made it seem like he wouldn't have to, even if he wanted. There was still a good chance his baby brother wouldn't be able to heal from his wounds, and the damage done to his internal organs would eventually be unfixable. They repaired him time and again, but the internal bleeding continued. As soon as they addressed one issue, another presented itself. The latest was sepsis.

Considering this, "all the best" just didn't fit at the

end of the letter. Sebastiano crumpled it up and threw it in the trashcan. He wanted to tell his brother how sorry he was, that he would give his life to bring her back in a heartbeat if he was able. But he wasn't like Johnny. He never had a way with words.

He stood and stretched. Despite having already worked his way through a pot of coffee before noon, he decided he needed another cup.

"Sebastiano, will you grab the paper?" his mother shouted from the living room, where the sound of her sewing machine could be heard ceaselessly.

"Yeah, ma." He walked to the front door, his limp lessening every day. When he opened the door, a dark figure stood before it.

"Oh shit!" the man shouted and doubled over. "You almost made me piss myself, Domingo."

Vincent Drucci.

Sebastiano exhaled. If he had been wearing his gun belt he would have drawn without thinking. "Mr. Drucci? What are you doing?"

"Just about to knock," Drucci said, shaking his head, and chuckling at how startled they had both been. "You should have seen your face."

Sebastiano looked over the boss's shoulder, where two cars were parked. Both were Cadillacs, one blue and the other black. They belonged to Bugs Moran and Drucci, respectfully. Cars like that were impossible to miss in Roger's Park.

"Can I help with anything?" he asked.

Drucci's face lit up with glee. "Can you help me? No, it's about what I can help you with!" He slapped Sebastiano on the arm.

All the empathy present a few months prior had

evaporated. The wild, crazed look in Drucci's eyes returned. Drucci smelled blood. They called him "The Schemer" for a reason.

"How's your leg? Good? Never mind that, can you walk?" Drucci said. He spoke fast, obviously in a hurry.

"Yeah, I can walk."

"Let's go then." Drucci waved him on.

Sebastiano took a step out the door, then hesitated. "Where?"

"Where? To kill those rat pricks, Domingo. On second thought, go put a hat on. Your hair looks like shit." Drucci grinned. He might have been a killer, but he insisted on looking dapper while he pulled the trigger.

Sebastiano considered it for a moment. He remembered what the old veteran told him on at the rally. "Leave it all there," he said. Then he remembered the crumpled letter, and how it felt to address his brother. "Yeah, I'll grab a hat."

The next time he wrote to Johnny boy, he would have more to say.

Chicago, Illinois—April 3, 1927

"Ever used one of these?" Drucci said, handing him the largest weapon Sebastiano had seen in years. Drucci chuckled when he saw Sebastiano's eyes light up. ".45 caliber, can pierce armor plates 500 yards away. This baby can fire 800 rounds in a minute."

The driver pulled onto Knox road as Sebastiano turned over the weapon in his hands. "Yeah, I've used one." He remembered storming the German pillbox with nothing but a Thompson machine-gun.

"In the war?"

"Yeah."

"Well, it's a little different here. Mainly the cost." Drucci shook his head. "Set me back 2,000 clams just to have the damned serial number shaved off."

"I'll treat it right," Sebastiano said, testing the weight of the drum, ensuring by sense alone it was loaded to capacity.

"I knew you would. That's why I wanted you here. Plus you're owed blood," Drucci said.

"Where are we going, boss?" the driver asked. "These streets all look the same."

"Just follow Bugs, dumbass," Drucci said, pointing to the blue Cadillac in front of them.

"Can I ask where we're going?" Sebastiano asked, anticipating a similar response.

"We're going straight to hell," Drucci laughed, but then sobered when Sebastiano didn't join him. "Before we can strike at Capone, we gotta get involved in a little politics."

"When can we get the guy who planted the bomb?"

Drucci shook his head. "No one knows who done that. It doesn't matter. Look, I get it. But we ain't gonna find em. Everyone in that outfit is 'Capone', understand?"

"I know how it works."

"You shouldn't worry about some two-bit rat who planted the thing. We have bigger fish to fry. We're going after the guys who allow it to happen, and let these assholes get away with it," Drucci said.

"And who is that?"

"You know what tomorrow is?"

Sebastiano considered it. "No, not really."

"You been stuck in that house too long. It's election day," Drucci said.

"Whole city is going mad," the driver added.

"Big Bill Thompson is trying to get back into the mayor's chair. He's going up against that prude, Dever."

"What's that got to do with us?"

"When was the last time you seen Al Capone around Chicago?"

"You serious?" Sebastiano furrowed his brows. "He's in every newspaper. The radio doesn't talk about anything else."

Drucci shook his head wildly. "I mean in person, Sebastiano. When was the last time you saw him—or even one of his top guys—in Chicago?"

Sebastiano declined to answer so the driver said, "Four years ago. When Big Bill Thompson was mayor."

"Capone and his goons up and moved to Cicero when Dever took office, because he cracked the Pharaoh's whip on every juice joint and still in Chicago. If we want Capone to come back to Chicago, we need Thompson to win," Drucci said.

"Do we actually want Capone to come back?" Sebastiano asked.

Drucci looked at his sidelong and smirked. "If you want blood we do. Once he's back in our territory we'll have plenty of opportunities to put these rat pricks in cement overcoats. Capeesh? But first we gotta make sure Dever doesn't remain in office. Not to mention if he gets reelected he'll have twice the ammunition to aim at our operations. He's a teetotaler and a puritan, Sebastiano. He'll cripple our way of life."

"So we're going to try and kill someone running for mayor?" Sebastiano said. He was surprised at himself.

He was actually prepared to accept if that was the case—he'd do about anything to punish his enemies.

"No, are you listening to me? We're going after one of his alderman. The asshole is rigging his whole district for Dever. As long as he's doing what he's doing, Dever is guaranteed to win the election, and that means we're guaranteed to all go to jail."

"I'm a bit surprised, Mr. Drucci," Sebastiano said. "I've never figured you to be so political."

"I don't give a shit about politics," Drucci waved the idea off. "I care about making money. And staying out of the Big House. Most of all, I hate that rat Capone for what he did to O'Banion and Hymie Weiss."

"That makes two of us," Sebastiano said. He didn't much care about O'Banion or Weiss, although he felt a debt of honor was in place because he had served under them. He could have let all that go though. He could have even forgiven the bullet to his leg, or how his brother had been shot. They were bootleggers, and violence came with the occupation. But what happened to his niece was unforgivable. If it was true that Capone's organization was behind it, then taking the Alderman was the first step of many he would take to making the bastard pay for what he did.

"So, what's the plan?" Sebastiano asked.

"Here's the plan . . ." Drucci set his gun down and used his hands to explain. "We got three shooters in Bugs' car. They're gonna pull up outside of the Alderman's office, and unleash the dogs of war on 'em, understand? But, here's the kicker. They're shooting blanks. It's gonna shake 'em up, and lure them out. After they stop pissing themselves and get to their feet, they'll open the door and we're gonna bust in. We shoot up the place, take the Alderman, and kill anybody who tries to stop us," Drucci said. "Easier than a South Side broad."

Sebastiano's face must have revealed his concerns. It was the dumbest idea he had ever heard. Drucci was called "The Schemer," but he was more suited for "the dreamer" if he thought he could get away with something like that.

"We've tried it before, and it almost worked last time," Drucci said, far less comforting than he assumed.

"You want to kidnap the Alderman?"

"Just until tomorrow. Once the voting is done, and this asshole can't strong arm the voters, we'll kick his ass out the door."

"Is there any other way to stop Dever from being elected?" Sebastiano asked.

"None that I can think of. What about you?" Drucci asked the driver.

"Not a chance."

"Then I guess we're going to kidnap the Alderman," Sebastiano said with a shrug. He received more ridiculous orders in the war and followed every last one of them. His lack of concern for his own welfare was the reason he lived through that. This quality grew even stronger since he lost his niece.

Drucci smiled and slapped him on the shoulder. "The bastards ain't going to know what hit them."

Bugs' car sped off like a bullet after firing a few thousand blanks.

"Alright, let's do this," Drucci said like a child before a schoolyard game.

Sebastiano followed his boss to the building, jumping out of the vehicle before it came to a complete stop.

As expected, there were screams coming from within. As the screams died down, the door was opened by some brave fool who thought he could look like a hero. He received the stock of a tommy gun as compensation.

As the man crumpled to the ground, Drucci grabbed the door before it could close and hurried in, Sebastiano following behind.

They followed the sound of screams to the Alderman's main office.

Around the room, the Alderman's workers were crouched behind chairs and under desks. Drucci let off a dozen rounds or so into the ceiling and Sebastiano followed his example.

"Where is he? Where the hell is Dorsey Crowe?" Drucci shouted as the echo of the gunfire calmed. "I'm not going to ask twice!" He spread more bullets across the room. Glass shattered and wood splintered, filing cabinets were punctured.

"I'm right here! Stop shooting!" a voice cried from across the room. It came from beneath a polished oak desk. A bottle of champagne was atop it, signaling that they had been celebrating a bit too soon.

"Stand up and no one needs to die," Sebastiano said.

The Alderman held his trembling hands above the desk and slowly stood to his feet. As he did so, another man stood across the room. He drew a revolver and fired several rounds errantly. Drucci turned and held the trigger down as bullets lit up the man's new suit. He collapsed.

The screaming of the women around the room was almost deafening.

"No more heroics, any of you!" Drucci shouted. Sebastiano's eyes were wide, feeling the adrenaline, horror, and fear he had experienced in France. He shouldn't have come. He should have stayed home.

"Don't shoot, please!" the Alderman finally stood. His lips were quivering, his thin frame shaking like he was having an epileptic fit.

"There you are, you bastard," Drucci hurried across the room. The Alderman cowered like Drucci was going to hit him. After toying with the man's fear for a moment, Drucci wrangled the man by his collar. "Come on," he said.

Sebastiano kept his Tommy pointed at the Alderman's chest, but prayed he wouldn't have to fire.

"What do you want? Money? I've got thousands in my desk. What do you want?" the man sobbed.

"I want you to shut the hell up. And I want you to stop looking at me!" Drucci shouted. He shoved the man forward and gave him a rap across the head with his tommy gun.

"Here, I'll give you this." The Alderman took two steps forward before his back was littered with bullets. He collapsed, crumpled bills in his twitching hands.

"Shit," Drucci said. It was his turn to have wide eyes.

"Why the hell did you do that?" Sebastiano asked, panicking.

"I thought he had a gun. He was reachin', reaching for something," Drucci began to tremble.

"Come on, we got to go," Sebastiano took the lead out of the door. He wished he had never trusted a hothead like Drucci.

As they exited the building, there was more to regret. The black Cadillac that was supposed to remain beside the curb for a quick getaway was noticeably absent.

"Shit," Drucci said, "No, no, no . . . shit," Drucci whispered to himself.

"What now?" Sebastiano said, wanting to shoot the man if he didn't give him a decent answer.

Sirens sounded in the distance.

"Someone called it in. We gotta run."

"To where, Drucci?" Sebastiano asked. They were simply two cornered rats, and there was no time for cordiality or respect.

"Bugs is supposed to be parked two blocks away." He took off in the direction of their last resort.

"If our driver got spooked, he might have too," Sebastiano shouted as he pursued the boss.

"We don't got no other options," Drucci was already out of breath. Panic had set in.

"Come on," Sebastiano grabbed him by his suit collar and led him down an alley. "We gotta stay off the road."

The sirens were drawing nearer.

"Ditch the gun," Sebastiano threw his behind a dumpster.

"I paid two grand for these!" Drucci pleaded.

"You can buy another if we make it out."

Drucci hesitated but finally tossed the weapon and followed after Sebastiano. It was clear who was now in charge. Drucci had lost that privilege.

"That way." Sebastiano pointed, as they continued to weave between old buildings.

They exited into a courtyard.

"Yeah, just up there to the right. He's parking behind an old bank building. I think," Drucci struggled to shout.

Sebastiano was infuriated by Drucci's incompetence, but hurried in the direction anyway.

A hundred yards in front of them, three men stepped into their path. They were nearly invisible in the black of night, but gold stars on their chest reflected the moonlight. They all had guns, but didn't even bother to point them. They had Drucci and Sebastiano cornered.

"Look who it is." One of the cops stepped forward, into the orange glow of a streetlight. Sebastiano instantly recognized the man. It was Dan Healy, the man who visited him at the hospital. Unlike the two others, his weapon was holstered. One hand was shoved carelessly in his pocket, and the other pulled a cigarette to his lips. He smiled when he noticed Sebastiano.

"Hello, boys," he said.

Chicago, Illinois—April 4, 1927

"Hello, boys," Healy said with a sinister grin. "If it isn't The Schemer himself." Then he looked to Sebastiano. "I see your leg is mending."

"What do you want?" Drucci asked, at a loss for anything else to say.

Healy looked over his shoulder at the two other policemen and laughed. "He asks me, 'what do I want?' I don't want nothing. You boys are under arrest."

"For what? Taking a stroll?" Sebastiano asked.

"Go ahead and put your hands on your head." Healy dropped his cigarette and smothered it under his shiny black boots.

"How'd you find us?" Drucci asked, following orders. He was capitulating quicker than Sebastiano would have.

"Your driver. Bought him off. Didn't take much."

"Yeah, if you're such a genius, why didn't you stop us?"

Healy chuckled. "We knew it wouldn't stick in court if a crime didn't take place. Crowe has acceptable collateral damage."

"I want to call my lawyer," Drucci said.

"I'm sure he's a Kike, brilliant, and expensive. But you aren't getting away this time, Drucci. You're going to rot in a jail cell. But if I have anything to do with it, you'll get fried in the chair."

"I'm gonna get you for this, you mick bastard." Drucci snarled. For once there was no door of escape.

"Is that right?"

"Yeah, I'll fix you for this," Drucci said.

Healy approached slowly, but didn't reach to restrain him.

"It is over, Drucci. Your whole gang is done for. We have an arrest warrant out for every one of your boys in Chicago."

The two other policemen paced over to Sebastiano to restrain him.

"You bulls are all the same, you know it? Full of hot air." Sebastiano shook his head.

Healy turned to Sebastiano and shook his head in mock disapproval. "'The war hero: returns to the States to kill the countrymen he fought for'. It'll headline in the papers. I should have smothered you in the hospital, Domingo," Healy said.

"But that detective had you on a leash right? You bark a lot more when your master isn't here," Sebastiano said as his arms were pulled tight behind him.

Healy smiled in triumph and didn't attempt to

explain himself. "Good thing that little girl is dead, Domingo. She'd be brokenhearted about what her uncle has become."

Sebastiano tried to jump to his feet, but a billy club cracked against his skull and the arms around him squeezed tighter.

"How much is Capone paying you, Healy?" Drucci asked.

Everyone stopped at the mention of Capone's name. Healy's smile faded and his eyes shone like fire in the streetlight. He stepped away from Drucci for a moment, and then slugged him in the jaw.

Drucci dropped to a knee, spitting up gobs of blood. Something solid fell with it, a tooth probably. "I'm going to kill you, you kid copper," Drucci said, composing himself. "I'll get out of this. And when I do, I'll fix you."

Healy straightened and took a step forward, towering over the kneeling Drucci like a victorious general. "Did you just reach for my gun?" Healy asked in a calm voice.

"What?"

"Did you just reach for my weapon?" Healy reached to his holster and brandished the state-issued pistol.

Drucci looked up, perplexed. Healy lowered the gun and shot Drucci in his knee. He collapsed, squirming in agony, as the detective put a boot on Drucci's chest.

"What the hell are you waiting for?" Healy looked over his shoulder at the other officers. "Put that bastard in irons."

"You shot me, you son of a bitch!" Drucci moaned.

"You resisted arrest. I had no choice." He locked eyes with the other officers.

"I think this will make newspapers, too, detective," Sebastiano said.

Healy stepped away from Drucci and hammered a fist into Sebastiano's rib cage. "Not likely, Domingo. No one gives a shit about scum like you. Better off for the rest of mankind if you're out of the picture."

Sebastiano sucked air, trying to catch his breath and not empty the contents of his stomach. "You're a real tough guy when you got two people holding your enemy back."

"You better not resist arrest too. We can probably still get you life in the big house." Healy lowered his voice in mock concern. "A pretty boy like you will be a fast favorite with those degenerates."

Drucci stood behind Healy, keeping all his weight on the one leg that wasn't destroyed. "I'm gonna get you for this. I'll burn down this whole city, and you with it."

Without hesitation Healy raised his pistol and shot Drucci through the chest, who jolted backward and hit the concrete.

The policemen fidgeted nervously to lock Sebastiano's handcuffs in place.

"He tried to kill me," Healy said, returning to Drucci. Rather than holstering his pistol, he pointed it again at Drucci's convulsing body.

The policemen behind Sebastiano froze as Healy lowered the pistol to Drucci's forehead.

Healy fired, the echo ringing off the tops of Chicago's financial district.

Sebastiano, without thinking, thrust a kick back at the bull behind him, and then turned to headbutt the stunned policeman to his side.

He broke into a sprint—or the closest thing he could managed with his old injury—arms still chained behind his back.

"Shoot him, damnit!" Healy shouted, followed by a few errant gunshots that narrowly missed Domingo's back.

He churned his legs forward as quickly as he could, not recoiling as the gunfire sped past. His bad leg threatened to collapse beneath him.

The gunfire stopped for a brief second, and then one more rang out. Sebastiano's hat flew from his head, a bullet passing threw it. Sebastiano continued to run, feeling only a brief sensation of burning atop his head where the bullet grazed. He ran down an alley and sprinted toward the main road. Sirens could still be heard in the distance.

Healy and his subordinates were close enough to be heard scrambling, but they lost his scent. He hunkered down beside a dumpster and prayed to God a way out would be shown to him. When he had almost given up hope, he spotted car lights turn on across the road.

The parked blue Cadillac glistened behind the headlights. Bugs Moran.

PART IV

39

SONNY

Bensonhurst, Brooklyn—April 15, 1931

The door guard rushed Sonny and Vico into the safe house, obviously noticing the blood splashed across their suits.

"It's over. Joe the Boss is dead," Sonny said, entering and his adrenaline still surging.

The room erupted into the cheers.

Cargo wrapped Vico up in a bear hug. Charlie lifted his hands in the air as if offering a prayer of thanksgiving. Bonanno shouted for joy and kissed Sonny on the cheek. Antonello jumped from the couch and wrapped his arms around his childhood pal.

Maranzano, however, remained seated. He closed his eyes, laid his head back and exhaled. He folded his hands as if in reverence. There was relief in his eyes, but if he experienced any joy, he didn't show it.

"You hear that, Caesar? It's over!" Bonanno said, hurrying to the boss's side to congratulate him.

Maranzano allowed himself a smile, but his face

contained careworn wrinkles. The war had taken a toll on him, caused him to age. Now it was over.

Everyone followed Bonanno's example and waited in line to kiss The Don and offer him a congratulations. It was his victory, after all. There wasn't another man in New York who could have taken on Joe the Boss, toe-to-toe, and come out on the other side.

When Sonny reached him, Maranzano finally stood. He stretched out his arms, and pulled him in. He kissed Sonny's head, ignoring the blood on Sonny's suit.

"I am so proud of you, Vincente," Maranzano said.

"Thank you, Don Maranzano. I just wanted to help the family."

It was true. They had become something of a family. His own family was destroyed by this life, but within it Sonny found another.

"So, it is over." Maranzano stepped away from the men present. He straightened his back and narrowed his eyes in thought. Everyone sobered as they prepared for one of Maranzano's famed speeches. "The war is over. Our enemy is vanquished, Gaul has been conquered. Now we, the Castellamarese, reign supreme in New York. And in America." They let out a collective cheer. Maranzano held out his hands to quiet them. "The war is won, but the hard work is only just beginning. Winning a war is the easy. Winning peace is difficult."

"We'll win that too, Don Maranzano!" Charlie said again, as the rooms cheered.

The door guards joined them and brought in a few bottles of champagne saved for the occasion.

"We will. We will win, I assure you," Maranzano said, again smiling for but an instant. "But we must create peace between the victors and the survivors alike."

"Lucky can help us out with that," Antonello added, anxious to remind everyone of the part he played.

"I have no doubt that he can. But we won this war by our own efforts and will have to secure the peace by our own efforts," Maranzano said. "We can't get reckless. We can't begin trusting outsiders." Maranzano accepted a glass of champagne and hoisted it into the air. "To those who aren't with us to taste the fruits of victory, and to those who have secured it!"

Sonny thought of Enzo and lifted a glass in his brother's honor. "Here, here."

"*Salute*!" the room shouted as the glass clanked together.

"We have been at war too long, stuck in these houses. Now, it is time to enjoy the fruits of our labor," Maranzano said and everyone laughed.

They spent a few hours sharing their favorite stories of the past few years, embellishing, and ensuring memories were solidified as far more humorous or courageous than they really were. Everyone spoke as if they knew the war would be won from the beginning. Sonny remembered that quite differently but said nothing to disrupt the good times.

As their conversations began to end, some of the boys wanted to go "enjoy the fruits," as Maranzano had said.

Cargo volunteered to drive a vehicle to the Rainbow Gardens, where the war heroes could be compensated for their hard work.

Vico, smiling for the first time in months, decided to go along with them. He hadn't been to his favorite bar since before Enzo died.

Sonny lingered behind. He was exhausted and would need a new suit before appearing in public, if he didn't want to be arrested. He contemplated leaving, perhaps to see his mother or sister, or returning to the apartment he owned in Williamsburg he hadn't seen in months. As he tried to decide what he would do with this strange feeling of freedom, he noticed Maranzano had settled back in at the kitchen table. It was here the war had been conducted. "Don Maranzano, I thought it was time to enjoy the fruits of our labor?" Sonny smiled, propping himself up against the kitchen doorframe.

The Don looked at his favored pupil and smiled sadly. "It is time for all of you to do so, but not me. There is no time to rest."

"You need any help? I can stick around."

"No, no. By all means, go enjoy yourself. Or get a good night's rest. You deserve nothing less."

"You sure?" Sonny asked, concealing his relief.

"Absolutely. I'm only going to make a few calls, and then I will get some sleep as well. I'm ready to leave this safe house, as well. But I want to return to Williamsburg, sleep in my own bed . . . bring my family back from Canada. It's been far too long since I've seen them."

"I can't imagine." Sonny nodded, thinking of his mother and knowing exactly how Maranzano felt. "There might be a lot more work to do, but give yourself a little rest, Don Maranzano. Even Caesar must have had an off day," Sonny said with a wily grin.

The Don laughed and waved him off. "Go on, Vincente. I will see you tomorrow."

"All right." Sonny rapped his knuckles against the wall and turned to leave. He gathered his coat and hat. As he began to leave, he heard Maranzano pick up the phone.

"This is Don Maranzano. . . . Yes, yes. . . . The glutton lies dead. We will have to celebrate. Call the heads of all the families, from California to Florida to Buffalo. We'll all meet here in Brooklyn. It's time to turn this into an Empire."

Sonny smiled as he threw on a suit top without drops of blood and plopped a fresh fedora on his head. He opened the door, and for the first time in a long time, he could go anywhere he wanted.

Printer's Row, Chicago- May 6, 1931

"Wow, look at that," Cargo said as Maranzano's private car pulled to a stop outside the Congress Plaza Hotel.

"You really are a little slow aren't you, Cargo? New York has hotels too." Bonanno laughed.

"Yeah, but I mean . . . come on. That's the most beautiful building I've ever seen."

"Stop acting like you care about architecture, Cargo. All you want is a quiff and a cheap drink," Charlie said.

Cargo shrugged as everyone laughed, except Maranzano.

This wasn't their first peace meeting since Joe the Boss had been eliminated, and it probably wouldn't be their last. Maranzano wanted to make sure all the I's were dotted and T's were crossed, as Charlie so eloquently put it. He wanted to make sure no one, on either side, would seek retribution.

"I've never been to Chicago, actually," Maranzano said, as he stepped out of the car, handing the driver a thick wad of cash.

"Oh yeah? Doesn't look like you're missing much," Vico

said, straightening his suit coat. He didn't really mean it. They had all been fascinated with Chicago since they arrived. The newspaper headlines were always filled with stories about the lawless city.

They'd all been anxious to come when Maranzano invited them. It was a party designated for VIPs only, but Maranzano made it clear that his "boys of the first day" were welcome wherever he was welcome. Only Buster refused to come. He had shuffled nervously when invited and declined. Everyone assumed Buster was still unsure of himself after he left them holding the bag on the Masseria hit, but Vico wasn't so sure. He thought he might have made some enemies in Chicago he wasn't keen on meeting again.

"Mr. Maranzano, welcome," a man said, stepping down from the steps to the hotel and offering a handshake.

Everyone was frisked, except the boss himself, and were then shown inside.

"How you feeling, boss?" Charlie asked Maranzano.

"I have a real estate company, a food import-export enterprise, a fleet of fishing boats, and a processing plant in New Jersey. On top of that, I have a farm in Upstate, and a family I haven't seen in over a year."

"I meant about the celebra—"

"I know what you meant, Calogero."

Clearly, peace taxed the father of their family more than war ever had. Sonny was worried for him, but he came to have faith in Maranzano's superhuman ability to succeed. He hoped it was just a slump.

As they were ushered into the hotel, a bear of a man approached. Wearing a flashy pinstripe sack suit, a Stetson fedora, and a pinky-ring that glistened in the hotel's florescent lights, it was impossible to mistake him. It was the host —Al Capone.

"The conquering hero himself," Capone said, wedging an unlit cigar in his teeth and shaking Maranzano's hand. The Don greeted the infamous racketeer with kindness, but not without formality.

"Thank you for hosting this event, Alfonso," Maranzano said. He gestured to the Sonny and the rest of the crew who waited anxiously behind him. "These are my finest men. I hope they'll be treated with the utmost respect during our stay."

"Of course, of course," Capone reassured him, nodding and sizing up each man in turn. "It's good to meet ya. I'm Al Capone."

His smile was charming as he greeted each with a handshake. His presence was just as intriguing as the newspapers claimed. "Let me show you fellas to our venue."

He led them down a marble staircase with gilded handles to the basement of the hotel. As they arrived on the bottom floor, two grand oak doors were opened to a marvelous dining hall. The room was filled to capacity with important men from across the country, and each of them stood when Maranzano entered.

"Everyone is chompin' at the bit to meet youse," Capone said, stretching out his arms to the dining hall, proud of the event he orchestrated.

Maranzano nodded but took a moment to breathe before he entered the room. As soon as he crossed the threshold, a smile creased his face, and he summoned up the charisma Sonny had always been so intrigued by.

Men around the room formed a line, a procession to greet the man who was now most famous in the *Onorata Societa*.

"It's an honor to meet you," Maranzano said, shaking their hands.

Hundreds of men accepted his introduction like a court before their king. After they greeted him, they fell in another line behind a table near the entrance. Here, each man pulled out a thick stack of cash and laid it on the table as tribute.

"That's a few simoleons," Cargo said, standing with the rest of them by the entrance to the room.

"Thinking about going back to your thieving days, Cargo?" Sonny said beneath his breath.

"No way. But hopefully part of that pot is ours after all we done," Cargo said, not removing his eyes from the collection.

Maranzano took the time to engage with each man individually, a politician greeting his constituents for the first time after an election.

Sonny spotted Stefano Magaddino from Buffalo, who was already jolly from the effects of wine, and greeted his nephew Bonanno like they hadn't seen each other in years. He also noticed the heads of the other New York families, and the dark imposing figure of Charlie Luciano. All others were strangers to him, but he was careful to treat each with respect, or otherwise might find himself on the wrong side of their newfound peace.

After introductions were made, all the guests were led to a massive table in the center of the room. It contained enough chairs for at least fifty men, and the remaining hundreds stood behind their respective leaders. Capone himself walked Maranzano to the head of the table, and pulled it back for him. He then sat in the chair to Maranzano's right.

The two made unlikely friends, Sonny thought. Capone was loud, boisterous, attention seeking. Maranzano valued discretion, and preferred honor over money or fame. It was a microcosm of the difference between the Sicilian old breed and the Italian new breed. But, after so many months of fighting, everyone wanted peace. If Maranzano had made peace with a man like Capone, who had formerly been aligned with Joe the Boss, there was hope for anyone.

Maranzano stood and waited for silence before he spoke. The only sound was of the beautiful waitresses who strutted around the room offering drinks to all the guests.

"You all know why you are here," Maranzano began in Italian, his voice calm but projected like he had one of those new microphones. "We, in our society, have endured hardship, and lean years as a result of the tyranny of one man. He condemned my people to die. He himself now lies dead." He paused and allowed his words to linger. "Many of you supported me in my efforts. Some of your fought against me. Because of this, I see many of you with smiles on your faces, bubbling with excitement. Others have pale, frightened faces."

Sonny and the others listened intently. Vico lit a cigarette.

"I want to make this clear, friends. You have nothing to fear from me. The war is over. Old enmities can now blossom into new friendships. Whatever has happened in the past, is now forgotten. There is to be no more ill will between anyone who now sits at this table. If your own brother was killed in this war, do not try to find out who did it, or attempt to get even. If you do, you pay with your life." Maranzano said. He looked around the table, and fixed eyes on Luciano, who was himself looking at the glass of whiskey in his hand.

"This a special time, comrades. We can now return to the way things once were, and also move towards a brighter future. We can return to our various enterprises, but we can also work together to form continuity in leadership and our operations." Maranzano took a sip of the wine provided him and gestured to the New York bosses who sat to his left. "Please, stand." When all were on their feet, he continued, "The men standing before you are the new leaders of the New York Cosce, including myself. This is Salvatore Luciano, better known as Lucky. He will now serve as the leader for the Masseria outfit . . ." Maranzano continued down the line, introducing each leader in turn. Gagliano beamed with pride to be formally inducted as a borgata leader.

After everyone had been introduced, Maranzano said, "These are New York's leaders. The rest of you are leaders of your own borgata throughout the country. By remaining here, you ascent to this hierarchy of leadership. There will be no more attempting to kill the man to your right or left in an attempt to take what they have built." Maranzano paused. "Is there anyone who wishes to offer an objection? If so, you may raise your hand, and you'll be allowed to leave. You will not, however, operate with the auspices of this body." No one dared move an inch. "Then we are one." Maranzano said and raised his glass. "Here is to the future,"

"Salute!" The men at the table cheered and raised their glasses.

Maranzano took his seat.

"He's 'letting the dice fly,'" Charlie said.

A few chuckled, as Maranzano was famous for quoting this line as well as many others by his hero Julius Caesar.

But Sonny didn't laugh. If he could tell by the look in his mentor's eye, he was expecting the dice to land poorly.

40

TURRIDRU

Williamsburg, Brooklyn—September 1, 1928

"The meal was delicious, dear," Turridru said, dabbing at his lips with a napkin.

"The meat was too tough," Elizabetta said, disappointment obvious in her voice. "I'll cook it less next time."

"That's not necessary. I think it was perfect." He reached across the table and took her hand. "What do you tell your mother, boys?"

"Thanks, Mama." Both sons said in unison as they sat on the edge of their seats, waiting to be dismissed.

"Go on now, loves." Elizabetta shooed them away, and they scampered away from the table giggling. "Finish your schoolwork. Papa will be up to check and make sure it's finished in a little while."

"Would you like some coffee, wife?" Turridru approached the kitchen record player and set down his favorite 45—Nessun Dorma by the incomparable Pavorati.

"No, I think I shouldn't. It's been keeping me up at night." She sighed.

"Too soft," Turridru jested, "you city—"

A knock on the door. Turridru exhaled and rubbed his temples.

"Are you expecting anyone, dear?" he asked.

"No, I shouldn't think so. It's probably one of the neighbors. They've been bringing over desserts lately. They want to meet you badly."

"I'd prefer not to,"

"Your reputation as a host proceeds you, I think." She wiped her hands on a kitchen towel and hurried to answer the door.

Turridru stepped away from the view of the entrance, hoping his wife would tell the intruders to bugger off.

"Husband, there are two men here to see you," she said, reentering the room.

Turridru smiled as if he wasn't annoyed at this disruption and followed her to the foyer.

"Paisanos, it's good to see you," Turridru said to the two men waiting there, summoning all the cheer left in his weary body. He gave them both hugs and a kiss on the cheek. Both were caught off guard by his cordiality. "Please, join me in my study." He winked at his wife before leaving for his office.

When the men arrived in Turridru's office, he made the full extent of his displeasure known. "I don't know what you are trying to pull, but it better not happen again." He kept his voice low, but the fire in his eyes intimidated them like he was shouting.

"Sir, we just—"

"Never set foot in my home again. Understand? My wife is here. My children are here." Turridru gritted his

teeth, and they lowered their heads. "Now tell me why you are here." He walked to the other side of his desk and poured them both some Scotch from a crystal decanter. They were low-level employees, nobodies, but he was determined to be a good host, regardless.

"We went to collect the vig from Consentino," one of them said before looking to the other.

The other said, "He wasn't there."

The fire in Turridru's veins froze.

"That's impossible. He knows when we collect."

The nobody on the left swallowed. "If he was there, he hid from us."

The glasses in Turridru's hand threatened to shatter in his grip. He stilled himself before passing the Scotch to his lackeys.

"We spoke with his wife," the other nobody said.

Turridru sat and waited to hear something useful.

"His wife said he was shopping."

"Shopping?" Turridru's heartbeat pounded in his ears. His teeth clenched so tight they might shatter.

"Yeah," one of them said.

"Car shopping."

"Car shopping?"

"That's what his wife said. She hushed her voice and said it was a birthday gift for their little girl."

Turridru sucked in a deep and heavy breath. His chin dropped to his chest.

"What do you want us to do about it?" the nobody on the right said.

"I don't want you to ever speak to his wife again, you understand me?" Turridru slammed a fist on his desk and pointed at them with a knifelike finger.

"We got it," they said together.

"He is shopping for a car. He wants to buy a car for his daughter," Turridru said, trying to make sense of it all.

One of the nobodies remembered something. "Mrs. Consentino said he's looking at the new Model A's. The girl always wanted one."

"And he decides to go shopping on the day I collect my payment. Spending money he owes me." Turridru drained his Scotch and slammed the empty glass on his desk.

"We can go to the barbershop if you want. We can break his legs." the nobody on the right said.

"That won't be necessary. Not at this time," Turridru said, forcing a cold smile. His decision wouldn't even be known to these lowlifes who worked for him. "Next month, go and collect my money as usual. Alonzo will know ahead of time that he will own me double the payment, with a 10 percent tax on top for the disrespect he has shown us. Understand?"

They nodded and departed.

Turridru poured himself another drink and approached the window. He watched their car pull away but could think of nothing but Alonzo. Turridru had shown the man forgiveness. For the sake of his family, Turridru had been willing to let the man live. What was he to do now?

There was only one thing. The thirst for revenge was now reignited.

There was only one way to quench it.

Little Italy, Manhattan—October 14, 1928

Turridru reclined in his leather office chair. Since arriving in the States, he maintained a real estate office in

Little Italy, just a few blocks away from where his estranged mentor lived, just down the road from where he cut hair. Up until September, he had decided to let the man live. But the car. That Model A. It was all Turridru could think about. He tried to show grace to the aging Sicilian and was spit on in return.

A few days prior, he had gone to the commission. It required calling in a few favors simply to arrange the meeting, and while there, he found himself more on trial even then Alonzo. That dusty group of old-timers were reluctant to give their blessing for Alonzo's murder. Even the younger Masseria, Gaetano Reina and Tommy Gagliano hadn't been ready to offer the nod. When finally Turridru acknowledged Mr. Consentino had missed out on his September vig did they relent.

Now, sitting in his office chair, he sipped a cup of espresso, and considered how he would feel when he received the news that Alonzo was finally dead. He recalled his time in Sicily, and what it was like to be alone and scared, up against a powerful enemy with his supporters either dead or missing. Alonzo did that to him, and he was responsible for the death of Turridru's mother. Alonzo's death wouldn't bring her back, and he wasn't even sure it would make him feel any relief. But his mind was made up. This was about honor now, not just revenge.

Three men were waiting in the foyer of his office, drinking water and whispering amongst themselves. Turridru only had to raise his hand, and they were to depart and take care of Alonzo as he was closing his barbershop for the day. He couldn't decide why, but he was reluctant to do so. Killing Alonzo had been the fixture of his mind for so long, it was too much to believe that it would all be over soon.

He considered whether his reluctance was because he wanted to kill the man himself. No, that couldn't be it. He had a wife and children now. No sense in bloodying his own hands and risking everything he was building just for a sense of satisfaction.

That couldn't be it.

Maybe he felt sorry for the old fool? He was a rather pitiful sight after all these years. Once the Don of a powerful Sicilian Borgata, he was now a barber in one of Manhattan's poorest districts. Turridru shook his head. He would prefer death to living like that.

"Sir." One of the cutthroats approached his office door.

Even when they approached with their squeamish reverence, he disliked it. In another life, he would have never even talked to such a man. "What is it?"

"A letter." The man stepped forward and placed an envelope on his desk.

"I receive a lot of mail. You interrupt me for this?"

"The courier wasn't a mailman. He was . . . someone like us." The man bowed and stepped out of the room.

Turridru used a letter opener to cut away the seal placed on the envelope and pulled out the enclosed letter. There were only three words, and all in Sicilian.

DON'T DO IT.

Below the words was an image, in black ink—a handprint with missing fingers. Threatening letters like this had circulated throughout Little Italy for nearly half a century, but men like Turridru didn't receive them. What made this one different was the missing fingers. Only a thumb and pinky finger were displayed.

It was a message that could have come from only one man: the Hook Hand, Giuseppe Morello, otherwise known as Piddu during his time in Sicily.

Turridru crumpled the letter between his fists.

The men outside noticed his reaction and turned away for fear of being seen as nosey.

It was clear his intentions had been relayed to the recently released Giuseppe Morello. The man lost much of his prestige during his time in prison, but his word was still law in the *Onorata Societa*. The Commission made it clear if Morello didn't ascent to the murder of Alonzo Consentino, Turridru should stand down.

Turridru's mind, which usually functioned like an oiled-machine, was now clouded by anger. He couldn't find clarity. He made up his mind, and all the pieces fell into place. Alonzo was supposed to die.

"Sir, are you ready for us to leave?" one of the bolder cutthroats said from the doorway.

Turridru realized he'd been sitting in his chair for some time. "No," Turridru said, tearing the Hook Hand's message in two. He placed it in the waste basket beneath his desk. "Why don't you three go home?"

"You sure?" The man stared back blankly, sadness in his eyes when he realized he wasn't going to be paid.

"Yes. And consider a new career while you're at it." Turridru stared down the man until he turned his back and departed. The others followed behind.

Turridru rubbed his forehead. Those cutthroats were dumb men and had allegiance with no one. He hoped they would talk. He hoped they would spend what little money they had at some bawdy speakeasy down the road. Once drunk, they would open their mouths and sing like canaries about how they had seen Turridru back down at the sight of a letter.

Exactly what Turridru wanted.

But he wouldn't back down. He wouldn't change his mind.

He would kill Alonzo Consentino. The man he would use would have to be an outsider, someone who couldn't be identified. But he would kill Alonzo. And afterward, if he had anything to do with it, he would kill Giuseppe Morello too.

41

ANTONELLO

Little Italy, Manhattan—May 19, 1931

He didn't want to let Sonny know he was hungover, so he sipped black coffee even as he turned the car onto Mulberry Street.

Sonny was such a good guy. Antonello didn't want to let him down. They were old pals, ran together as kids, and Sonny stuck his neck out for him. Antonello just didn't know how to stop once he got started. If he ever sampled the dope he was selling on the side, it stole whatever little willpower he usually had.

Sonny was looking over his files in the passenger seat. He looked more like a businessman than a gangster. He was never any fun on days like this. He hated making collections, but now that the war was over, Maranzano decided it was important Sonny showed his face to all the business owners in Little Italy who paid up to them for protection. During the war, Antonello did it alone and got a cut from everything he brought in, which suited him just fine.

Usually he'd like riding with Sonny, but he didn't laugh like he used to. Maybe it started when Alonzo met his end. Or maybe it was Enzo. Maybe it was something else entirely. Regardless, Antonello missed the way they used to joke.

When Antonello was growing up—right there in Little Italy—his father used to beat him. Bad. Between punches and whips of the belt, Mr. Balducci would tell him how he'd grow up to be a bum.

And he was probably right. He was a bum. If it wasn't for Sonny, he'd be a nobody. By now, he'd probably be up the river in some prison for some petty crime or another, and he'd probably be happy for it too. He'd have a roof over his head and food in his belly. More than his father usually had.

"We need to visit the confectioner on Houston," Sonny said, almost to himself.

"Oh yeah? He late on payment?"

"No. If he gives something, that's a bonus." Sonny leaned back in the passenger seat and exhaled. "But we need to get some sugar for one of Maranzano's stills in Upstate."

"Poughkeepsie?" Antonello asked, trying to appear more informed than he really was.

Sonny nodded. Either way, Antonello drove the rest of the way in silence to Houston Street.

When they parked, Antonello hurried to hold open the door for his old pal, the caffeine starting to remove the headache and shakes from his past night of binging. He hoped for a thank you or a job well done. Sonny gave him another nod, which was probably the same thing.

They'd only been inside the candy store for a few seconds when the clerk was dabbing his head with a handkerchief.

"*Buona Sera*, gentlemen," the clerk said. Not only was he sweating, he shook too. Most fellas were uncomfortable when they showed up for collections, but this seemed excessive.

Antonello turned to his old pal, and Sonny gave him a nod. That meant he should carefully draw his revolver. Antonello did so without delay. He didn't want to hurt this old-timer, but if it meant protecting his pal, he'd do anything. And something strange was going on.

"Ennio, we just came by for some sugar," Sonny said.

"We have plenty of that. By the door there!" The clerk gulped like somebody from those ridiculous old silent pictures.

Antonello looked at Sonny. He should leave. Why was he staying? He didn't have to risk anything. But there wasn't fear in sadness in Sonny's eyes. Only sadness.

Sonny whispered. "What's behind the counter?"

"Nothing, I swear!" Ennio shouted. "We never keep guns in the store!"

"Who said anything about guns?" Sonny said. He hung his head and nodded again.

Antonello knew what that meant. The ballgame was about to start like it was opening day at Fenway. Antonello put his finger in the trigger well and stepped closer to the counter. He peered around the corner, gun drawn and pointed. He saw skin and nearly shot, but gasped. Kids. Dirt-covered kids. Three of them.

Antonello shook his head, panicked, and relieved in the same instant he hadn't pulled the trigger unwittingly.

"Please," Ennio said, his voice shaking. "Don't hurt them. Their mothers told them to run when they saw black cars."

Antonello turned to Sonny, who looked more deflated than the balls they played with growing up on Mulberry.

Antonello thought he could even see tears in the eyes of his oldest pal when he said, "You think I would harm children, Ennio?"

The kids jumped out, holding their hands up like the bulls were arresting them.

Sonny hung his head. He fished out a roll of dollar bills and separated several. "I'll take three of the biggest bags of candy you have. One for each of them."

"Right away, Mr. Consentino." Ennio hurried to fill the bags, and Sonny knelt to their level. He took off his fedora and met their eyes. "I want you boys to take these bags to your mothers. Let them decide how much you can have, and when. And always share with your siblings—family is everything."

Sonny looked at the linoleum beneath him as the boys continued to stare, wild-eyed and mystified.

"You don't ever have to scared of guys like me," Sonny said. "Unless you *become* guys like me. But you're not going to do that are you?"

They shook their heads, newsboy caps drooping to the side.

"Go to school, go to Mass. Find a pretty girl and a regular job."

The tallest of the three boys smiled. "I've got my eye on a pretty gal, mister."

The little one chirped up. "And I'm gonna play shortstop for the Yanks!"

"Good." There was a quiver in Sonny's voice Antonello never heard before.

He turned and made for the exit, Antonello trailing behind.

"What about my collections?" the clerk shouted after them.

"No collections today, Ennio," Sonny said. "Just wanted to stop by."

The clouds had broken and the sun shone brighter when they walked out.

As they reached the car, Antonello said, "You're a regular Al Capone." He chuckled.

Sonny entered the car and exhaled. "I'm not doin' it for the papers."

Antonello laughed again and almost replied but saw Sonny had pulled the fedora over his eyes and he was weeping. Antonello hadn't seen him cry anywhere outside St. Patrick's cemetery. "You all right?"

Sonny coughed and dried his eyes. "Just drive."

42

SEBASTIANO

Chicago, Illinois—October 28, 1928

Sebastiano woke to the sound of his grandfather Girolamo entering the shed. It had been his own little prison cell since he escaped Healy and his cops. With nowhere else to turn, he went to his grandfather and told him he needed boarding. He couldn't go back home.

His grandfather, the old quiet type he was, gave consent without any questions. Sebastiano was shown to his grandfather's work shed, where he would live for the next year.

He lived there, slept there, ate what his grandfather brought him there. He left the building only to help his grandfather in the yard. As the months passed by, he considered leaving several times, but occasionally his grandfather would enter with a newspaper in hand and accidentally leave it behind. The headline often contained Sebastiano's name, updating the Illinois populace about the pursuit of the North Side Gang member.

"I appreciate it, but I'm not really hungry yet," Sebastiano said as the thin stream of light poured in from the open door. His grandfather stepped into the building and shut the door behind him. He wiped oil from his hands onto a dirty old towel. When he wasn't at his distillery, he was often working on one of his boats in the backyard. He didn't often disturb Sebastiano except with food and the rare but cherished bit of company.

"I don't have any food for you, boy," his grandfather said, looking down.

Sebastiano scrambled to his feet. "Looking for a tool? I'll help you find it."

"That's not it either."

He looked at his grandfather. "What is it then?"

He hoped it wasn't what he had long dreaded—the moment his grandfather would ask him to leave. He knew his grandparents well, and although his grandfather would have let him live there forever, Sebastiano knew his grandmother's nagging would eventually become unbearable for the old man, and Sebastiano would have to go.

"There is someone here to see you," his grandfather said.

Sebastiano's heart raced. Men had come and gone since he had been there, police even, searching the premises. No one had been ushered into the shed which was several acres behind the house. His mother and sister-in-law had visited but were never alerted to his presence. If they had been, they would have rushed out to see him no matter how much grandfather tried to stop them. He'd never come to Sebastiano with news about a visitor.

"Who is it?"

"He says he knows you are here and wants to help," Girolamo said.

"Well, what's his name?"

"Joseph Aiello."

Sebastiano racked his mind for a moment, before finally remembering a Mr. Aiello who was once a neighbor of his Roger's Park."He says he knows me?"

"He says he wants to help. He's like us. Should I bring him?"

Sebastiano thought about it. If jail was to be his fate, or even the electric chair, he was ready to accept it. The police weren't giving up the pursuit and living in a shed was no life at all.

"Yeah, send him on in. Thanks, Grandfather," Sebastiano said.

He slipped suit pants over his long johns and threw on his coat. After living in a shed for over a year, there wasn't much he could do to look decent, but he would do his best. He recalled what Healy said and decided that if Chicago's "war hero" was to be paraded through the newspapers, he wasn't going to look like a bum.

The door opened again, and this time a visitor stepped in. He wore a pinstripe suit and a porkpie hat. He was young but had the distinguished look of someone with vast life experience.

"Good morning, Mr. Domingo," he said.

"Mr. Aiello," Sebastiano said, unable to hide the shame of his appearance.

"Do you remember me?"

"We were neighbors once."

"We still are, if anyone can judge from your address.

But you haven't been home in a while." Aiello stepped close. His face was mostly absent emotion, but there was sympathy in his eyes.

"That might be the case."

"And I know why," Aiello said, nodding. "All of Chicago knows."

"How is my family? Are they okay?" Sebastiano asked. He had been anxious to know since he went on the lamb but couldn't bring himself to ask any information of his grandfather.

"They're all right. They were heckled a little bit for the first few weeks after you left. People were lining up outside your house, since the address was in the papers. But everyone stopped caring a long time ago. The only bastard who still cares is that detective Healy. Every once in a blue moon he still puts out word that he'll find you if it's the last thing he does."

"That bastard didn't go to jail? He shot Drucci in cold blood," Sebastiano said.

"I figured as much. The story goes that Drucci attacked him. 'Reached for his gun,'" Aiello said with air quotes. "Drucci's widow tried to get an investigation, but they minted a medal for Healy instead."

Sebastiano lowered his head. "What can I do for you, Mr. Aiello?"

"From the looks of ya, there isn't much you can do for anybody," he said, his voice soft and without judgement. "But I can do something for you."

"And what is that?"

"We have a mutual enemy, Mr. Domingo. Capone and me . . . we don't get along."

"He isn't my enemy anymore. I gave up caring about

that shit. I just want to get back to my family." Sebastiano shook his head.

Aiello took a few steps closer and placed a hand on Sebastiano's shoulder.

"We both know that ain't true. And we both know you can never go back to your family." Aiello stepped back and lit a cigarette. "Want one?" He held out the pack, and Sebastiano grabbed a Lucky Strike. "Those days are over, Domingo. But, seeing as you're a neighbor, and we hate all the same people, I want to help you out. We might have the same enemies, but we don't have the same friends. That is what I can do for you."

"You're gonna find me some new friends?" Sebastiano said, more sardonically than he intended.

Enjoying his cigarette, Aiello stepped to the workbench in the middle of the shed, where a phone sat. He picked up the phone and asked the operator to put him through to an address in Brooklyn. Without addressing the person he called, he extended the receiver to Sebastiano.

"Someone wants to meet you."

Sebastiano hesitated before taking the phone and placing it to his ear.

"Hello, Sebastiano," the voice on the other end of the line began before Sebastiano said anything.

"Hello."

"My friend Joseph tells me you're having some trouble." The man spoke in Sicilian. Sebastiano was rusty so it took him a moment to respond.

"You could say that. Yeah. In a manner of speaking."

"I can help you." The voice on the other end of the line was clear, calm, and collected.

Sebastiano, on the other hand, was not. "How could you do that?"

"You need a way out. I can provide that."

"You can?" Sebastiano asked, trying to temper his enthusiasm.

"Yes, I can. Don Aiello is a friend of mine. And he is a friend of Bugs Moran, who let us know about your situation. You need to leave Chicago, Sebastiano."

"I do?"

"Yes. The time is running out. Your presence is burdening those you love."

"Maybe I can go back to Benton Harbor. I have friends there."

"You know that isn't possible, Sebastiano. You're a smart man. It's a simply ferry ride from Chicago to Benton Harbor. You'd be arrested before you could blink."

"You think so?"

"I know so, Sebastiano. I've read the papers. You know this, too, or you would have already left."

Sebastiano had dreamt of leaving for Benton Harbor, but knew it was nothing but a fantasy for some time. He could never go back.

"Where do you suggest I go?"

"New York. You'll be my guest," the man said.

Sebastiano still didn't even know who he was talking too, but didn't dare ask. Aiello continued to watch him as he smoked his cigarette.

"And you think I'll be safe there?"

"You will. You'll be safe because everyone will think you are dead."

"They'll think I'm dead?"

"That's correct. Don Aiello knows some of the

policemen in Chicago. They'll make a report that you were found washed up on the side of the shore. They'll say you took your life after your run-in with the law. The war hero will have his last newspaper headline, and some semblance of honor can return to your name, and some peace can return to your family."

"You think so?"

"We know Chicago reporters as well. They'll say what they're instructed."

Sebastiano blinked the tears from his eyes and tried to compose himself. It had been a year since he escaped Dan Healy, a year of living in a shed. He had dreamt of a better life waiting for him, but it was quickly becoming apparent that his life would never return to normal.

"What happens to my family?"

"That is simple. If you aren't paraded before the courts to be convicted for violation of the Volstead Act—along with murder charges that will certainly bring about your execution—your assets will remain intact. The money you earned through your hard work will remain with your family."

"It will?"

"Yes, it will. And I have arranged that a $10,000 payment be made to your mother, for various expenses. Your brother returned home recently, and your family could use the money."

"He's all right then?" Sebastiano always believed his brother would recover, but evidence would set his heart at ease.

"Stay on track Time is running short."

"So you want me to come to New York?"

"Yes."

"And I'll be safe there?"

"As safe as a man can be."

"What if someone finds out who I am?"

"The men in our line of work don't ask questions. But you won't be able to use your name, not frequently at least. Most of the simple men who live in Manhattan would find your name difficult. 'Buster' could suit you just fine."

"Let me get this straight." Sebastiano found himself becoming angry with the man, but didn't know why. "You want me to pretend I'm dead, come to New York... and then what? Then what happens?"

The man on the other end of the line went silent for a moment.

"I have a favor that I would ask, in return for the service I have given you."

"And that is?"

"To kill a man."

"You're saying that you want me to kill a man while trying to escape murder charges?"

"That's right. But, in so doing, you'll have the full backing of a powerful man. I'm giving you the opportunity for new life. I am offering you new birth."

"You're out of your mind," Sebastiano said, ignoring the glare from Aiello.

"I only offer this once." The voice remained calm but contained a coldness Sebastiano hadn't noticed before. "Look around you. What choices do you have?"

Sebastiano did as the man asked and looked around. The shed was cold and dirty. It had been his home for so long he had become accustomed to it. The man's voice reminded him of what it was like to have a clean home and nice cars.

"I'll do it. Okay? I'll do it," Sebastiano said.

"Don Aiello will arrange the details."

"Wait," Sebastiano said. "What's your name?"

"You aren't the only refugee living under an assumed name." Before Sebastiano could respond, the man hung up.

43

SONNY

Bronx, New York—July 18, 1931

"Give me one more, fella," Vico slurred to the barkeep. "As a matter of fact, go ahead and make that two."

"Maybe you should slow down, Vico," Sonny said, placing a hand on his brother's shoulder.

"Or what?" Vico spun to him, his eyes drooping in a way that they only did when he drank.

"Or nothing . . . I just meant maybe you've had enough."

"Or you just can't keep up," Vico said, sipping the whiskey from one of the glasses placed in front of him.

Sonny signaled for another drink as well. The Rainbow Gardens wasn't his favorite leisure location, but Vico favored it. It beat being stuck in hideouts. At least the war was over.

Their brother had been avenged. Joe the Baker was dead, as was his boss Joe Masseria. All survivors surrendered and joined them under the leadership of Lucky

Luciano. Everything was set right except the murder of their father. Nearly three years had passed since Sonny received the telephone call that would change the trajectory of his life forever.

As he sipped his neat whiskey, he wondered how things might be different. He would have finished college, likely with honors. Maybe he would have continued to date Rachel, the dame who like to spend time with his fraternity. He would have graduated and taken a job on Wall Street, where he would have earned a stable income and paid to move his mother and father out of their cramped tenement in Little Italy. He would have married, and had two kids, maybe three. Preferably one of each gender. He wanted a boy to carry on the family name—Enzo and Vico weren't the settling down types. He had also wanted a girl. He knew he would dote over her, and she would have been spoiled. The apple of his very eye.

But that hadn't happened. Even with the war over, he felt it was likely never going to happen. Other members of the *Onorata Societa* seemed perfectly able to have a wife and children on the side and still maintain their obligations to the family they were apart of. Sonny didn't want that. He wanted his children to have a father. One who wouldn't be called up to leave and hide for a year, while his very life was threatened.

An image flashed before his eyes of a nice home with a picket fence and baseball gloves in the yard from a recent game of catch. He pictured his own little family, smiling, as the police came to the door and placed him in irons. They'd probably abandon him when they discovered the truth, and they'd have every right to do so. Orphaned children and a widowed wife. He couldn't ever allow that to happen.

He could get out of the life. Maranzano had even hinted

that he would allow it, that he would set up Sonny with enough money to open up another investing company, perhaps one of those new mutual fund even. He could be a big shot and rule New York like his father once told him he could.

But what about Vico? What would happen to him if Sonny turned around? And ultimately, what about their father? Was he not worth retribution, no matter how long it took?

"You ever heard of a cocksucker named Turridru?" Vico asked the bartender.

"Never heard of him." The bartender leaned in to hear better.

"Come on, Vico," Sonny said, intervening on the nervous bartender's behalf.

"No, I mean it. Don't lie to me, dirtbag. You heard of a fella named Turridru?" Vico asked again.

The bartender shook his head and glanced away.

Vico slacked in his chair. "Well, you ever meet him, tell him that the Consentino's are looking for him. And we'll kill him," Vico said.

"Where's Gagliano's crew? Don't they usually hang around here?" Sonny tried to change the subject.

"Hell if I know. Cargo is still bodyguard to your Old Caesar. The Gap and Gagliano are probably too good for places like this now." Vico gestured to the old entertainment venue around him. "I mean look at this place. It's a piece of shit," he said, too drunk or uncaring that the bartender was within ear shot. "Look at these girls, these whores. Don't give a damn about nobody. They just want your money." He scoffed.

"It's their job, Vico. Can't fault them for that."

"Don't give a damn about nobody. I been coming here

for over a year, and nobody even knows my name. Not even my fake one. Gagliano's the big boss and nobody gives a damn about anyone but him."

"Yeah, he is the boss. This is still his joint, so keep your voice down." Sonny whispered.

"My father died, you assholes!" Vico shouted. "My father was killed! Got murdered by some two-bit hood while he was earning to put bread on my mother's table. You like that? Huh? That important to you?" The room silenced and everyone stared. "And my brother too! They cut him up like a fish and stuffed him in a sack. They gouged his eyes out. What do you think about that?"

Sonny was panicking but couldn't do anything to stop his brother once he got started.

Some of the girls snickered and whispered to their patrons.

"See, nobody cares." Vico turned his attention back to his drink. For a moment, his eyes shimmered with tears.

Sonny wished there was something more he could say. Maybe he could tell his brother they could move on, that they could reopen their father's barbershop, spend more time with their mother, settle down. They could get out of that life. But his list of suggestions was growing thin, and in the end he didn't even believe it himself.

"You Vincente?" The bartender approached Sonny.

"Yeah, who's asking?"

"Some guy on the phone." The bartender returned to the telephone and stretched the cord until it could reach the bar in front of Sonny.

He picked up the receiver. "You got Sonny."

"Vincente, it's good to hear your voice."

Don Maranzano. He was the only person Sonny knew

who would call him at a speakeasy and talk in Sicilian, let alone call him by his Christian name.

"You, too, Don Maranzano. It's been a while."

"Indeed it has. Nearly a month now."

Sonny tried to interpret the Don's tone, but couldn't tell if he was upset with him, or merely calling to check in. "Yeah, I know you've been busy. I didn't want to interfere. Everything going all right?"

"Yes. The restructuring of this Thing of Ours has been difficult. I wish I had you by my side throughout this. I could have used your wit. That being said, everything is going just fine."

"I'm glad to hear it," Sonny said. When silence lingered for a moment, Vico asked who it was, and Sonny hushed him. "There anything I can do for you?"

"Are you sober?"

"Yeah. I've had a few drinks, but I'm fine. What is it?"

"Nothing serious, " Maranzano said. His voice was melancholy, like he was dealing with a late-night case of nostalgia. "Not like the things I used to call you about. If you have the time, why don't you join me at my house? I'm about to put on some coffee to brew, and my wife baked some wonderful tiramisu. I'd just like to see you."

In truth, Sonny had missed his mentor a lot. He'd only stayed away for fear he'd be asked to commit more sins, and he knew if he was asked he would say yes. Hearing Maranzano's voice, he felt foolish for that fear. The boss had always looked out for him and tried to keep him from the worst parts of the life. "I'd like that," Sonny said.

"I'll see you shortly." Maranzano hung up.

Sonny stood and pulled out his billfold. He counted through his cash and set down more than enough to cover his tab, then pulled out a few dollars and handed it to the bartender directly. "Call him a cab, make sure he gets home all right."

"Fine." The bartender sighed.

"Hey, did you hear me?" Sonny got bug-eyed and pointed at the barkeep. "If anything happens to him tonight, I'm holding you responsible. I hope he gets home safe for both our sakes."

Vico's head rested on his arm and his words were slurred. "I'll be fine. Don't worry about me. I'll walk back to Harlem . . . I don't give a shit."

"I love you, big brother." Sonny bent over and kissed Vico's head before he turned to leave.

Wappinger Falls, New York—July 18, 1931

Sonny was greeted at the door by Mrs. Maranzano and the smell of her tiramisu.

"Good evening, ma'am." He took off his fedora and tucked it under his arm.

"It's nice to meet you, Vincente. My husband has told me so many nice things about you." Mrs. Maranzano smiled and accepted his hand gingerly. She had a noble beauty to her. She was the perfect Cleopatra, albeit a modest one, to Maranzano's Caesar.

Sonny noticed a little fellow peaking from behind his mother. "And this must be little Maranzano," he said as he leaned over to shake the young boy's hand.

"Little Maranzano is in there," he pointed to an office

connected to the foyer, "He was running and got hurt. I'm Ignazio, the older brother."

"Nice to meet you. You can call me Sonny."

"I'm in here, Vincente," Maranzano hollered from his study.

"Go right on in," Mrs. Maranzano said. "The desserts will be ready any moment."

Sonny placed his fedora on a hat rack and walked into Maranzano's office. It was as immaculate as Maranzano's real estate headquarters in Manhattan, filled with rows of leather-bound books and a massive mahogany desk.

Maranzano sat in a red leather chair in the corner of the room, the youngest of his two boys curled in his lap. Maranzano's arms were stretched around his child, delicately bandaging a bloody knee.

"Oh, what happened?" Sonny asked.

"He was playing too rough, weren't you?" Maranzano asked his boy. With a pouted lip, the boy nodded. "Boys will be boys though, won't they?"

"That's right. Me and my brothers used to come home bloody about every other day,"

"As any young man should." Maranzano dabbed rubbing alcohol on his handkerchief. "This is going to sting a little. Hey, look at me."

The young boy, fear in his eyes, looked up at his father.

"Keep looking at me. Don't let me know that it hurts."

Maranzano's youngest nodded. His body jolted as Maranzano dabbed the alcohol onto the fresh wound, but then he steadied himself, never losing the fixed gaze into his father's eyes.

"I think he's as tough as his old man," Sonny said.

The boy looked up, his fear replaced with pride.

"Tougher, even," Maranzano said, placing a bandage over the wound to seal it. "While his papa was away on business, my boys had to be the men of the house. Didn't you, little pal?"

He nodded. "We took care of mama."

"Go on. Wash your hands before dessert. You have blood on them."

The boy limped out of the room in dramatic fashion.

Maranzano stood and smiled at his protege.

"It's good to see you, Don Maranzano." Sonny embraced his mentor.

Maranzano kissed his cheek. "And you as well. Please, sit." He extended his hand to the red leather chair opposite his own. "What do you think of my home?"

"It's perfect for you, Don Maranzano."

Maranzano nodded and peered out his window. "I came to this country later than most and made a name for myself even later. Manhattan and Brooklyn were teeming with stills run by *pezzonovanti* from every culture imaginable. And I let them have it." He inhaled deeply, his shoulders relaxing. "I'll take my countryside, my forests. Peace and quiet. Away from law enforcement and jealous eyes."

Like he was before a king in court, Sonny listened intently, hopping for the morsels of wisdom Maranzano so often doled out when he was in the mood to do so.

The Don returned to his leather chair. "I've missed this room. It's been nice coming home. To my books, to this statue." He gestured to the marble bust beside his chair. "Do you know who this is?"

"Not certain, but I could venture a guess, if I know you as well as I think. Julius Caesar?"

"That's right," Maranzano said. "I look at it often and reflect. He was near my age when he first conquered Gaul. Most believed that the bulk of his life's work was completed, but he knew that wasn't true. Most men would have wanted to retire and enjoy the spoils of war, but Caesar knew his war was just beginning."

Sonny listened carefully.

"I'm sure you have wondered about the money that was laid out at our meeting in Chicago, and why you haven't been given any of it," Maranzano said, turning his gaze from the statue to Sonny.

"I haven't. I didn't expect any of that."

"You're a better man than most, then." Maranzano sighed. "Others have begun to grumble. You're better than most, but your also too humble for your own good. Some of that money belongs to you for the work you did during the war. If I was in a position to distribute it, I would."

"Don't mention it, Don Maranzano. I didn't do any of that for money."

"And that's why it should be you to receive it." Maranzano returned his attention to the statue. "But none of the money can be distributed yet. We will soon be going to war again, and we need it to fund our campaign."

Sonny gripped the arm rest of his chair. "Another war?"

"That's right."

"With who?"

"There are many who still plot our destruction. They smile at us in public but meet in secrecy to discuss how they can destroy what we've built."

"Who, Don Maranzano? Who?" Sonny asked. Was this just a loyalty test? He prayed it was.

"I've been reading more since I returned. Recently I've begun to read 'The Sertorius Scrolls.' Have you heard of them?"

"No, but—"

"The author tells of a battle, called the Battle of Arausio. In one day, 90,000 Romans were slain." He fixed his gaze on Sonny again. "Then, after his wounds were healed, he returned to the field of battle, to finish what needed to be done. We are the descendants of the Romans, Sonny. But we have become coddled by leisure and excess." He gestured to the room around him. "The war isn't over."

"We're going back to the mattresses?"

"We are," Maranzano said with a hint of sadness in his voice. "We can have no rest until our enemies are dead. Luciano, Genovese, Capone too if he doesn't get locked away . . . they were never meant to be apart of our society. Drug dealers, brothel owners, pimps, cutthroats . . . they care only for money, and what it can afford them. They will turn on us the moment they see an opportunity."

Sonny lowered his eyes and tried to hide his dread.

"But we had a deal, Don Maranzano. I thought the past was the past, and no one was to seek retribution?"

Maranzano's eyes glossed over, his face becoming as stone-like as the bust of Caesar beside him. "This isn't about retribution. This isn't about the past. This is about the future. A better, more secure future for our people."

"I see." Sonny didn't know what to say, or what was expected of him.

"Joseph Bonanno will be heading our war efforts. We hope that this campaign will be a shorter one than against Masseria. As soon as our enemies have been eliminated, we may finally have rest."

"Do they know? Luciano and them, do they know?"

"Not yet. And I hope that I can count on your discretion," Maranzano said. "I do not expect you to join me in this war, but if the time comes, I hope you would never side against me."

Sonny's jaw dropped. He shook his head and waved

his arms. "I would never side against you, Don Maranzano," he said, offended that such a thing could even be suggested.

"It was Caesar's friend Brutus who held the knife that killed him. One can never be too sure."

Sonny looked down, and for a long, awkward moment, silence settled over the room. "I am not a traitor."

"And I didn't mean to insinuate that you were." He leaned across the desk and took Sonny's hands within his own. "You are like a son to me, Vincente. I can fight the whole world, but I couldn't bear the thought of losing your friendship."

Sonny found it difficult to maintain eye contact. "Of course, Don Maranzano. I'll do whatever is asked of me."

"Would you like to smoke?" Maranzano asked.

Sonny's eyes narrowed. Another test? The boss hated smoke.

"You tap your feet when you need a smoke. I notice these things." Sonny noticed his bouncing leg for the first time himself and was quick to stifle it. "And I want you to listen to what I'm about to say very carefully."

"You sure?" Sonny asked.

Maranzano nodded. Sonny fished out his gold case and lit a match.

"I want to ask you a question." He pounced to his feet, clasping his hands behind his back. "Joe Masseria led by fear. Most insecure men who seek to validate their importance do. But others may rule with love. For a boss, what do you think is best? Fear or love?"

Sonny took a long drag of his Lucky Strike as Maranzano materialized a makeshift ashtray.

"Is there a right or wrong answer?" Sonny asked. Maranzano gave no indication he heard him. Sonny thought hard and blew smoke away from his boss. "Seems like it'd be tough to keep all the boys in line with love."

"So fear then?" Maranzano raised a brow.

"No . . . well, not like Masseria. I don't know."

"The correct answer is love," the Don said with finality. "Fear can be transferred from one man to the next. Today they fear me, tomorrow they may fear another. Today they may fear This Thing of Ours, tomorrow they may fear the government or law enforcement.

"But love, love is permanent. With it there is absolutely loyalty. There are no doubts or fears." He returned to his seat and met Sonny's eyes as the cigarette burned out. "Do you love me, Vincente?"

Sonny swallowed. "I love you, Don Maranzano."

Maranzano leaned back in his chair and exhaled deeply. He rubbed at his neck and blinked.

"And that's why you're the only one I can trust." Maranzano suddenly looked so human, fragile. Like all the sleepless nights and the weight of orchestrating a war collapsed on him at once.

As if his lungs were filled with fresh air, he reanimated. "Unfortunately, Vincente, there are some whose egos are too large to fear another man, and some whose hearts are too cold to love. And these men must be eliminated before we're ever going to be safe."

Sonny nodded. He already knew he would probably join the war the moment his mentor asked him to. He was incapable of refusing him. Boy did he hope he was wrong though.

Mrs. Maranzano arrived at the door to the office. "Gentlemen, the dessert is ready. Vincente, do you prefer milk and sugar in your espresso?"

"What? Oh, certainly. However you make it is just fine," Sonny replied, still lost in his own thoughts.

"Let's go, Vincente, and speak of more pleasant things." Maranzano stood.

"Lead the way," Sonny tried to force a smile. He followed his mentor into the kitchen and was greeted by the warm aroma of tiramisu.

It made his stomach turn. He was now decidedly less hungry than he had been previously.

Little Italy, Manhattan—August 3, 1931

Sonny found the Father playing ball with some of the orphan boys who hang around the church. The heat was oppressive, and the black pavement beneath them baked. Sonny smiled. Sammy must be dying in that black cassock, but he looked to be having the time of his life.

"Hey there, batter up. Batter up," Father Sammy said with his best radio announcer impression. He wound up the pitch like was going to throw lightening, but he tossed the ball lightly and the teenager smacked it past him and took off running. "Slow down, Babe Ruth, you're making me look bad!" Sammy shielded his eyes from the sun as he watched the boy round the makeshift bases—tires of nearby cars that were probably in great danger.

As he continued to follow the runner, his gaze passed over Sonny and then bounced back. His mouth opened and he looked him up and down for a minute, not quite believing his eyes.

"Hey, Father. It's good to see you." Sonny took off his newsboy cap.

"You too, you too." Sammy nodded to the kids to indicate he was stepping away. They groaned for a moment but then jumped back into their game. "You want to step inside?"

"Wouldn't mind to. I'm frying out here." Sonny smiled and kissed him on either cheek.

Sammy shook his head. "You're telling me." He tugged at his collar.

Sonny followed him into Old St Patrick's courtyard, passing between the burial plots on either side of the path where his father and brother were buried. The greenish stone of the chapel made Sonny feel at home—it brought back memories of a time when he actually had a home—and that was an unusual but welcome feeling.

Inside, the female choir was practicing *Ave Maria* near the altar and under the blue stained glass.

"This is kinda like our theme song." Sammy nodded to the singer.

"If you're gonna have a theme song, that's not a bad one."

"She's no Elisabeth Rethberg, sure, but who is?" Sammy led the way into the clergy room which served as his office, which was completely bare save a desk and an image on the wall depicting the crucified Savior, his blessed mother by his feet. "Sit on down." Sammy pulled out a chair for him.

"Appreciate it. It's good to see you," Sonny said.

Sammy looked stunned for a moment. "Yeah, yeah. I'm glad to see you. Surprised, but glad . . . hey, Sonny, I want to apologize for what I said last time. I hope I didn't overstep or hurt your—"

Sonny held up his hands to stop him. "It's all right,

Father. I think you were right." Sonny exhaled and prepared for what he was about to say. He'd never uttered the words before, and generally avoided thinking them. "I'm going to get out."

Sammy nearly jumped from his simple leather chair. "Yeah? I'm relieved just . . . surprised."

"I'm just as surprised to hear myself say it." Sonny stood and placed his hands in his pockets. He ensured the door was closed behind him. "Maran . . . the boss I mentioned asked me to go to war again. I don't want to do it. Don't think I *can* do it honestly," Sonny said. He hoped it was true. The Father was still wide eyed, but he was smiling like he believed him. That made Sonny feel better.

"What will you do then?" Sammy asked.

Sonny made himself sit back down or he knew he'd continue pacing. "I want to get back into the financial business. This market will come back eventually, and I want to ride the wave up."

The Father's spun toward the depiction of Christ behind him, and Sonny thought he heard Sammy thank Him. "What will your, uh, 'family' think about this?"

That was the one element Sonny was especially reluctant to consider. Since he met with Maranzano in mid-July, he couldn't resist the desire to get out, but the thought of offering goodbyes terrified him. And not just because he anticipated reprisal. If they would ever turn on him, they were no friends of his anyway.

"I don't know," Sonny said. "My brother Vico will be relieved—he doesn't want me tied up in all this anyways. My pals Bonanno and Buffalo will be disappointed, but they'll move on quick. Cargo won't even notice." He paused and Sammy waited for him to continue. "My old buddy Antonello will be despondent. He's the one I'm really worried about. But he's got an in with the 'family' now."

"Maybe he'll follow your lead?" Sammy said. "From what you've said, he's joined you in everything you've done."

Sonny smiled sadly at the pleasant thought but knew it would never happen. "He doesn't know any other life. I hope, but . . . another war will probably give him an opportunity to move up. Gain some respect, maybe even authority. He'll be all right."

Sammy nodded. "What about that brother-in-law of yours? What's his name? Buster?"

"Yeah, Buster." Sonny considered it and shook his head. "Honestly? I have no idea. He's an enigma, that guy. I don't think he'll care. Only thing he's concerned with is my sister, Maria," Sonny said. "I've never seen a fella love a woman like he loves her."

Sammy sobered. "What about the big boss man?"

Sonny felt a slight tremor in his hands at the thought but was quick to stifle it. His eyes felt misty, but he blinked them dry. "I've never been afraid of him before. He really has been good to me. Never made me feel anything but safe and protected. Like I had someone who really had my back. But the last time we talked . . ."

"What happened?" the Father.

"Our last conversation just made me feel strange," Sonny said. "Like he was looking at me different. Like he might find himself at the end of my revolver instead of the guys we fought."

Sammy crossed his arms and leaned back. "Man like that is bound to protect himself no matter what. Has to, if he wants to stay alive.

"You think he'll consider me a threat?" Sonny knew the

Father couldn't possibly offer an answer to that, but he felt his breaths become rapid and stinted.

Sammy shook his head. "No. No. No way, right? I can tell he thinks a lot of you. Most of the fellas you ran with probably didn't feel 'safe and protected' all the time."

Sonny sighed. "I wish we could still be pals . . . maybe grab coffee every once in awhile."

"Think that's wise?"

Sonny's voice became quiet and weak. "I just don't think it's possible." He exhaled, and the fresh breath in his lungs allowed him to speak more confidently. "The life is everything to him."

Sammy leaned across the desk and placed his hand on one of Sonny's. He waited till Sonny met his eyes. "If I'm out of line here, you tell me to go jump in a lake. But what about the guy who got your dad?"

Sonny smiled. "That's what I've thought about more than anything. The rage . . . that terrible rage in my gut it just . . . vanished. I've even tried to search for it, but I can't summon it up."

Sammy grinned and leaned back in his chair.

"The guy who killed my dad might even be dead already. If he's not, he will die. When you live by the gun and by the knife, you die by the gun and by the knife."

"Vengeance is mine, saith the Lord," Sammy said. "You're right. Justice will be served one way or the other."

Sonny felt a tinge of doubt, feeling like it should be a Consentino to exact that justice. If the killer was eliminated for any other reason, would it really avenge his father's death? But, unlike the past few years, Sonny quickly found answers to that question that satisfied him. The spark of anger was snuffed out before it could light.

"That's it, Father."

Sammy cocked an eyebrow and smirked. "There's something you aren't telling me. Despite the weight of everything you're saying, I can tell you're light. Your spirit is radiating joy. I can feel it, unless it's still the heat of this cassock. Tell me I'm wrong."

Sonny laughed. "You know, you're pretty good at this."

The Father shrugged with feigned humility. "Who would have guessed, right? Almost like I do it for a living."

Sonny couldn't help smiling now. He hadn't told anyone else but was bursting at the seams to do so. "There's a girl."

"I knew it!" Sammy's voice echoed off the high walls of the cathedral office.

"Calm down, calm down." Sonny laughed. "I've had my heart set on her for awhile, but I couldn't put her in harms way, ya know? Now that I'm leaving . . ."

"Look at you." Sammy reached across the desk and pinched his cheek. "Like a school boy in love."

"I'm gonna marry her, Father." Sonny nodded, more sure of that statement than anything in his life.

"If you don't let me marry the two of you, I'll be the one you gotta worry about!" His joy was genuine, and Sonny felt a weight off his back he hadn't known was there. The Father's eyes watered as he stood and embraced Sonny. He tried to let go, but Sammy held on tight. "I want you to know—if you were *my* son, I'd be pretty damn proud of you, kid."

Sonny wrapped the Father up in a bear hug like Alonzo used to give, and fought back his tears with laughter.

44

LUCIANO

Garment District, Manhattan—August 21, 1931

"Go fish, asshole." Luciano threw up a middle finger to Costello. He wasn't going to fall for his bluff. He doubled his bet. He had two-pair in hand, and knew Costello bet wildly when he didn't have anything.

"I think you're playing the wrong game, Charlie," Costello said, chomping down on his cigar.

"I think you forgot who you're playing with, Frankie," Luciano said, irritated at his friend's jovial behavior. Luciano's nickname might have been Lucky, but when it came to cards, fortune generally sided with Costello.

"Let's see what you have, gentlemen," Genovese said, having already folded.

The remaining players laid out their hands, and, of course, Costello won with three-of-a-kind.

The phone rang just in time to distract everyone from Luciano's angst.

Meyer Lansky answered the phone. "This is Meyer. Okay. All right. I hear you." He hung up and turned to Luciano.

"Who was that?" Costello asked, collecting his winnings.

"Our friend from Brooklyn,"

"Joe Bananas?" Genovese asked.

Lansky shrugged.

"Just spit it out, Meyer," Luciano said, still irritated about losing another hand.

"Yes, it was Joe Bonanno."

"Did he have anything good for us?"

"He can confirm that Maranzano is planning a hit on you. On all of us, actually," Lansky said, exhaling. Everyone watched his reaction, and he was careful to show them as little emotion as possible.

"We already figured as much. What else?" Luciano said evenly. He pretended he was paying attention to the cards he was being dealt, but his feet tapped beneath the table.

"Bonanno doesn't wanna go to war. He just got married. He wants to help us end it before it starts."

"Maranzano still rolls around with a small militia. How are we supposed to get to him?" Genovese asked.

Lansky held up a finger. "This is where it gets interesting. He says that Maranzano doesn't allow guns in his real estate office."

"That can't be right. We would have knocked him off during the war if he was that stupid." Luciano threw out his ante.

"Back then things were different. His worst enemy was Joe the Boss. He considers us small fries in comparison. His biggest enemy now is the IRS, and he's been planning for an audit. He thinks they'll be visiting soon, so he doesn't want guns around."

Luciano finally looked up at his associate.

"Joe Bonanno said all that? I thought the two of them were peas in a pod?" Luciano narrowed his eyes.

"That's what he said."

"And what does he want in return?" Costello asked, figuring there had to be a catch.

"His safety guaranteed. If we go after Maranzano's faithful, he wants to make sure he isn't touched."

"That it?" Genovese asked.

"Well . . . and he said that naturally he would become the boss of the family after Maranzano was out." Lansky shrugged.

"Trade out one asshole for another." Luciano shook his head.

"At least that asshole doesn't want us dead." Costello peeked at his cards and raised the bet.

"He can be handled easier, Charlie," Lansky agreed.

"All right then," Luciano folded, unwilling to let Costello take any more money from him. "We need to find some badges then. Have somebody make some fakes for us. One of those chinks in China Town probably. Meyer, send some of your boys to his office. Maranzano will bring them in and start to show his ledgers. Then we knock him off." He looked around. Everyone had been in favor of eliminating Maranzano since the war had ended, but now that it was a reality they squirmed. "Capeesh?"

"Yeah, I got it." Lansky nodded.

"I'll call someone about the badges," Genovese said.

"Fellas," Luciano said, halting his crew before they could disperse. "We need to take care of his pals too.

Bonanno can live, but those others . . . they gotta go. Consentino, Bobby Doyle, Buster from Chicago. Understand? All of 'em. Buffalo, Balducci, and that Cargo too."

They nodded and departed to do his bidding.

45

MARIA

Westchester County, New York—September 9, 1931

The nurse down at the women's clinic said she wouldn't deal with much discomfort until later in the pregnancy. Well, that had been a wicked, foolish lie.

Now five months into her pregnancy, Maria couldn't find a comfortable position no matter how much she tried. Her mother was right after all, she should have eaten better growing up, so maybe she wouldn't be so slender. That baby in her was an active little fella too. She swore up and down that it was a boy. He fought in there like a boxer.

Buster wasn't so sure. He might not have told his friends, but Maria could tell he wanted a baby girl. A girl could be the apple of his eye and take some of his attention away from Maria.

While Buster had been gone on his "business," Maria had cried most nights, and prayed for him to come home. Well, she got what she wanted. He was home now, and hardly left her side. Unfortunately, she got more than she bargained for. He was constantly pining for her, doting on her, kissing her, and carefully tending to her every need.

It annoyed the hell out of her. She couldn't get one moment's peace. When she'd complain, he'd offer to rub her feet or go to the store to pick up a remedy. She just wanted him to shut up and listen to her complain. The more ornery she became, the more patient he was. Sometimes she wished he was a brute and would just fight with her, throw something, or yell at the top of his voice. In her more sentimental moments, she wept when she considered how lucky she was to have a husband like Buster, but she dared not let him see this.

On a day like today, when Buster had work to do for his "employers" in New York, she could finally get some peace. A little independence went a long way to improve her mood.

She searched through the overflowing dirty clothes hamper for her keys. She could never keep up with them, despite how often her husband begged her to hang them on the key ring beside the door, where the keys to the Buick remained when he was home.

Finding them, she smiled. It wasn't too cold out, but having been locked in that damn house for so long, she knew she'd catch a cold if she didn't wear a coat. She threw a jacket over her shoulder and started out the door.

She wasn't certain where she would go, but she wanted to do something on her own, for herself. She had an odd, yet uncontrollable, craving for butternut squash. That would be the target of her journey outside the home, although she might take the long way to the nearest grocer.

As she stepped out onto the city streets, she spotted that beautiful Model A, it's baby blue coat glistening in the sunlight. Even though it belonged to her husband, she had become the de facto owner. He'd taught her how to drive like her father had promised to do, just so she could take it out. She hadn't been out driving much for some time, but Buster always took that old Buick regardless.

She held her belly still, and she slipped into the front seat.

As she pulled out onto the neighborhood street, the car jolted. She tested the gas and the breaks, readjusting from a few weeks away from the driver's seat. Getting a grasp on the controls, she fixed the rear view to her sight.

Unfortunately, she caught a view of herself. She used to feel like the most beautiful girl in New York when she drove that Model A, with the windows down and the wind blowing through her hair. Now she was absent makeup, her hair filled with split ends, and had a plump little belly hanging from her otherwise thin frame like a fanny pack.

She turned her eyes back to the road and slammed on her breaks. Traffic was coming to a dead halt in front of her. She came within a few inches of the car bumper in front of her before the tires stopped screeching.

She laid her head back and tried to catch her breath. Buster would have been furious at her if she got hurt. *Why didn't you call me? I could have brought anything home for you!* He would have said. But she would show him she could still do anything she wanted.

The light turned green, and she followed the procession through the stop light. She spotted the grocer in the distance, her belly grumbling at the thought of all the strange delicacies she might find inside.

Tires screeched so loudly that it deafened her.

She turned. A Chevrolet. Careening toward her.

Her head whipped against the window. Glass shattered and rained down in bits.

Everything went so fast. Then everything went silent.

Her vision was hazy and her senses numbed.

The baby.

The baby.

Her trembling hands felt for wounds along or around her stomach. She felt no pain, but as the light faded out of her eyes, she noticed the bright red blood running down her hands.

46

SONNY

Little Italy, Manhattan—September 10, 1931

"Eat your peas, Ma," Sonny said placing a napkin on his own plate to signal he was finished.

Rosa shook her head. "I'm not hungry. I can't sleep anymore. Those neighbors are always keeping me up. That dog of theirs is always yapping, howling at the moon. I heard he smokes reefer you know," she said.

He tried to make up for his months of absence by visiting his mother for dinner a few times a week. She seemed determined to make it as unpleasant as possible, but he kept returning regardless. He understood why she was like this. She was widowed and all her children had left. One of her sons was dead at thirty. It was remarkable she wasn't worse than she was.

Instead, their cramped tenement just kept getting smaller, as new knickknacks and old keepsakes lined the hallways and the floor of the living room. Her way of coping.

"Well, don't let the neighbor's iniquities keep you from getting a good meal." Sonny encouraged her to continue eating. It was strange how their rolls had reversed over the years.

She took a few bites. "They're too soft now."

"Easier on your teeth, Ma. Come on, finish up. I brought you a cannoli from Ferrara's for dessert."

The phone rang, to Sonny's relief. He rose and kissed his mother's head. "I'll grab it, Ma."

"Consentino's residence," he answered.

"Sonny?" The familiar voice was weak, and hard to understand through sobs.

"Yeah? Sis? That you? You all right?"

"Sonny, I got in a wreck," Maria said.

Rosa said, "Is that your sister? She hasn't visited me in weeks."

Sonny picked up the phone and moved it further away from his mother so she couldn't overhear.

"Slow down, Maria. What happened?"

"Oh, Sonny . . . Sonny, it was so bad."

"The baby?" he asked. He felt guilty for not asking about her health first.

"It's fine. The doctor's said there was some tissue bruising but . . . but the baby was unharmed."

"What's wrong? What's your sister saying?" Rosa asked. Sonny turned his back to her.

"Oh my God, Maria. What can I do? Does Buster know?"

"Yeah . . . he knows cause I didn't come home last night. He's been here most of the time."

"Why are you just now calling? You should have let me know immediately. I would have been there."

"Is Vico there?" Maria asked.

"Ah, no."

"You can't tell him what I'm about to say, Sonny. Okay? He'll do something bad. You can't tell him. Promise?"

He stepped as far away from his mother as possible and pressed the receiver to his ear. "I promise."

"When they took the car in . . ." she began to cry more.

"Come on, Maria. What is it?"

"When they took the car in, they said the title . . . they said the title was in dad's name."

Sonny listened to his sister's sobs in silence. He tried to decipher what that meant.

"How is that possible?"

"I don't know, Sonny! I don't know." She sniffled. "The date of purchase was a few months before my birthday . . . a few months before he died."

"What are you saying?" Sonny's stomach turned.

"I don't know . . . but I'm scared, Sonny! I'm really scared . . . what if . . ."

"Don't say it, Maria. Don't say what you're about to say."

The inflection in her voice changed suddenly. "Oh okay, well it was good talking to you, Mama," she said. "Buster just got back. He's taking really good care of me. Don't worry about a thing!" She hung up.

Sonny continued to hold the phone to his ear. His fingers were numb, and his limbs shook. He contemplated what he could tell his mother, but couldn't think of anything.

"You tell that girl to come see me," Rosa said, still picking at her food.

"All right, sis. You stay inside and try to keep warm. It sounds like just a cold," he said to the dial tone. "Love you,

Maria. Mom sends her love as well. Bye now." He hung up and set the phone back on the table.

"She's cold? I always tell that girl to cover up. That's bound to happen when your hemline is above your knees."

"Yeah, that's it." He gathered his coat and fedora. "She needs me to bring her some cinnamon and quinine tablets, and some broth."

"What about that husband of hers?" Rosa said.

"Giving music lessons," Sonny said. He placed the cannoli on the table and kissed his mother again on the cheek. "I'll be back real soon. Eat that dessert. It's caramel, your favorite."

He hurried out the door before she could pester him about it.

Headlights flashed before him on Mulberry Street. His vision blurred, he seemed to watch everything from afar, outside himself.

Could Buster have been behind Alonzo's death? Why? An old war buddy of Vico's, moving to New York to kill his father? Could Buster be Turridru?

It wasn't possible. No. No way.

He hurried to his car and slammed on the gas.

If there was one person who would know, it was Salvatore Maranzano.

47

SEBASTIANO

Little Italy, Manhattan—November 11, 1928

"Do you understand what needs to be done?"

"I do," Sebastiano, now called Buster, said.

The man was barely visible in the office chair before him. The lights were dim, and a homburg was pulled low over his face. "Kill him, and him alone. Make sure no one sees, and no one is around to identify you. If they do, I'll deny ever making your acquaintance," the man said.

"I don't even know your name. How could I possibly rat on you?" Buster said. Dread coursed through his veins like a shot of morphine. There was a physiological response to the thought of killing again. Images of Private Franklin and his death in France flashed through his mind as clear as a studio photograph.

But he knew it had to be done.

"What happens after?" Buster asked.

"You'll be pronounced dead tomorrow morning. It will make Chicago headlines. Everyone will be much too intrigued by Al Capone's involvement to do any real digging."

"And my family?"

"You won't be paraded before the courts, so your assets will remain intact. As promised, I will sign a $10,000 check tomorrow morning, and ship it to your mother's front door. They will never know you are still alive. For all intents and purposes, you are now dead. When Alonzo dies, you are born again."

The words stung like a knife. "What am I supposed to do after I kill him? I can't go back to Chicago."

"No, you can't. Do you know anyone in New York?"

"No . . . well, yeah. A war buddy."

"Call up your old companion then. Make acquaintances. But never let them know who you really are, or what you've done."

"That's it?"

"Yes. I would only engage with those you trust. We won't speak again, not until I have further use for you."

Buster shook his head.

"This deal seems to work out in your favor."

The man shrugged.

"That's the only kind of deal I make. If you'd like to return to Chicago, I can have it arranged. A noose will be waiting for you."

"I'm going to do it. I'll do it."

"When you're done, return to me just once. There is something on the man's person that I want. A razor, with the man's initials on it."

"War trophy?" Buster scoffed.

"A symbol of my victory."

"Why don't you kill him yourself then?" Buster asked.

The man turned his back. "I am a businessman, Buster. I want to control New York. If I'm to do that, I can't involve myself in these kinds of affairs," the man said. "Are you prepared?"

"Yes."

"See him out, Calogero."

A suave and charming young man came to Buster's side and led him from the office.

"One last thing," the man shouted after him. "Take that damned Model A. It's existence insults me. Do with it what you will."

The door shut behind Buster. Turning, he noticed a gold name plate on the door. The words etched into it were clear and distinct: S. MARANZANO.

48

SONNY

Manhattan, New York—September 10, 1931

Sonny declined to use the elevator. Instead he rocketed up the nine floors of the Eagle Corporation building to the real estate offices of Salvatore Maranzano. He burst through the doors.

"Whoa, Sonny, slow down," Charlie Buffalo said.

"I need to see The Don."

"He's busy. Take a breather. You're beet red. Let me get you some coffee, and I'll let him know you're here."

"No, I need to see him now," Sonny said, pushing past Charlie.

"Damnit, Sonny." Charlie followed close behind Sonny hurrying toward the boss's office.

Sonny opened the doors. Maranzano looked up from his desk. And frowned.

"I told him not to interrupt, Mr. Maranzano. He wouldn't listen."

"That's all right, Calogero," Maranzano sat back in his chair. "Take a seat, Vincente."

Sonny crossed his arms. "We need to talk."

"Then talk," Maranzano said, his fatherly smile overcoming his irritation at being interrupted.

"Alone." Sonny looked at Charlie.

"What? What the hell can't you tell me?" Charlie said, offended.

"Go on, Calogero. Just give us a moment," Maranzano said. Charlie glared at Sonny when he turned to leave. "I'll admit, Vincente, I'm surprised to see you acting like this. Something must be very wrong." Maranzano crossed his arms.

"I think Buster had something to do with my father's death," he spit out before thinking. He had planned on being more tactful, but the thought of his brother-in-law being his father's killer was too much to contain.

"You do? And what evidence do you have? Where did this come from?"

"The car . . . the Ford he gave my sister, it was in my father's name."

"I see." Maranzano laid his head back and stared at the ceiling. "That would have been very foolish of Buster."

"What?" Sonny asked, perplexed.

Shouts came from the office lobby.

Maranzano strained to see through the glass door to the entryway.

He shot up.

"That's the IRS. I've been expecting them. They're going to try to get me like they're getting Capone. We'll continue talking, Vincente, just give me a moment."

Sonny peered out the frosted glass windows. Maranzano's employees were lined up against the wall, hands on their head.

"You have a gun? This could be a setup." Sonny felt his coat, realizing he'd forgotten his pistol in his haste.

"No guns. This is strictly business." Maranzano opened his office door and prepared to meet the agents.

Sonny didn't like the look of this raid. He hurried to Maranzano's desk and fumbled through the drawers. If the agents were phony, and tried to pull another St. Valentine's Day Massacre, he would put a stop to it.

So close to answers. Nothing could stop him from getting them now.

He fumbled through several drawers, finding mostly folders of paperwork, and general office supplies.

He reached into the lowest drawer on the right side and spotted the shiny nickel of a revolver. He grabbed it and tucked it into his waist band.

As he went to shut the drawer, something else shinned in the candescent office light. He leaned back down and found a straight razor within the drawer. The initials A.C were engraved on the ivory handle.

His father's.

EPILOGUE

Little Italy, Manhattan—November 11, 1928

"Need any help?" Oscar asked, throwing on a wool Lindberg jacket.

"No, don't worry about it. I'll finish sweeping and lock the doors," Alonzo said.

His friend and employee Oscar sheepishly looked at him.

"Go on, now! Go eat some dinner with those girls."

"We'll see you tomorrow, A.C.," Oscar said, fixing a fedora on his head and departing.

Alonzo continued to sweep up the remains of the last haircut. He missed the days when Sonny had been there working with him this time of night but wouldn't change it for the world. His boy was in college and would be the world's smartest man on Wall Street one day. Alonzo was nothing but a fifty-year-old barber, with not a lot to show for his life. But his son was making something of himself, and that was enough.

Given where they started, in Castellamare del Golfo,

he was pleased with that. His children wouldn't have to do the things he'd done. They wouldn't have to be the man he'd been. The twins had messed up, sure, but they were smarter than they acted, and had good heads on their shoulders. Eventually, they would get on the right course.

The bell attached to the front door jingled.

"Sorry, we're closed for the day," Alonzo said, bending down with a dustpan to collect the hair.

When the bell didn't ring again with the man's departure, Alonzo looked up.

The man walked slowly into the barbershop, a fedora low over his face, and a cigarette in between his lips. He walked with a noticeable limp and turned the sign from open to closed.

Alonzo propped his broom up against the barber chair and sized up the intruder. "Who sent you?"

"I don't know who he is. Or why." The man spoke in a calm, even tone. He wasn't aggressive or insulting.

"Turridru?"

The man grimaced like he'd already been shot.

"Or, is he called Don Maranzano, now? He was my protege once. I loved him like a little brother, like a son even."

The man pulled out a revolver.

"My family . . . will they be all right?"

"He doesn't want anything bad to happen to your family. He'll find work for your boys and make sure your wife is fed."

"Tell them . . . will you tell . . ." Alonzo realized how foolish he was. He straightened himself and met the eyes of the man before him.

He had made many mistakes. In Sicily. In America.

He should have never associated with a man like Morello, and he should have never borrowed from a man like Turridru. But everything he had done, he did for his family. And he would do it all again if he had to.

The man raised his gun.

Alonzo said one last silent prayer.

The gun fired.

Alonzo fell, finished his prayer, and memories of his family danced before his eyes while the light began to fade.

If you want to be the first to hear about the release of Book 3 in "The Consentino Crime Saga," be sure to Join the Bureau!

Just scan the QR code below!

ABOUT THE AUTHOR

Vincent B. Davis II is an author, entrepreneur, and soldier.

He is a graduate of East Tennessee State University, and has served in the United States Army since 2014.

He's the author of eight books, four of which have become international bestsellers. When he's not researching or writing his next book, you can find him watching Carolina Panthers football or playing with his rescued mutt, Buddy.

Made in United States
Orlando, FL
09 May 2023